Dead And Buried

This book is dedicated
to my parents for
their support and for
pushing me to finish.

Dead And Buried

A Martha's Vineyard Mystery

By

Crispin Nathaniel Haskins

1

She was aware that she was awake...but only vaguely. She had been asleep forever, or at least, that's how she felt. Her joints were so stiff... Had she been at a party? She couldn't quite remember. She remembered Christmas shopping, but that might have been the day before... was it? God, she still had so much to do before the holidays. The food had been ordered, but it had yet to be picked up from Edgartown Meat And Fish. All of her gift shopping was done except for little things—stocking stuffers mostly. Rather brilliantly, she thought, she had bought—some of the family—theatre tickets. They all had so much crap already, so much clutter. Who needed more junk? Giving people the gift of making memories—that was the way to go. Besides, they were easy to wrap. She just stuck them in a card and put them on the tree! Had she put them on the tree yet? She was pretty sure that she

7

had. Had she put up the tree, yet? God, she felt so out of it.

She still needed to wake up. Maybe she'd make some coffee. Had she been napping?

Her in-laws were coming for the holidays and that was never an easy thing. They were great people, make no mistake, but they were still in-laws. She never felt quite good enough when she set the table for example. She always did it differently that her mother-in-law would. She made gravy that was thinner, or thicker, or lumpier than her mother-in-law did. Once her mother-in-law had actually commented on just how smooth the gravy was. Naturally, her tone was such that it implied just how much everyone preferred lumpy gravy, but she shouldn't worry about it. Was she paranoid? She really needed to let it go. It was gravy.

The air was so heavy. It smelled sweet. It smelled wet. Maybe 'dank' was a better description. Was that the ocean that smelled like that? She listened for the waves at Wasque. She couldn't hear them. Funny. She could always hear the waves at Wasque. That was one of the reason she had asked her husband to build so far down on Chappaquiddick. The walks on Wasque were one of her favourite things in the world...

She could see the beach now. The colours were so vibrant on the beach. Funny, she could see the beach, but she couldn't hear it. It was so beautiful—what a warm, sunny day.

8

Her throat felt dry. Her breathing was hoarse.

She ran along the beach. Her bare feet were wet and cool in the sand. Chappaquiddick on a hot day was the best thing in the world.

Wait, it was Christmas. She was on Chappaquiddick for Christmas. It wasn't hot out—it was cold. What was the matter with her? She needed to focus…it was so hard…

She looked back over her shoulder at her Daddy. He was chasing her down the beach. Daddy was so handsome. She loved that he was the youngest, most handsome, Daddy of all of her friends. He was shouting at her, but she couldn't hear him. He was too far away and the waves were too loud. She laughed. It was a little girl laugh—a giggle with a lot of life in it. She liked the sound, even in her own head. There wasn't a happier sound in the world than that of a child laughing, she thought.

She knew her eyes were open. She opened her eyes and closed them. She could feel the tickle of her eyelashes brushing against each other. There was no light. She couldn't see, she couldn't see a thing. She ran her hands along her body. This was real. Her hands were cold, clammy. Dirt stuck to them when she felt her legs. It smelled so earthy—sickly, sweet.

As she ran toward the ocean, the sand got harder, wetter, easier to run on. Her Daddy was bigger but he couldn't catch up. She looked behind her and she could see him. He was running and getting farther and farther behind her. How was that possible? They were supposed to be playing tag. He was still screaming at her. Was Daddy crying? Maybe he was laughing. She had never seen her Daddy cry.

Warm stickiness ran into her mouth. It ran from her face, from her nose. She licked at it instinctively. Its metallic tang told her it was blood. She definitely had a nosebleed.

She looked at her to-do list. She made a Christmas checklist every year. It was really the only way to stay organised. All of her groceries were on the kitchen counter. She loved it. What a feast! This was definitely going to be the best Christmas ever. They had never hosted it on Chappaquiddick before, thinking that it would be too much trouble for everyone, but this year they had said, to hell with it! It was going to be worth it. She could tell. Her feet were so cold. She looked down to see the ocean wash over them. She was up to her ankles in the surf.

With both hands, she felt her face. It was cold and covered with grime. She brushed off the dirt. Her throat really hurt now—burned. Her chest burned too; it burned from the inside out. Her lungs were tight, restricted. She tried to breathe deeply, but there just wasn't enough air. With the last attempt, she convulsed in a heavy cough. She lurched forward and hit her forehead on something hard. Her body shook. Blood ran down the back of her throat.

She waded deeper into the surf. She had never been scared of the ocean. She loved its big waves. She giggled her little girl laugh as the cold ocean rushed at her, inviting her in. Her long, sun-bleached hair stuck to her

10

cheeks in salty clumps. Her pink summer dress slapped to her skin. It was her favourite dress. She hoped it wasn't wrecked. Mommy would fix it. It would dry. God, she hadn't seen it in ages. She reached out into the waves and saw her small pink hand. It was the hand of a child. A large wave crashed over her—consuming her.

Sand fell in her eyes when she hit her head. Reflexively, her eyelids shut, but only succeeded in grinding the sand in deeper. She tried to get up, but there wasn't room. She tried to roll over, but there wasn't room. She felt the walls around her. They were wood—planks of wood. She felt as far as she could reach. The occasional nail pricked her finger. She coughed again—more blood. She was getting colder.

She looked down and saw her pretty pink dress floating in the sea around her. It was such a nice dress. It had frills at the bottom. She loved the way they floated in the water. Her dress ballooned in the wave; it looked like the jellyfish that sometimes washed up on shore. Mommy told her never to touch jellyfish, no matter how pretty they looked. The water swirled around her. She could see her underwear. There were so many bubbles everywhere. They tickled.

Her hands and feet were heavy and impossible to lift. She could feel them lying beside her like wet sandbags. Her head lay on the wooden slat beneath her. She could feel something crawling in her hair. Her throat stopped hurting and she could see the ocean, she could see the sun. She

11

was running. She could see her Daddy. He was so handsome, like when she was a little girl. Daddy had been dead so long. God, how she missed him. It was so good to see him. They were running on the beach...

The water pulled her down. The blues got darker. The water got colder. Her pink dress looked purple, then navy, then black—everything was going black. The last thing she could see was her hand...it was so small.

2

Chief Laurie Knickles stared at the wall in front of her. Thick sweatshirts of every colour bulged from the wood and metal shelves. They all had one thing in common—The Black Dog logo. Her husband may be a washashore, but he insisted on dressing like a tourist. Laurie couldn't remember the last time that he had worn an article of clothing that wasn't blazoned with the words Martha's Vineyard, Edgartown, or Oak Bluffs, or embossed with the iconic Black Dog logo. On a really banner day, Charles might be wearing a sweatshirt with a Black dog on it, board shorts that read Martha's Vineyard, and a hat that read Vineyard 1642. That's what he had come down wearing to go out for dinner a week ago. Laurie had been adamant. *"You have to take something off and replace it with an article of clothing that I can't read. I don't care which one it is, but one of them has got to go, or we're not leaving*

this house! I'm sick of eating dinner with a billboard!"
Charles had gone back upstairs and put on a plain blue T-shirt. It was a Slip77 shirt with a small white seagull and orange sun—representative of the secession flag—tastefully dyed on the left breast. Laurie knew he'd selected it on purpose—it was her favourite shirt. It looked great on him. In fact, Laurie had just left Slip77 where she had loaded up on Christmas gifts for Charles. Their stuff was top quality and there was plenty to choose from that didn't have that touristy feel. Now, to appease his touristy heart, Laurie was at Black Dog looking for something Charles would like, but wouldn't make her crazy. She had seen a beautiful black full-zip hoodie with red and white trim, but Charles hated wearing black—he thought it was depressing. Laurie set down her bags and reached into the shelf in front of her. She pulled out a moss green, full-zip, hoodie with cream and burnt-orange trim. It was very soft and the colours were Charles' favourites—warm and earthy. Not only could she could live with it, she rather liked it. Pleased with herself, she picked up her bags and headed toward the cash. She still had time to walk down the street and get a bowl of chowder at The Wharf for lunch.

Having paid for Charles' present, Laurie stepped out onto Edgartown's Main Street. She inhaled deeply. The air was cold and fresh. It felt good in her throat and in her lungs. When she took a deep breath like that, she got the salty tang of sea air in her nose. It reminded her of when she had first moved to the island, when the ocean had filled every breath. Now, she only caught it here and there, when she took an extra deep breath or went for a walk in the early morning after a rainstorm.

Big snowflakes fluttered toward the ground as Laurie walked toward Water Street. A snowfall on a sunny, windless, afternoon was one of Laurie's favourite things. It reminded her of being a little girl in Canada. Laurie and Charles had grown up together in Toronto before losing touch in their teens. When they had bumped into each other again, both literally and figuratively—neither of them had been looking where they were going—you could have knocked Laurie over with a feather. She couldn't believe it was Charles. Eventually, it seemed, everyone came to Martha's Vineyard. Three years of long distance relationship had been enough for both of them. They had married last year. The wedding, organised by their dear friend Edie at The Edgartown Inn, had been beautiful; however, the days leading up to it had been harrowing. Someone had tried to kill Charles because they believed Charles knew something about their involvement in the death of a young man. Charles had ended up in the hospital, but they got through it. The guilty parties were imprisoned and the wedding had taken place. After taking some time, they had honeymooned on Nantucket, only to come back early and find themselves in the middle of a case of multiple murders. Someone had decided to take care of their personal problems by removing three women from the island permanently. Charles and Laurie had helped their police friends Chief Jefferies and Detective Jack Burrell, wrap that case over a year ago. The peace and quiet of bucolic living that had drawn them to Martha's Vineyard in the first place, had returned. All was well.

The past summer had been beautiful and the shoulder season had been quiet. Laurie's favourite month on the island was September. The September sun burned as bright, and warm as it did in August, but the island moved at a much slower pace. Now, it was December. This weekend would mark Charles' first *Christmas In Edgartown*. They had been married and living on-island last Christmas, but the second weekend in December was the island's *Christmas In Edgartown* celebration and Charles had been in Toronto visiting family. This year, they had plans to do it up proper! Laurie and Charles both loved Christmas and Christmas on Martha's Vineyard was picture perfect. The wrought-iron lampposts were trimmed with pine garland and Christmas lights. The town hall, local businesses, and the Memorial Wharf were all trimmed in lights. Christmas trees on green wood lattices garrisoned the street corners, and tonight would be the lighting of the Edgartown Lighthouse marking the beginning of Christmas In Edgartown. Hundreds of people would gather at The Shore Line Hotel, many arriving by horse-drawn wagon, for eggnog, hot toddies, and carolling. The evening would climax with a countdown to the

Edgartown Lighthouse being lit with Christmas lights. It was like having an entire weekend directed by Frank Capra. Laurie loved it—a weekend of pure schmaltzy perfection.

Laurie was hungry. As she headed up Main Street toward her truck, she was sure that every passerby could hear her stomach growling. She would have gone directly in for lunch from shopping, but she was carrying far too many bags to manage sitting at a table. Laurie would unload everything, then relax, and have lunch at The Wharf in comfort. It was a short and pleasant walk to the parking lot just past Edgartown Books.

Edgartown was bustling with holiday excitement in contrast to the stillness that had blanketed the island for months. The entire island had been populated with no one but islanders since Columbus Day. Until twenty-four hours ago, the now bright and energetic storefronts had been dark. Restaurant doors now swung continuously, emitting bursts of laughter and music into the streets; they had been bolted and silent only a day prior. Every hotel room was booked for this weekend and had been for quite some time.

Laurie watched young couples and families bounce their way down Main Street. Their expressions were those usually worn by children in toy stores. They laughed and wore Santa hats; they bought roasted chestnuts and hot cider from pop-up street vendors.

"Merry Christmas, Chief!" called out a blonde woman with large sunglasses and a fur hat.

"Merry Christmas, Sandra!" Laurie called.

"I hope you and Charles will be at the Minnesingers Concert at The Old Whaling Church tonight!" called Sandra. "Katie's nephew is singing!"

"We wouldn't miss it! We already bought our tickets! I want Charles to get the full *Christmas In Edgartown* experience!" The two women waved and Laurie continued toward the parking lot. She passed Edgartown Books and cut across the parkette toward her truck. Laurie pulled her hand out of her mitten. She dug around in her coat pocket for her keys, found them, and popped the back hatch. It opened with a click. The cargo space was large and there was more than enough room for her packages. She laid them in gently and closed the hatch again. Laurie had left the squad car at home opting for their new Toyota Land Cruiser instead. It was "new" to them, but in fact it was a 1993. Laurie loved it—it ran like a champ. Sometimes, when she was off-duty, she just didn't feel like driving a squad car. She certainly couldn't take the squad car fishing on Wasque or through the bush out toward Quansoo. Having 'Chilmark Racing Stripes' on the Land Cruiser was one thing, but having them on the police cruiser was quite another. Laurie chuckled to herself. When Chief Philip Squanto of the Chilmark Police Department had first explained to her that 'Chilmark Racing Stripes' were actually scratches from the bush and

18

not auto-detailing like she'd thought, he'd laughed so hard that he had dropped his fishing rod, and had to chase it into the surf. The image of the big man lunging into the ocean still made her laugh. That was a long time ago. She had still been considered an outsider then—a moniker she was slowly shedding.

Packages stowed and the hatch shut, Laurie headed back down toward The Wharf. There was a bowl of chowder and maybe a clubhouse sandwich waiting with her name on it.

*   *   *

"Jesus H. Christ! Fenway! You're going to drive me to distraction!" Fenway The Beagle stared up at Charles with big brown eyes that tore right through Charles' heart no matter what the dog had done. *"Give me that shoe!"* Charles reached for the shoe in the puppy's mouth, but Fenway was too fast for him. Fenway The Beagle yelped with a mouthful of Nike runner, and bolted for the back door. Without breaking speed, he head-butted his way through the trap door that Charles had installed only a week ago. Bubbas, the mackerel tabby, lay on the desk beside Charles' laptop. She absorbed the situation with large green eyes and an expression of bemused disapproval.

Charles, who had started to give chase, gave up when the dog made it outside. "Fine. That's another pair for you, Fenway." Charles shook his head. No one had warned him that the biggest expense for dog owners was footwear. The phone on the desk vibrated. Bubbas reached out her paw, smacked the phone, and connected the call. "Thanks, Bubbas." Charles moved her paw and picked up his iPhone. "Hey, babe."

"Hi!" said Laurie. "Did Bubbas answer the phone again?"

"She did."

"I love that! We need to put that on YouTube! What are you up to?" she asked.

"Writing," said Charles. Charles could hear the smile on Laurie's face; it was contagious.

"How's it going?" Laurie asked.

"Pretty well, I think. I'm not really sure. I've never written a book before—maybe it sucks," Charles chuckled.

"I doubt it," Laurie said. "I read your short stories and they were pretty great."

"I'm not sure that I can trust you for an unbiased opinion," Charles grinned.

"Then stop asking me to read them," Laurie said. Her tone wasn't even half-serious. "I laughed at all the right places, didn't I?"

"True," agreed Charles.

"Exactly," Laurie stated. "Stop being so goddamn needy! It's exhausting. Are you still coming down to meet me?"

"Absolutely. Are you done your shopping for me?"

"Yes, but I've kept all the receipts. If you keep up this level of neurosis, I'm taking back all of your presents and buying you therapy sessions instead!" Laurie laughed.

Charles laughed in spite of himself. "Hey, when I get down there, let's go to Shirley's Hardware on the way home—I want to buy a shelf or something. Fenway got another Nike. We're going to have to keep the shoes off the floor. That damned dog—I swear he's going to grow up thinking his name is Jesus H Christ!"

Laurie laughed, "You can't blame a dog for being a dog!"

"The hell I can't," said Charles.

"He's not even full-grown yet. Sweet little man is still a puppy."

"They were your runners."

"What? Which ones?" yelled Laurie.

"Your new purple and pink Nike's." Charles' tone was mildly smug.

"Jesus H Christ!" Laurie barked. *"That little bugger!"*

"That's what I said," Charles chuckled. At the sound of the trap door's swing, Charles turned around. Fenway the Beagle trotted into the room and sat down. "I'll be in Edgartown in an hour. Where should I meet you?"

"The Wharf? Bar side?"

"Sounds good. See you soon." Charles hung up. He looked down at Fenway. "It's not good, buddy—you got mommy mad at you now."

Fenway The Beagle cocked his head to the side and whined sweetly.

Charles shook his head. "It's a good thing you're cute."

*   *   *

Charles walked into The Wharf and spotted Laurie immediately. She was dunking a sandwich into seafood chowder and watching football highlights. Charles liked to watch her when she wasn't looking. She was so beautiful. Her naturally streaked blonde hair fell around her shoulders and her expression was one of happiness and contentment. The fact that she had agreed to team up and face life with him still blew him away. He wasn't sure exactly why she thought she got a good bargain, but he wasn't questioning it—he thought he got the deal of the century. He walked toward her with an unconscious smile, pulling his arms out of his coat as he went. "Hey!" he said.

Laurie turned at the sound of his voice. "How bad is my shoe?"

"I'm not really sure," said Charles. "He bolted outside with it. It's probably under the porch. I'll get it later."

"Okay. Thanks," Laurie smiled. "Here, want half? I can't finish it. My eyes were bigger than my stomach."

Charles reached for the sandwich half and took a bite. The bacon, turkey, cheese, and bread worked magic on his taste buds. Maybe he was hungrier than he thought. "Are we staying for a while?"

Laurie shrugged. "If you want."

"I'm going to order a Bad Martha's and a bowl of chowder. You want a beer?"

Laurie nodded with her mouth full.

Charles turned to find the bartender. Catching his eye, he called out, "Two Bad Martha's and a bowl of chowder please, Sam. When you have a moment. Thanks a lot." Charles returned to Laurie. "Did you get all of your shopping done?"

"Mostly. I just have stocking-stuffers left now, I think." Laurie smiled. She was quite pleased with herself.

"Wow! I'm impressed!" Charles said.

"So am I. I'm usually running around like a crazy woman on the twenty-fourth of December!"

"Really? You'd never be able to tell from your heart-felt gifts. I will never forget the Christmas of the chainsaw and the edible underwear!"

Laurie laughed out loud. "Shut up! I never got you a chainsaw *or* edible underwear!"

"I know and it's all I've ever wanted," Charles frowned and clutched at his chest melodramatically.

"Oh my God, you're such an idiot," Laurie chuckled. "But you're *my* idiot."

"True story."

The bartender brought their pints and Charles lifted his glass to Laurie. "To my first official *Christmas In Edgartown!*"

Laurie picked up her glass. "Cheers!"

They clinked glasses and each of them took a healthy gulp. Setting their pints down, they looked at each other with smiles of pure pleasure. Neither one of them said anything—they didn't have to. They just smiled and they both knew what the smiles meant. Laurie turned back to her chowder and Charles finished his sandwich. When his soup arrived, Charles ate it in silence while Laurie nursed her pint and watched the football highlights. Charles asked Sam the bartender for The Boston Globe and rifled through to the book reviews. Seeing that the new Stephen King book had been reviewed, he folded the paper for easy handling and started to read.

After almost an hour had passed, Laurie stretched and looked at her watch. The football highlights were over, Sam the bartender had cleared away their dishes, and Charles had finished his second pint. "Are you about ready to go?" she asked.

"I am." Charles nodded.

"Good, because if you want to go and buy a shelf and bring it home before we go to the Minnesingers concert, we'd better get moving," said Laurie. She stepped down from the bar chair and put on her coat.

"Oh, good point," said Charles. "Where did you park?"

24

"Over behind Edgartown Books," she said.

"Why all the way up there? That's not like you."

"It was all I could find! This town is crazy this weekend," Laurie explained.

"No kidding." Charles put on his coat and hat and followed Laurie out of the restaurant. They headed up the street. "Who is going to this concert-thing tonight?"

"It will be packed! Everyone is going," said Laurie.

"No, I mean, are we meeting anyone there, or is it just us?" Charles elaborated.

"We're meeting Edie and Jeff and Chris." Laurie smiled with holiday excitement. "It's going to be a great concert—you wait and see!"

"I'm sure it will be awesome. I love choral music. I grew up with it. My mom sang in a choir, remember?" Charles reached out an arm and put it around Laurie's shoulders. She leaned into him.

"Oh, that's right. I'd forgotten," said Laurie. "The Amadeus Singers?"

"That's right! I'm impressed."

"I had totally forgotten about them," she said.

"Jack!" Charles called to a young couple across the street. The couple stopped, looked in the direction of Charles and Laurie, waved, and crossed Main Street in their direction.

Detective Jack Burrell was in his uniform, complete with winter coat and hat. Beside him a girl was bundled into a black winter coat with a fur-lined hood. She was

25

wearing a pink hat, mitts, and scarf. Her face barely peeked out from behind all of her defences against the cold.

"Virginia is that you in there?" Charles laughed.

"I don't like the cold!" Came a muffled and distressed voice.

"No kidding!" Charles said. "Are you guys going to that concert-thing tonight? The Old Whaling Church was heated last I checked."

Jack shook his head. "Nah, we're skipping it. We'll be at the lighting of the lighthouse though. You guys going up for that after?"

"I don't know." Charles looked at Laurie. "Are we?"

"If the concert lets out in time, absolutely—but we'd better get a move on!"

"Where are you guys heading now?" Charles asked Jack.

"We're meeting some friends at The Newes," said Jack. "Then we're all heading up to The Shore Line Hotel. Maybe we'll see you there?"

"Sounds good!" said Charles. Charles patted Jack on the shoulder as the two couples separated. When Jack and Virginia were out of earshot, Charles turned to Laurie. "I like them as a couple," he said.

"Don't get too used to the idea," said Laurie.

"Why not?" asked Charles. "Has the island's broken telephone told you something?"

26

"No, nothing like that. I'm just saying Jack's a cop," Laurie said. "Being a cop makes starting a relationship hard on young people. Don't hold your breath."

"Well, aren't you the prophet of doom!" Charles and Laurie crossed the street and made their way across the small parkette beside the bookstore. The parking lot was just behind it. "You and I made out alright and I didn't even live in this country!"

"They're not even a couple yet, Charles." Laurie shook her head.

"I know but still—"

"Charles!" Laurie cried and ran across the parking lot.

"What's the matter?" Charles' eyes followed Laurie. She stopped on the other side of the lot and turned to look at him. Her eyes were wide.

"Our truck's been stolen!"

3

"Pass me the blown-glass Santa Claus. The one that's just a head," asked Chris. "Please?"

"Where is it?" asked Jeff. He picked up a box and tossed it onto the couch.

"Would you be a little more careful with those, please?" snapped Chris. "You just tossed about three-hundred-dollars worth of hand-painted, blown-glass ornaments across the room!"

"Three-hundred-dollars?" exclaimed Jeff.

"You didn't spend it—I did. So, don't get all bent out of shape. Why do you always have to be such a jerk at Christmas?" Chris looked at his husband with exasperation.

"I don't like Christmas," Jeff mumbled.

"Why not? There's no reason for it. No one has asked you to do anything except show up! Yes—you're "helping" me decorate the tree, but if it weren't Christmas, you'd be helping me clean up. We're having company over—we do it all year—there are always things to do! So, get over yourself. If you *decide* to be pleasant, if you *decide* to be happy, there's a very good chance that you actually will be." Chris came down from the stepladder beside the enormous pine tree. "You know what? Go upstairs, have your shower, and wash away all of your crap. Come back down with a positive, happy attitude or don't come down at all."

"Aren't we going to the Minnesingers concert with Charles and Laurie?" asked Jeff. He stood awkwardly in the centre of the room like a chastised child.

"*I'm going to the Minnesingers concert* and so are Charles and Laurie and we would absolutely love to have you there—honestly Jeff, we would—I mean it. It's Christmas and I love you, but I shit you not, Peter Jefferies, if you don't get a positive attitude, I'm leaving you here. It's bad enough that I have to deal with you like this at the holidays, I'm not inflicting your lousy disposition on our friends!" Chris glared at Jeff until he skulked out of the room. "Honestly!" said Chris.

Chris walked over to the couch and picked up the box of ornaments from where Jeff had tossed it. He moved the tissue paper around with his hand and inspected the ornaments inside. As he suspected, they were fine. The

29

painted glass ornaments were so light that they practically floated in the box. Chris would have been shocked if Jeff had actually damaged any of them—that wasn't why he was so angry. Chris was angry because they could be having a really happy holiday; they could be laughing and enjoying Christmas, but they weren't because Jeff was moping around like a grounded teenager. What was even more irritating was that Chris couldn't figure out why. Jeff wasn't like that, not normally. Oh sure, he could be grumpy. Chris actually liked Jeff's grumpy, quiet guy routine—he thought it was kinda sexy—but this was completely different. Something got under Jeff's skin every year at Christmas and he wasn't telling Chris what it was. As far as Chris knew, Jeff had never told anyone what it was. All Chris knew was that each Christmas was worse than the last, and he was fed up. Funny, when Chris had been a defenseman on the Chicago Blackhawks, if a teammate was being a jerk, Chris would get into a fistfight with the guy and everything would sort itself out. Within hours, they'd be laughing about it over beers. Now, if he tried that, he'd be arrested for spousal abuse. Chris chuckled. That didn't seem fair.

Chris reached into the box of ornaments and lifted out the Santa Claus that he had asked Jeff to pass to him. Light as a feather and trimmed with a white and silver beard, the jolly face sparkled. Blue eyes twinkled, and pink cheeks glowed under the red Santa hat. Although it was difficult for Chris to commit, he was fairly certain that this one was his favourite ornament. That was a bold statement as their tree was trimmed with some real beauties—a royal blue peacock with a real peacock feather tail was a close runner-up. Chris slid a hook through the loop on the Santa hat and hung it strategically at eye level for optimal exposure. He stepped back. All he had to do now was place the star on the top. He decided to pour himself a rum and eggnog first.

The kitchen in the Johns/Jefferies household opened onto the family room and dining room. Chris walked around the island counter that acted as both a partition and a breakfast counter and pulled open the refrigerator door. With a carton of eggnog in one hand and a bottle of rum in the other, Chris kicked the door closed with his foot. He mixed a drink that was heavy on ice and even heavier on rum. He swirled the cocktail with his finger and—when it had been blended to his satisfaction—sprinkled it with nutmeg from a tin on the counter. Chris licked the bold mixture from his forefinger. He raised the glass to his mouth and took the first mouthful, letting a rough chunk of ice slip past his lips. The ice rolled around on his tongue before he crushed it between his teeth with a pleasing crunch. Chris walked back into the living area and flicked on the gas fireplace. The hearth flickered to life, bathing the room in a warm and comfortable glow. The light from the flames danced on the metallic and shimmering Christmas tree ornaments, tossing light across the room. Chris sat down and took another mouthful of the creamy, vibrant cocktail and dimmed the lights. How could Jeff hate Christmas when it brought such delights as rum and eggnog? On that score alone— Christmas was worth it. Chris picked up his iPhone, opened the remote app for his AppleTV, and then returned it to the coffee table. Peggy Lee purred out of the surround sound bar. A lot of people didn't realise that Peggy Lee sang all of Rosemary Clooney's parts on the original *White Christmas* soundtrack album. The soundtrack was released on Decca Records and because Rosemary Clooney had an exclusive contract with Columbia, she was not allowed to appear. Peggy Lee stepped in. It was a win/win for Chris. *White Christmas* was his favourite Christmas movie and he had always preferred Lee to Clooney. Eventually, iTunes released *The Ultimate White Christmas* that was a hybrid of the original and re-recordings, but Chris still liked the songs by Peggy Lee best.

"The tree looks great."

Chris turned toward the sound of the voice behind him. Jeff stood in the archway. He was wearing a clean pair of jeans and a winter sweater that Chris had given to him last year for Christmas. His hair was tousled and a still little wet.

"Is that rum and eggnog?" asked Jeff.

"It is," Chris nodded.

"It looks good. Can I refresh yours?"

"Please." Chris took the last mouthful in his glass before raising it over his head for Jeff.

32

Jeff took the glass and ran his fingers through Chris's hair. His socks padded into the kitchen barely audible over Peggy Lee singing *White Christmas*. He mixed two drinks and returned to the living room.

"Thank you," said Chris, accepting his drink.

"You're welcome." Jeff sat in a chair beside Chris. He reached out his glass. "Cheers."

"Cheers," said Chris. They both took a sip and then sat in silence for a moment, looking at the tree.

"Are you putting the star on top?" asked Jeff.

"I was waiting for you."

*   *   *

Mike Walker made the last delivery on his route that evening and headed home. He drove his white pick-up truck down Beach Road in the direction of Oak Bluffs. With any luck, Trish would be pretty close to being ready, but not quite ready yet. Mike would need five minutes to shower, five minutes to shave, and five minutes to dress— fifteen minutes in total. Add that to the ten minutes that it was going to take him to drive home, and that gave Trish twenty-five minutes to finish getting ready. If she was pulling her boots out of the closet when he walked in the front door, they'd be fine. On the other hand, if she was still blow-drying her hair—they would never get out of there. Mike loved Trish to bits, but he had never seen a girl so slow at getting ready. He had threatened to put a chalk outline around her once just to make sure she was actually moving. Trish had failed to see the humour in this remark and she had been quite vocal about it. Mike hadn't mentioned it again. Damn it all to hell though, this was his first Christmas in Edgartown and he didn't want to miss it! They were supposed to go and meet a bunch of friends down at The Newes From America. Then, they would head up North Water Street in a horse and wagon to watch the lighting of The Edgartown Lighthouse! Mike thought it all sounded great. Mike loved Christmas and this was his first one with snow! He had come up from Austin, Texas less than a year ago—not long before the kidnappings and the murders. In fact, Mike had delivered a package to Trish's store—Pretty Vineyard Girls—that had been pivotal to that case. That's how he had met Trish. They had hit it off right away. Now, they lived together in Trish's blue and white, gingerbread cottage in Oak Bluffs. It was cosy. Sometimes, Trish thought it was a little too cosy, but Mike liked it. If they were ever going to start a family though—which was big on Mike's list—they were going to need a bigger house.

Mike pulled up to the front of the house and shut off the engine. He collected his bag, thermos, empty Mocha Motts cups, and everything else he had collected over the course of the day. Satisfied that he was leaving the truck in the same state in which he had found it that morning, he got out, and closed the door behind him. Mike hated a dirty truck. He always thought that you could tell a lot about a person by the way they treat their belongings.

Mike's heavy work boots clomped up the short steps to the front door and with the two fingers he had available, he turned the knob. The door swung open easily. Right in front of him, on her hands and knees, Trish foraged in the closet for her boots. Her denim-clad behind aimed directly at him while her face was buried deep in a closet of coats and shoes. Mike smiled and heaved a heavy breath.

"I'll be ready in a minute, honey! You'd better hurry up!" Trish's muffled voice called out.

"I won't be long," said Mike. "Can you help me with this stuff so I can get my boots off please, babe?"

"Oh, sure!" Trish wriggled herself out of the closet and turned around. She assessed Mike's predicament. "Actually, why don't I just take your boots off and then you can walk that stuff right back into the kitchen. Okay?"

"That would be great," said Mike. He waited as she fidgeted with his bootlaces and one foot at a time, pulled him out of his boots.

"Jeez!" exclaimed Trish. "Do these boots have a hole in them already? They're brand new!"

"No. They don't have holes in them. Why?"

"You're feet are soaking wet!" Trish exclaimed.

"The boots are fine—they're just sweaty."

"Oh, gross!" Trish scrunched up her nose. *That's lovely.*"

Mike laughed. "You're the one who offered to take my boots off for me! It's not like I sit at a desk all day." He headed back into the kitchen and set down the contents of the truck on the counter. "Just let me go and have a shower and I'll be fresh as the morning dew."

"Okay, hurry up. I just need to find my other boot..."

*　　*　　*

"*What do you mean, 'It's been stolen'?*" asked Charles. His eyes were wide with disbelief.

"What's to understand, Charles?" Laurie exclaimed. "I left the truck here and it's not here anymore!" She kicked at the ground to prove her point. "It was right goddamn here!"

"Well, what do we do now? Do we call the police? You are the police!"

Laurie pulled out her iPhone, made a few deliberate taps to the screen, and brought it to her ear. "Jack. Can you come back to the parking lot off of South Summer—across from Alchemy? You know where I mean? My truck's been stolen!" She hung up and looked at Charles. "Christ!" she said.

"It will turn up, Laurie," Charles said calmly. "Where are they going to go? We're on Martha's Vineyard for God's sake. It's not like they can leave the island. All of the guys at the Steamship will recognise that it's your truck, right away. Even that short squat broad who hates your guts—the one who thinks she owns the Steamship Authority—wouldn't let anyone leave with your truck!" Charles smiled and took Laurie by the shoulders.

36

"That's not the point," she said. She shrugged his hands away. She wasn't ready to be consoled just yet. "All of my Christmas presents were in the back!"

"You'll get them back," said Charles. "Christmas is still two weeks away. That's plenty of time to recover your truck and your presents. Kids probably just took it for a ride—they wouldn't even realise that your packages were in the back. Did you cover them up?"

Laurie thought about it a moment and then nodded. "Yeah," she said.

"Well, there you go; they don't even know your packages are there."

Jack Burrell half walked/half jogged into the parking lot and stopped when he had reached Laurie's side. "What happened, Chief?"

"I told you my goddamn car has been stolen!" Laurie barked.

Jack took a step back. "Ok. Your truck?"

"Well, no one's going to steal my freaking squad car are they? Give your head a shake, Jack!"

Charles stepped between them. "Give us a minute, would you please Jack?"

Jack's face was a mix of surprise and relief. "Oh— sure, Charles. Where was the truck parked?"

Charles motioned toward the spot where Laurie had indicated she left the truck and Jack took a few steps over to inspect the area. Charles took Laurie by the arm and guided her in the opposite direction. "What the hell is the matter with you?" he asked.

Laurie glared at him and began to wrench her arm free. Charles wouldn't let go. His grip was firm. Laurie looked down at her arm and then at Charles. Her eyes softened and her face relaxed. Tears of emotion welled in the tiny troughs of her lower lids. "I just so wanted your first Christmas in Edgartown to be perfect. Now, all of your presents have been stolen by some asshole that felt like joyriding in my truck." She spoke softly to hide the tremble in it. For the most part, she succeeded.

"My first Christmas in Edgartown will be perfect because I'm here with you and we're here with our friends. The only thing threatening to make it *not perfect* is you freaking out like a crazy woman on one of our closest friends in a way that you'll regret later." Charles smiled at her. "Jack is just trying to help."

Laurie nodded and wiped at her eyes. "You're right. I hate it when you're right."

"Don't worry, I'm planning to screw something up big time between now and the holidays. You know, kind of an early Christmas present!" Charles' grin became more mischievous.

"Thanks," Laurie said. "I'd like that." She turned, looked toward Jack, and then back to Charles. "Look, I got this. Why don't you go on to the concert and meet Edie. I wouldn't be able to concentrate on the concert anyway. Maybe I can catch up with you at intermission."

38

"You sure?"

"Absolutely." Laurie nodded and smiled a genuine smile. "Thanks." She kissed him.

"What for?" Charles asked.

"Just for being you. Go."

Charles turned and headed toward the church. Laurie patted him on the bum as he walked away.

4

Edie sat on a wooden pew in the Old Whaling Church. The sanctuary had been decorated for Christmas and she was impressed—it looked terrific. She wasn't sure who had been on the Preservation Trust's decorating committee this year, but they had done a really great job. The white Greek revival architecture had been trimmed with boughs of pine and red velvet ribbons. The stage had been set up for The Minnesingers' who by Edie's estimation had sold out the Whaling Church's four hundred and seventy seat capacity. It was filling up quickly.

Edie started to feel mildly uneasy. She was the first of their group to arrive and she was holding seats for Charles and Laurie. There was no assigned seating, just pews. She didn't relish the idea of having to tell someone that she was saving seats for friends who had yet to materialize. Something about those words brought her right back to middle school. She hadn't liked confrontation then and she didn't like it now. She didn't think anyone would give her a difficult time over it—especially if she dropped the Chief's name—but it would still be uncomfortable. When she was married, she had always let her husband do those things. He had been so good with people. Edie had no problem taking charge when she was at The Edgartown Inn, but that was her domain, her home turf. This was different. Edie spread out her coat on the pew beside her as a deterrent. She hoped the coat would give the illusion that it was not her coat at all, but rather one belonging to someone who had just slipped out to use the washroom. As if on cue, a tall man slid in beside her and sat down. She barely had a chance to get her hands out from underneath him. Edie was taken aback. He hadn't said, 'Hello' or even nodded in her direction. He just sat down. There would barely be room for one person between them let alone two. As Edie gauged the space between herself and the tall stranger, she noticed to her horror that he was sitting on her coat. Splaying it out to ward off unwanted company had been an exercise in futility. In fact, it seemed to have quite the opposite effect. It was as if Edie had padded the pew and made it look all the more inviting. The tall gentleman didn't seem to notice at all. He removed his hat, opened up his program, and began to read.

Edie tugged gently on her coat with what she considered to be a universally accepted, passive-aggressive hint. It had no effect. The man didn't acknowledge her. Instead, he turned the page of his program and continued reading.

Edie felt her face flush. She stepped up her game. As loudly as she could muster, she cleared her throat, and pulled a little harder—still nothing.

Finally, she had no choice. "Excuse me, but you are sitting on my coat," she said to the tall stranger. Edie felt her face get hotter and she was embarrassed at her own timidity. She talked to new people all the time at the Inn. She had even been known to kick a drunk out of the library that had inadvertently gone to the wrong hotel! Why, when taken out of that familiar environment, should she be any different?

"Was that so difficult?" asked the tall man.

"Pardon?" asked Edie.

"You've been trying to get my attention since I sat down. I just prefer to be addressed like a civilised human being." The man turned and looked at Edie and smiled broadly.

Edie was taken aback. She hadn't realised from his profile just how handsome he was. His skin was smooth, dark and unblemished. His smile revealed perfect teeth. His eyes were onyx but not cold—quite the contrary. There was heat in his smile, in his eyes.

"I assume you would like your coat back?" the tall stranger asked. His voice was deep and smooth.

Edie regained her composure. "Yes, I would!" Hearing the sound of her own voice strengthened her resolve and she spoke again. "I consider it very rude of you to ignore me if you knew you were on my coat! Did it not occur to you that I was saving those seats for my friends? You could have asked before you sat down."

"Why didn't you just ask me to move instead of going on yanking, and pulling, and clearing your throat? A bit juvenile, don't you think? You're not a school girl anymore—far from it, in fact." He raised an eyebrow. "I mean didn't you feel just a little silly?"

"I beg your pardon?" Edie glared at the tall man.

"You were yanking on your coat like one yanks on a dog's leash. Clearing your throat like a character in a Noel Coward farce—such theatrics. I did not see your coat when I sat down on it, but when you started with your dramatics, I was intrigued to see how far you would take it." The man lowered his eyebrow, smiled again, and held out a hand. "My name is—"

"I don't give a damn what your name is! You are the rudest man that I have ever met! If you will excuse me!" Edie exclaimed. She stood up. "I think I'll sit somewhere else."

"Suit yourself. It's a big church." He shrugged.

"Histrionics!" Edie slid past the tall man without waiting for him to stand. His long legs pressed into her as she struggled past, but she made it into the aisle. "I am not hysterical—thank you very much!"

"That argument would carry a lot more weight if you weren't yelling at a total stranger minutes before a children's Christmas pageant. Don't you agree?" Unruffled, he turned back toward his program.

Edie turned away from the tall man, made her way back a few rows, noticed a vacancy, and slid in. She could feel her eyes misting up. She always cried when she got mad—she hated it. Her heart pounded in her chest. *Calm down,* she thought. *Don't let that jackass spoil your evening. For Christ's sake where the hell were Charles and Laurie?* Edie tilted her head up toward the ceiling in an effort to stop any tears from rolling down her cheeks. Blindly, she fished around in her purse for a tissue—she knew there was one in there somewhere.

*   *   *

Charles sprinted up the front stairs of the Old Whaling Church and hurried between its stately, Doric columns. The sanctuary was swarming with people overheating in their winter coats, milling about, and chatting with friends and neighbours. There were quite a few people whom Charles recognized. He reached up and gave a wide, friendly, wave to his friends, Marnely, Hali and Nate, and a few others. Some people had already taken their seats—elderly people who wanted or needed to

44

sit and people who didn't give a rat's ass whether they were seen or not. Charles knew that Edie fell into the latter category. Edie had lived on Martha's Vineyard for forty years. She already knew everyone she wanted to know, and more importantly, knew who she didn't want to know. Almost at once, Charles spotted the back of Edie's golden blonde head. It was tilted back; her face lifted toward the ceiling. Her posture was more rigid than usual. Charles excused his way down the centre aisle. As he went, he craned his neck in search of Jeff and Chris. They were supposed to be there somewhere but he couldn't see them. He made his way along the pew toward Edie and sat down beside her in a vacant space.

"Any sign of Jeff and Chris? They're supposed to be here tonight too." There was no response. "Edie?" Charles turned toward Edie. One look at her and he knew that something wasn't right. Edie's warm face was rigid. Her eyes were glassy, her lips tight. "Edie?" Charles asked. "Are you alright?"

Edie turned her head down and wiped her eyes with a rumpled but clean tissue. "Oh, I'm fine! I'm just pissed off! That's all. I cry when I'm mad—I hate it."

Charles smiled warmly at his friend. "I do too...and I hate it too." He put his hand on her shoulder. "Why are you pissed off?"

"That man!" Edie pointed subtly at the tall man seated a few rows up on her right. "He's the rudest man I think I've ever met!"

"Who?" Charles craned his neck to try and see where she was pointing.

"The tall, bald, black guy in the sweater," Edie said.

Charles found the man and looked him up and down—what he could see of him. "I don't recognise him. Who is he?"

Edie shook her head. "I've never seen him before and I never want to see him again!" Edie's face flushed.

"Well, don't think about him. Don't let him ruin our night. My night has already taken a bad turn. In fact, I was relying on you to cheer me up!" Charles rolled his eyes.

"I don't know what I can promise you in my current state." Edie paused and turned to look up at Charles. "Why? What's the matter with you?" she asked.

"Laurie's truck was just stolen," said Charles.

"What? Stolen from where?" Edie exclaimed.

"Just now in that small parking lot behind the Yellow House across from Alchemy—you know the one," Charles explained.

"Of course, I use it all the time," said Edie. "I don't mean to sound redundant, but did you call the police?"

Charles nodded. "We happened to just pass Jack on Main Street. I left the two of them together. Laurie is skipping the concert."

"I don't blame her," Edie said. "I wouldn't be able to concentrate on a concert if my car had been stolen!"

"She says we might see her at intermission but I'm not holding my breath."

"I'm glad you came, Charles. I'm already not as upset as I was." Edie smiled at her friend.

"We'll be good for each other," said Charles. He put his arm around her in spite of the heat in the room.

People settled in their seats and the choir stepped up onto the stage. Young men in black suits and young women in long black dresses took the stage followed by their conductor. They stood in silence waiting until they had the full attention of the crowd. When the conductor was satisfied, she turned toward the choir and cued them to begin. Thirty young, perfect voices softly began 'Silent Night'.

Watching the choir sing under the large evergreen wreath wrapped in red velvet ribbon, Charles couldn't help but feel the Christmas spirit. It was a warm and generous feeling. He looked down at Edie and she had seemingly forgotten her altercation with the tall man up front. She was smiling her usual warm and friendly smile. Edie had a beautiful face. In the back of his mind, no matter how delicately the choir sang, his thoughts were on Laurie. He hoped she was okay. He knew everything would be alright in the end—it almost always was—but he wished she was with him now. He wished she was holding his hand, and enjoying the concert like she had hoped to be. Between songs, Charles turned his attention toward the tall man a few rows up on the right—the man who had upset Edie so badly. Who the hell was that guy?

*   *   *

Mike Walker drove his truck down Main Street in Edgartown, slowed to an almost dead stop at Water Street, and then continued to Dock Street. He turned up Mayhew Lane and entered the parking lot that sat just below Among The Flowers Cafe. He manoeuvred his truck slowly through the lot. Mike and Trish both twisted left and right in their seats in the hopes of discovering an available spot.

"Over there!" Trish exclaimed. She tapped her forefinger against the window. "That truck is leaving!"

"Where?" asked Mike.

"In the other row by The Kelley House!" she said.

Mike exited back onto Main, turned sharply, and re-entered the lot where he had come in the first time. The other truck disappeared up Kelley Street just in time for Mike to slip into the vacancy.

"Perfect!" he said.

"I know, right?" Trish released her seat belt and opened the door. Cold night air filled the cab.

"Do you have everything?" asked Mike. Mike patted down his own pockets to see if he had everything. Finding what he was looking for, he decided that he did.

"I think so," said Trish. She stepped out into the night air directly under a lamppost wrapped in Christmas lights and garland. Snow fell lightly in big flakes. "Look! It's a Charlie Brown snow!"

Mike locked up the truck and put his arm around Trish's shoulders. "It is!" he said. "It totally is!" Mike tilted his head back and caught a few snowflakes on his tongue. He looked down at Trish and grinned. "I'm loving this place at Christmas! All these decorations and the snow! I'm so excited about the snow!"

"You're so funny," Trish smiled up at him.

"Stupid, I know."

"No, it isn't! It's your first Christmas with snow—I get it. I'd be excited too!"

Mike and Trish entered The Newes From America and scanned the pub for their friends. The Newes was their favourite place to hang out—especially in the winter months. It was just so cosy. The perpetually burning fire enhanced the rich colour of the red brick walls, the well-worn wood floor, and the matching furniture. The conversations of the restaurant patrons were punctuated by the snap and crackle of the sparking fire. Its smoky scent filled the restaurant. Walking into The Newes was like stepping back into the whaling days of Edgartown's yesteryear. All of the wood and exposed ceiling beams convinced every tourist who walked in that nothing had changed for centuries, that they had rediscovered a time and place where whaling captains would discuss the terms of their bounties, but it was all a ruse. Even though The Newes sat in the base of The Kelley House, which had been in operation since 1742, The Newes had only opened its doors in 1993. Yet, it was the pub's old world, colonial British feel that made it an island favourite. So much so that unlike most of the restaurants in Edgartown and across Martha's Vineyard, The Newes stayed open year round.

"Hi Kurt!" Trish called across the pub to a corner table where two men nursed a Guinness. One man was bald and the other had dark hair and a beard. The bearded one gave Trish a broad smile and a wave.

"Who's that?" asked Mike.

"Captain Kurt Peterson. He owns Catboat Charters. You know, that sailboat with the American flag sail in Edgartown Harbor?" Trish looked up at Mike's face for signs of acknowledgement.

"That's a charter boat?" asked Mike with excitement.

"Totally! A friend of mine works as a deckhand for him sometimes."

"Oh, we are so doing that next summer!" exclaimed Mike.

"Cool! I'd love it," said Trish. "Look, Virginia's back by the bar. I don't see Jack though."

The two of them made their way back to Virginia. She was seated alone at a table for four.

"Where's everyone else?" asked Trish. "Where's Jack?"

"He got called in. We were on our way here when Chief Knickles' truck was stolen! He had to go over and meet her in the parking lot. I don't think we'll be seeing him again tonight."

"Someone stole the Chief's truck?" asked Mike. "What an idiot. There's no way they could have known that it was the Chief's. I mean, it must be kids, right?"

Trish nodded. "I would have thought that everyone around here would know the Chief's truck—although she hasn't had it very long and it is just an old, beat-up, truck." Trish chuckled and shook her head. "I wouldn't want to be them when it's found!"

"No kidding," agreed Virginia. "Laurie will kill them. In fact, if I find out who did it, I may kill them myself. They've screwed up my evening pretty badly and it wasn't even my truck."

"Let's get you ladies a drink," Mike said. "White wine?" Mike looked from Trish to Virginia and back. They both nodded. "Okay, I'll go to the bar; it'll be faster that way." Mike stood and walked up to the bar at the back of the room.

*   *   *

Laurie exploded through the front door of the Edgartown Police Station. The doors sprung a lot faster on their hydraulics than they were supposed to and Jack reached out to brace them with his hands. Without breaking stride, she strode down the white hallway toward her office and, once inside, slammed the door behind her.

Jack, who had been racing to keep up with her, leapt backwards to avoid losing his nose in the jam. He sighed in relief that he had ended up on the outside of the office and not the inside when the door shut. Jack liked Laurie a lot, but her temper was terrible. He would wait a while and then, if she didn't call him in or open the door, he would call Charles. Charles always knew exactly what to say to her.

5

Victor Helm laid the last stone that he was going to place that day. He had made great progress—the wall was really coming along—but his calloused hands were cold and sore. The light was fading. When his day had begun, the pastures behind him had been a rich green sparked by golden streaks of morning. Now, those very same fields were deep purple smouldering with pinks and reds. It was time to call it a day.

Stone walls were a tradition in New England, and on the Eastern Seaboard of Canada, that dated back hundreds of years. Settlers had come and cleared their land. They removed stones from their future pastures as they went, and used them to divide their territory from that of their neighbours. Chilmark, West Tisbury, and Chappaquiddick in particular were laced with miles and miles of them. Stone walls divided properties and secured livestock. The older the walls were—weathered by the flux of hundreds of seasons—the more beautiful they became. Most stone walls on the island were dry-built; larger boulders had been laid in position while smaller stones, acting as chinking, filled the gaps without the aid of cement. Victor was proud to carry on the tradition of his mason father, grandfather, and great-grandfather. He was actually the ninth generation of his family to live on the Vineyard. In fact, he was the ninth generation of his family to live in the West Tisbury Helm family home. That was a long history even by Martha's Vineyard standards.

The crunching of steps on the gravel driveway behind him stirred Victor from his thoughts. He stood and turned around. Wrapped in a sweater, Edie walked down her drive carrying a fair-sized traveller mug in her hand. "Edie! What are you doing here? I thought you were gone for the evening? Didn't you go to the Minnesingers Concert?"

"I did. It's over. I came right home. We were going to go out for supper and to see the lighting of the lighthouse, but frankly, I wasn't in the mood. Then the chief's car got stolen so I came home."

"*The chief's car was stolen? Her squad car?*" exclaimed Victor.

"No. Her SUV," answered Edie. "I left them to deal with it." Edie eyed the wall up and down and then, eager to change the subject, she said, "Victor, it's really coming along! I'm impressed!" A beautiful stone wall had always framed Edie's property since the day she bought it. In fact, the wall was centuries older than the house itself, but it had needed some maintenance for quite some time. Victor's work could be seen all over the island, especially along Middle Road, and it was very highly regarded. During high season, Edie could never seem to find the time to get anything organised outside of The Edgartown Inn. Every time she drove in and out of her driveway, she would look at the wall and tell herself, *I've got to get that damned wall fixed,* but as soon as she walked into the inn, she lost all track of the outside world. Now, with the season over, she had made a list of all the things that she needed to get done. Slowly, but surely, she crossed items off her list and when she came to "Wall", she had hired Victor for some much-needed mending and extending.

"Thanks, Edie. I'm glad you like it." Victor smacked his gloved hands together out of habit. Dust puffed out in a cloud, but it didn't make his gloves any cleaner. "I think it's coming along alright myself."

"Oh, this is for you." Edie passed him the YETI traveller mug. "Coffee," she said. "With a little something extra." She smiled and winked at him. "This is hard work."

"Ah, you're a good woman," Victor took the mug and brought it to his lips. He sipped. The warm liquid immediately began to do its work.

"Ha! I'm glad someone thinks so. Just bring the mug back tomorrow. Okay?"

"Fair enough," Victor agreed.

"Would you like some supper before you go?" asked Edie.

"Oh no, Violet will have something on. That's for sure." Victor turned to cover his wall with a tarp before he packing up his tools.

"Why do you always cover up the wall before you go?" asked Edie. "You're just coming back in the morning."

"Protects it from frost and precipitation," he said. "We're supposed to get snow tonight and it sounds like it might just be enough to stay on the ground this time."

"It's already snowing down-island." Edie rubbed her shoulders against the cold and looked skyward for any sign of snow. The sky was grey and cloudy, but that wasn't unusual at this time of year. Edie returned her focus to the stone wall surrounding her property, and narrowed her gaze in thought. "You know, when I head over to America, I see stone walls everywhere—especially when I head up to my friend's place in Connecticut, but there's something different about our walls here on the Vineyard. They're prettier somehow."

"It's the rock," said Victor matter-of-factly.

"What do you mean?" asked Edie.

"Martha's Vineyard is a terminal moraine." With one hand, Victor set his full-size toolbox down on the bed of his pick-up as if it were a Fisher Price plastic toy.

"You're losing me Victor. Pretend I'm not a mason for three or four minutes," she chuckled teasingly.

56

"Sorry," Victor grinned patiently. "Martha's Vineyard was created by the last glacial push of the ice age. The land mass created by the furthest reach of a glacier is called a 'terminal moraine' because it's the end of the push. It's the ice age's last hurrah, so to speak." Victor chuckled at his lame attempt at a joke before continuing. "Imagine a glacier pushing across the Earth's surface, forcing a pile of residue to collect in front of it. By the time you get to the end of the push, and the glacier retreats, all that remains is the strongest of rock formations. That was how Martha's Vineyard was formed. The glacier would have destroyed any softer rock in its path which is why our rock is mostly granite."

"That makes our walls look different?" asked Edie.

"Yes, because it means that even though our walls might be only a couple of hundred years old—just like everyone else's—the stones we use could be over twenty-five thousand years old. It makes a difference." Victor looked at his watch and his face tightened. "I should run. Violet won't hold supper forever!"

"Oh, I'm sure you'll be okay," said Edie. "I'll see you in the morning, Victor. Thanks again!"

Victor shut the door of his blue pick-up and drove off in the direction of his West Tisbury home.

*   *   *

After Victor's truck disappeared onto Old County Road, Edie walked back toward her log cabin home. Her driveway was easily two hundred feet long but even at that distance, the night air was rich with the sweet smell of the wood fire burning in her hearth. She could even see the flickering light emanating from the front windows. The last of the evening glowed beyond the tree line. The evening light faded quickly and when it did—so did its warmth. Its brightest point was behind the peak of her tin roof. The whole house was silhouetted by an orange and yellow halo. The smoke from the chimney swirled toward the night sky. Edie pulled her sweater close as the cold began to filter through her clothing. She quickened her pace.

Edie had lived out here now for forty years. She was the true definition of a 'washashore'. Like so many others, she had come for a two-week vacation, got a job, and never left. Edie had never regretted that decision. She loved the Vineyard. She loved the hectic pace of the summer season, and she loved the charm of the shoulder seasons. She even loved the endless quiet of the off-season. Not long after she had moved on-island, Edie had met and married a young man named Mark Sparks. They bought this land and built this house together. They had shared a wonderful life here. Mark had been an islander—a fisherman—and one night, his boat, Ellen Jane, went out and didn't come back. The vessel had sent an S.O.S. but the response team hadn't been fast enough. Ellen Jane had sunk and the men were never found. The reason for

58

the sinking was as unclear now as it was then. The forensics team's results had been inconclusive. That had always bothered Edie. It had also bothered the fishermen in Menemsha—they were a superstitious lot and they didn't care for their people "turning up missing"—but that was a long time ago. So long, in fact, that people no longer whispered about it when they saw her in the grocery store, nor was it still a topic of speculation at the rare social gathering that she chose to attend. In a lot of ways, losing Mark had been Edie's rite of passage with the locals. Losing your loved one to the unforgiving power of the sea had connected her to the island and its people. It took a really long time to get to that point on Martha's Vineyard, but Edie had finally reached it. She had reached it a long time ago. Now, she was the owner of The Edgartown Inn. The Inn was steeped in island tradition and with it came a lot of respect; therefore, so did the widow, Edie Sparks.

Edie smiled inwardly, momentarily warmed with memories. It had been a long time since she had allowed herself to think about Mark. He had been a lot of fun, a lot of laughs, and devilishly handsome. Rich brown hair, eyes that were dismissed as brown, but were really copper, and a broad smile full of strong teeth. He hadn't been overly tall—one inch shy of six feet—but that was certainly tall enough for her. Like all fishermen, he was incredibly strong. His back was broad, and his arms were thick. She blushed in spite of herself when she remembered how hairy his chest and stomach had been. Despite all of this, she hadn't liked him at all in the beginning, but he wore her down. When she finally stopped putting so much energy into hating him, she had discovered that she actually loved him and doted on him every day that they had been together. That was a long time ago.

Edie realized that she was still smiling. She had, once again, loosened her sweater. The air really did feel a little warmer. A spark danced past her nose and she smiled at its fairy-like movement...then another...and another. She looked ahead, her eyes widened, and she stopped in her tracks.

In unison, Edie's kitchen and living room windows shattered. Long ravenous orange flames licked out of the glassless panes like tongues hungry for fuel. On the second floor, she could see light gnawing from one room to another. She realised the light she had taken for the fade of evening was actually the rise of flame behind her house. The air was filled with a sizzle now, like that of a barbequing steak.

Everything she owned was in that house. Her phone was in her purse, and her purse was in the kitchen. Her closest neighbour was over a mile away. Edie just stood there. Immobile. What was she supposed to do? She couldn't run into the house—the front door was gone. It was all happening so quickly. She couldn't run away—there was nowhere to go. Thirty years of history was disappearing in front of her. She heard the yawn of metal—a beam buckling or perhaps the fire gaping for

60

another bite. Soon, everything would just be gone. There was a crash inside, somewhere behind the external wall. It was hard to tell whether it was the cabinets containing her mother's china collapsing or the entire second floor. Maybe it was the staircase. Edie had never watched her world go up in flames before. It was both gut-wrenching and mesmerizing. There was too much to feel all at once. Two windows were still intact on the second floor but they were black with smoke. It was all too much. Edie was numb. That was it. End of story.

In the distance, she could hear the sirens of fire trucks.

"Someone must have called 911," she said aloud. "That's good." There wasn't a single emotion in Edie's voice. She felt neither cold nor hot. Edie didn't feel anything at all.

*　　*　　*

Victor pulled up on the dirt driveway beside his house. He sat there for a moment collecting his thoughts. He didn't see the boy's truck—that was something. He cupped his hand over his nose and mouth and exhaled. He could smell no alcohol from Edie's coffee. Still, it wasn't worth the risk. Victor reached into the glove compartment and pulled out a half a pack of Juicy Fruit gum. He pulled out a stick, peeled off the wrapper, and popped it into his mouth. He chewed vigorously. He took a deep breath and then another. It was time to go. Victor opened the door and stepped down onto the lawn. He reached for the coffee cup and then looked at the cup in his hand. He thought better of bringing it into the house at all. He poured out the remaining liquid, and put the cup in the back under a tarp where it wouldn't be seen. Slowly, with plodding steps, Victor made his way toward the front door of his home.

*   *   *

Corey drove the truck down Edgartown-Vineyard Haven Road as fast as he dared. He was not used to driving such a big vehicle. Ever since high school, he had driven sports cars—small cars. Now, aided only by the occasional streetlamp, this rig was too much for him to manage. He glanced quickly at Tina. She was asleep. He didn't know if that was good or a bad. It was probably bad—she had lost so much blood. He was trying not to think about that—he was trying to stay focussed—but the truck was filling with that metallic smell. He was starting to taste it on the back of his throat. They would be at the hospital soon. It had begun to snow and the road was getting slippery. The truck skidded, but only slightly. Theirs was the only vehicle on the road. That meant no one was there to notice how erratically he was driving, but it also meant that there was no one there to help them if he drove into the ditch either. Corey focussed on the road as best he could. It would almost be a relief if the police pulled them over. Police involvement would absolve him of responsibility. That might be the best thing for him. It would certainly be the best thing for Tina. Corey took another quick glance in Tina's direction. He had really made a mess of things. How had he gotten them mixed up in all of this? This wasn't who he was and it definitely wasn't who Tina was. He didn't steal cars—at least not before tonight, he didn't. But things got out of hand and Tina got hurt. The truck wasn't locked. He wasn't planning on keeping it. He didn't know how he was going to return it. Maybe he could just leave it in the hospital parking lot? No harm, no foul. A security guard was sure to check the lot and call someone to tow it away. The rightful owner would have called it in by then and they could just come and pick it up. That wasn't a bad plan. No one had to know that they had taken it at all. Corey looked back over at Tina. She was still asleep. Her head was resting against the window. Her breath fogged the glass. That was a good sign—at least he knew she wasn't dead. This whole trip to the Vineyard had seemed like such a good idea at the time. Now, it was such a mess. Everything was such a mess.

Corey turned right onto County Road. There were even fewer lights on County than there had been on Vineyard Haven Road, if that was possible. Corey turned on his high beams. He tried to figure out where all of this had backfired. Deliver some packages—that was all he had been asked to do. His boss couldn't do it himself and it was very important that these packages get to the island before the holiday season. So important that Corey's boss, Cameron, was willing to pay him a thousand dollars just to deliver them. He told Corey that he should consider it his holiday bonus. Corey had assumed that there were expensive Christmas presents in the box. It was the season. Cameron had a lot of cash. At least, Corey assumed he did. In the summer, he drove a Corvette—a nice one too—for Christ's sake. The garage was busy and Corey's boss needed to stay and get some of the jobs out before they shut down for the holidays. Cameron told him that he had been doing great work and had earned this holiday bonus. He just had one more job for him to do...deliver these packages to Martha's Vineyard.

"It's the holiday celebration out there on the Vineyard!" Cam told him. "You and Tina will love it. Go, drop this off, I got family out there. Enjoy the day, and come home. If you can find a place to spend the night, stay and keep your receipt. I'll reimburse you—just one night though! Have fun, buddy."

Corey shook his head at his own stupidity.

The streetlights were becoming more frequent. A car passed him and flashed their high beams. Corey turned his lights down and steered the truck onto Eastville and then Hospital Road. He could finally see the hospital in the distance.

Corey stole a glance in Tina's direction. "We're almost there, babe. Just hold on for one more minute."

64

6

Charles walked into the Edgartown Police Station to find Jack working quietly at the front desk. Jack looked up with an expression of nothing but relief.

"Hey, Charles," Jack said. "Am I glad to see you."

"She in her office?" asked Charles.

"Yep. We haven't heard a peep out of her."

"Any luck on the truck?" asked Charles.

"Our officers are out looking for it. The other five towns have all been notified too. It will turn up—sooner rather than later too. They can't get far," said Jack.

"Did you tell her that?" Charles asked with a sly grin. He already knew the answer.

"You tell her!" Jack shook his head. "It's nothing she doesn't know already anyway."

"I know...sometimes, it still helps to hear it." Charles headed down the white hall. "I'll tell her."

When he reached the wood door with the name plate that read Chief Laurie Knickles, Charles knocked lightly on the door. There was a pause before he heard the lock unlatch and the knob turn. Laurie opened the door an inch, leaving Charles to do the rest of the work. He waited a beat before slowly pushing the door open. Laurie was behind her desk. Her face was flush. Her eyes puffy. Charles stepped into the office and closed the door gently behind him. He found his usual seat. When he spoke, his tone was soft and measured.

"So...how are you making out?" he asked.

Laurie snorted at the absurdity of the question. "Never better," she retorted. "Never better."

"You know that they'll find the truck. They're out looking for it right now. Whoever took it can't get very far—it's an island, babe."

"Oh, for Christ's sake! I know it's a goddamn island!" Laurie reached for a fresh tissue from the box on her desk. "I don't care about the truck. The truck was a piece of crap anyway."

Charles stared at her with narrowed eyes. "Is it the presents? The presents in the truck?"

Laurie wiped at her nose with the tissue and then grabbed another one to wipe her eyes. "Not exactly...sort of...god, this is all so embarrassing. Some police chief, huh?"

"What is it? You can tell me? I think you're the best police chief there is—and I'm not alone in that. What's

66

going on in that head of yours? Laurie, honey, you always do this. You get yourself all wound up about something in your head. If you don't tell me what's bothering you, I can't help. But I promise you, tell me and it will get better."

Laurie sat behind her desk, breathing softly, and staring at the wall. She wiped at her eyes again, took a deep breath, and exhaled. She turned to face her husband and spoke in an uncharacteristically, soft voice. "I just wanted everything to be perfect for you. That's all. I wanted Minnesingers, and presents, and lights at Donaroma's, and our friends, the lighthouse, and everything just perfect. I had this idea in my head—like you said. I was so excited about everything going perfectly as planned. Then, the truck was stolen with the presents in it and I was too upset to go to the concert, so you had to go alone. Really, I'm the one screwing it all up. If I had just kept my cool, left Jack to process the truck and gone to the concert with you, things would be a lot better."

Charles started to grin.

Laurie stared at him in disbelief.

He tried to suppress his smile, but it kept broadening until he started to laugh.

"Are you serious right now?" Laurie asked. "You're laughing at me?"

Charles stood up and walked around the desk. He reached down for Laurie and pulled her close to him. Laurie's eyes were wide; her expression was one of bewilderment. "Do you know..." Charles started, "I couldn't

67

love you more if I tried?" Charles held her tightly. "How many people do you know would get themselves this upset—not because their truck or presents were stolen—because their husband's first Christmas on Martha's Vineyard wouldn't be Norman Rockwell perfect. You have to be the sweetest person I know." Charles felt Laurie soften into his embrace.

"I'm an idiot," she said.

"Yeah, but you're my idiot," said Charles.

A sharp knock at the door jarred them back into reality. They broke their embrace and Laurie took a more professional stance. "Come in," she called.

Jack opened the door and stepped into the office. His face was pale.

"What is it, Jack?" asked Charles.

"We just got a call from West Tisbury. There's been a fire. Edie's place just burned to the ground."

*   *   *

Edie was standing at the foot of her drive when Charles, Laurie, and Jack drove up in two squad cars. She wasn't crying. She wasn't yelling. She wasn't even pacing. She wasn't doing any of the things that she would have expected herself to be doing under the circumstances. Edie was just standing there awash in the strobe of the fire engine lights. Edie tried to focus on what she was feeling but she kept drawing a blank. There were so many

68

thoughts racing through her brain that she didn't know where to start. Her home was gone. So, where did she go? Her clothes and belongings were gone. So, she had nothing to pack even if she did figure out where she was going. She had insurance, but where was her policy? She couldn't remember whether it was at her lawyer's office or in her safe in the den—or what was her den. In movies, safes always survived house fires. She hoped that was true because the other thing she always saw in movie was insurance companies looking for any excuse not to pay up. Maybe they wouldn't if she couldn't find her policy.

Her limbs all felt too heavy to function. Her face felt heavy. She wasn't even sure she was blinking. Every inch of her body was exhausted, but she knew that if she tried to lie down she would come right back up like one of those inflatable, punching clowns. There was just so much to do... but what?

"Edie?" Laurie ran up to her with Charles and Jack right behind her. "Edie? Are you okay? What happened?" Laurie's eyes welled with tears and her voice shook.

"I'm okay. Thanks," said Edie in a very matter-of-fact tone. "I don't know what happened." She motioned toward the fire engines that were still dousing the remnants of her home. "They haven't told me anything yet." She turned and looked toward the blaze. It was half the size that it was when the fire fighters had first arrived. "They're really good at what they do." Edie's voice was flat, almost robotic. "I should get them something for all of their hard work."

"Honey, don't worry about them right now," said Laurie. "Let's worry about you." Laurie took Edie by the shoulders. Edie was so cold that Laurie let out an audible gasp. Laurie turned toward Jack. "Jack, go and turn the heat on in your squad car. Turn it on high."

Jack turned toward the car without question.

Laurie turned back toward Edie. "Edie, honey, I want you to get in the car with Jack. Okay?" Laurie bent down until her eyes were directly in Edie's line of vision. "Okay, Edie? Charles and I will follow you in our car."

Edie stared blankly at Laurie for a moment before responding. "Where are we going?"

Charles walked up beside Edie, put his arm around her, and began to guide her toward Jack's squad car. "We're going to take you home." He said.

*   *   *

Victor walked in the side door of his West Tisbury family home. He was hoping to be met with the comforting, homely smells of a hot, home-cooked meal, but that was not the case. He didn't smell anything. He took off his boots on the covered porch before stepping inside the kitchen proper. The room was dark, cool, and quiet. He listened. He could hear the sound of the television coming from the den. Someone was home. Victor walked across the tile kitchen floor and opened the refrigerator. There wasn't much to eat in there either. There was wine—Violet always had a few chardonnays in the fridge. There was a jar of mayonnaise that had been there for a while. It was probably expired. Victor couldn't remember the last time he had eaten mayonnaise. Victor opened the freezer door. There were frozen dinners stacked on top of each other. He closed the door again. The only ready and edible things were three jars of pickles. Victor was starving. He opened the jar of dills, pulled a large one out with his fingers, and stuck it in his mouth. He put the jar back and closed the fridge door.

Violet Helm was slumped in a gold wingback chair watching The Real Housewives Of Beverly Hills. She was still in her work clothes—a white shirt and black pants—that didn't fit her as well as they did when she had first started wearing them. She'd put on some weight since then. When Victor walked in, she did not look up.

"Hi Hon," Victor said. Violet offered no response. "How was your day?" Violet gave no indication that she was aware of his presence at all. "What did you want to do about dinner?"

"I ate," Violet said matter-of-factly.

"You did? There's nothing in the kitchen," Victor said. He knew what was coming.

"I ate at the hotel," Violet said.

"I thought we talked about that. It's so expensive, Violet," Victor said. "With Joey at home, we really have to watch our spending."

"What do you expect me to eat—Hungry Man meals every goddamn night from the Stop & Shop? That might be fine for you but I'm not eating that shit." Violet pointed at the women in eveningwear on the television. "They don't eat that crap. They eat steak in nice restaurants. I never get to go anywhere without a lecture."

"Did you have steak at the hotel?" Victor felt his stomach tighten as he started to calculate just how much her dinner was going to set him back. If she ordered a steak that meant she ordered a bottle of wine too. He wondered if she had invited Joey to meet her for supper. Actually, the boy probably showed up at the hotel to meet her after her shift. Joey would have been all to eager to suggest they stay and eat in the restaurant. Violet wouldn't need much convincing and Joey could eat more than anyone Victor knew. He was a big boy.

"Yes, I had a steak! Do I not deserve a steak? I work hard all day, Victor. When Joey showed up at the end of my shift and suggested dinner, I thought it was a great idea. At least my son is supportive. I'm the front desk manager, Victor. The Shore Line Hotel is the nicest fucking hotel on Martha's Vineyard." Violet's lips peeled back from her teeth like an angry dog. Her eyes, that had at one time had been hooded and sexy, were beady and accusing. "People expect me to live a certain lifestyle! What would people think if I was the only manager at The Shore Line who shopped for second-hand clothes at Chicken Alley, stayed home, and ate the crap you want me to eat every night?"

"Violet, I don't buy those frozen dinners. We could eat home cooked meals, together, as a family. That would be more economical," said Victor.

"So, I'm supposed to cook for everyone after a long day at the hotel too. Yes, that works out nicely for you, doesn't it?"

"I don't want to fight every time I come home Violet. We didn't use to."

"Well, you come home and cook a goddamn meal for Joey and me then. How about that?"

"Where is Joey? Is he home?" asked Victor.

"No, he's not home," Violet spat. "He's out enjoying himself. At least one of us is."

Victor spun around and walked back out the way he came.

"Where are you going?" yelled Violet.

"Grocery shopping," said Victor. Victor put his boots back on and walked back out to his truck.

7

Corey parked the truck as close as he could to Martha's Vineyard Hospital's emergency entrance. He jumped from the vehicle and ran to the passenger door. Tina's head was still pressed against the window, her ash-blonde hair glued across the glass with the condensation. It was impossible to tell, at this point, whether the condensation was fresh or from breaths taken a long time ago. *God,* Corey thought. *I hope I'm not too late.* Corey reached for the door handle, but jerked his hand back. If he let the door swing open, Tina was going to fall to the ground. He had to get her conscious. Tentatively, he knocked on the window. There was no movement. He knocked a little harder. Nothing. Corey felt his stomach knot.

"Tina?" he called out. "Tina, honey—we're here. We're at the hospital."

Tina did not move. Her face was pale. Her skin was discoloured, almost yellow. Thoughts ran through Corey's mind. Not good thoughts. Horrible thoughts. He tried to stop them, but they just kept coming. Thoughts that he wasn't prepared to think—not yet. Corey ran back around to the driver's side of the truck and opened the door. He climbed in and reached for his girlfriend.

"Tina?" Corey pulled her into an upright position. "Tina!"

Tina's head rolled forward. She slumped in her seat like a marionette whose strings had been cut.

Corey pulled her head up and slapped her face as hard as he could. The sound of his hand hitting her cheek, the impact of his palm on her flesh, made his chest tighten. For a moment, he couldn't breathe. Tears welled in the corners of his eyes. "Tina!"

Tina moaned her disapproval.

"Tina?" Corey said excitedly. It wasn't much, but it was distinct. He had heard a moan. He jumped out of the truck, slamming the door behind him. He ran to the passenger door and pulled it open. The force of the door made Tina slump toward him, but Corey caught her. She was heavy. Corey's clammy fingers tried to get a good grip, but they just got tangled in her clothing. She began to slip to the asphalt. "Goddamn!" Corey yelled. He propped Tina's body against his legs and she slid gently to the ground. Corey straightened her as best he could. Lying flat out on the pavement, Corey could see the extent of the blood stain on her dress. The dark stain ran from the top of her navel to the lace trim at the bottom. The swell of her belly made everything worse. Funny, how twenty-four hours can change everything. Less than twenty-four hours ago, that swollen belly made his entire life worth living. It was the major reason Corey had taken the money for this trip in the first place. Kids were expensive. Now, that swollen belly made everything worse. Tina was due in less than a month, but now she was lying swollen and bleeding on an asphalt parking lot. Corey got into a squat position, shoved one arm under Tina's thighs, and the other under her shoulder blades. With everything he had, Corey drove his heels into the pavement and forced himself into a standing position. As he stood, Tina's head lolled like that of a new born. Cautiously, Corey headed toward the port cochère that read EMERGENCY in capital letters.

*   *   *

The Old Whaling Church cast ample light over its front steps for its patrons. Nineteenth century lampposts comfortably lighted the red brick sidewalks of Edgartown's Main Street. Each one aided by their trimmings of evergreen boughs and Christmas lights. Beyond the reach of the street lamps, unaided by stars, the night was black. Chris and Jeff walked down the steps of The Old Whaling

76

Church into the cold December air. Chris inhaled and exhaled deeply. Someone, somewhere, was burning a wood fire. Probably more than one somebody, he thought. 'Tis the season, after all. He pulled on his toque and gloves.

The night air felt particularly cold after being in the church, wedged between all of the hot bodies for over an hour. That was the thing about winter that Chris liked the least. The best way to beat the cold was to layer up. Unfortunately, when you went inside, you could never entirely layer down; therefore, you overheated. That was the irony of winter—being inside was sometimes the most uncomfortable part of the entire season. Chris always layered up. He spent a lot of time outdoors in the winter. He and Jeff hiked all of the trails in the off-season. Jeff even enjoyed that. Jeff really enjoyed it now that he had installed the TrailsMV app on his iPhone—he was such a gadget guy. If it meant that Jeff got out, got some exercise, and was excited about it, Chris was more than happy to let his husband pick the trails, direct them through the woods, and follow their progress on his screen. If he was being honest, it did drive Chris a little crazy that they went out to walk in the woods, to spend time with nature, and Jeff spent just as much time staring at his bloody iPhone as he did looking at the goddamn trees, but he figured it was better than spending the afternoon cooped up indoors, staring at a TV screen. Besides, Chris figured that eventually Jeff would spend less time looking at his phone and more time at his surroundings. It would take a little time.

"Did you see Charles and Laurie in there anywhere?" Chris asked Jeff.

"No, but I wasn't really looking," said Jeff.

"Oh," said Chris. He studied Jeff's face. Chris didn't know exactly where Jeff was, but it wasn't standing beside him that's for sure. Jeff was doing his best to keep it under wraps—Chris gave him credit for putting in the effort—but Chris could tell something was up. "I was looking, but I didn't see them. I'll text Charles. Shall we walk up to the lighthouse?"

Jeff looked at Chris and gave a smile with everything but his eyes. His eyes remained distant. "Sure," he said. "That sounds great."

"Great," said Chris. Chris smiled a genuinely warm smile at Jeff. The irritation he had felt back at the house was growing into genuine concern. Something was upsetting Jeff and he was bottling it up. Jeff knew the holidays were important to Chris and he was putting on a brave face, but there was definitely something eating away at him from the inside. Chris reached out and took Jeff by the arm. They started down Main Street in silence.

"Jeff! Chris!"

The two men turned around to see Jeff's dad, Peter Jefferies, lumbering toward them. Retired Fire Chief Peter Jefferies was a big man. He was as tall as his son but a lot heavier. His once handsome features were now weighted

78

down and fleshy, framed by a full head of white hair. He and his son shared the same broad smile and the Fire Chief's eyes sparkled like those of a man half his age.

"Hey Dad!" Jeff called out. He walked back up Main toward his father. "What's going on?"

"Hey Peter! Good to see you," As Chris followed Jeff up the street toward his father, Chris could see the pall lift from his husband. There was a visible change in Jeff. "We're looking forward to seeing you for Christmas dinner."

"Me too! Wouldn't miss one of your holiday dinners, Chris!" the big man said. "I'm just heading out to Edie's now. I know I'm retired, but the boys might need an extra hand. Damned shame that, damned shame. That poor girl."

"What are you talking about?" asked Jeff. "What happened at Edie's place?"

"You didn't hear?" Peter Jefferies asked. "Oh, Christ. I thought you would have heard. It burned—it's gone. Nothing left."

"*What?*" Jeff and Chris exclaimed in unison.

"Edie's place burned down? You're heading out there now? We'll go with you. We'll follow you out," said Jeff.

"You're more than welcome to, but if you're going out to see Edie, I have it on good authority that she's on her way to Laurie and Charles' place now. I think they'll be putting her up... for a while at least," Peter said.

"Maybe we should go there instead, Jeff," said Chris. "There's nothing we can do out at the site except get in the way."

"Yeah, that's a good idea," said Jeff. "Okay, thanks Dad. Call us as soon as you know anything, okay?"

"Will do, son," said Peter. He planted a large, meaty hand on Jeff's shoulder. "It's good to see you, Jeff."

"You too, dad," Jeff smiled at his dad, but then quickly looked away.

"Chris," Peter took his hand off of Jeff's shoulder and extended it toward Chris. "Always good to see my son-in-law. Am I going to get you out on the ice this winter?"

"It would be a pleasure, Peter. I'll kick your ass!" Chris grinned slyly and shook the large man's hand. Chris had been a defenseman in the NHL—he was not a small man—but still his hand all but disappeared in the grip of his father-in-law.

Peter shook his head. "Goddamned hockey players—you're all too cocky for your own good!" The big man turned and walked away. "I'll be talking to you soon, boys."

Chris turned to Jeff. "So much for the lighthouse. Let's go get the car." The two men crossed Main toward the parking lot. "Poor Edie, fire scares the hell out of me. Every time we go away, that's my biggest fear."

"I know," Jeff said.

"I'm going to call Charles and see if they want us to pick up any food on our way. We could stop at Stop & Shop or get everyone some pizza or something."

"That's a good idea," agreed Jeff.

"Your dad is such a nice man," Chris said. "I wish we saw more of him."

Jeff didn't respond.

Chris looked at Jeff and saw that Jeff's face had settled back into the same distant stare that had been there for most of the evening. Chris shoved his hands into his pockets and began to think. Maybe it really was time that he got out on the ice with Peter Jefferies.

*   *   *

Karen Malone walked out of The Shore Line Hotel with a pile of dry-cleaning over her arm that she had picked up on her lunch hour. Her shift at the front desk had been a long one. She was tired and her feet hurt. She had eaten—the hotel was required to feed all employees who worked a full shift—but that had been a long time ago and her stomach felt hollow and achy. When her replacement, Amelia, hadn't shown up for her shift, the hotel manager had asked Karen to stay an extra four hours. They had talked the night auditor into coming in early to cover the back half of Amelia's shift. So, they had asked Karen to stay to cover the first half. She had. Her boyfriend, Sam, hadn't been very happy with her when she had called to tell him, but he had agreed when she pointed out just how much they could use the money—especially, with Christmas coming. The holidays were always marketed as the happiest time of the year, but you know who did that marketing? Rich people, that's who. If you were barely getting by financially, Christmas was an entire month of stress and embarrassment. That's what Karen thought anyway. She had already backed out of two Christmas parties this season because she couldn't afford anything to wear and didn't want to spend the money on a bottle of wine nice enough to take to a party. Two bottles of wine would run her thirty or forty dollars. She and Sam could eat a homemade chilli or stew for three or four days on that kinda money—lunch and supper! She thought of everything in terms of how many meals it equated to these days. Sam knew that was one of the main reasons she was working as much as she could—aside from the extra money—was that she was getting free meals. Gift giving was going to be tough. Especially, if Sam didn't get a contract. Karen and Sam had agreed to buy only for immediate family this year. Luckily, there were no kids on either of their lists. Kids were so expensive at the holidays. Karen specifically told her friends that she didn't want to exchange any presents this year. Maybe they could all just get together for a pot luck dinner instead? Not that a dinner wouldn't be expensive enough. In fact, Karen was starting to think that a dinner wasn't such a great idea either. Everything just cost so much money. Cyndi Lauper was right—money changes everything. Still, making a turkey for six people would probably be cheaper than having to buy six presents and wrap them. She tried not to make too much of a big deal about it at home. Sam felt bad enough about being between contracts and not helping financially as much as his male ego thought he should. It was certainly true that Karen would love it if he could, but she didn't hold it against him. It wasn't his fault. His last job had wrapped up early and he was waiting to hear back on a few bids he had out there. That was the nature of contract work. Winter was bad too. Like everyone else on Martha's Vineyard, summer was his busy season. Still, they'd get through it. They had been through worse. At least, they weren't asking their parents for help. They hadn't had to do that in a few years and Karen and Sam had both sworn that they would never do it again. When she looked at it from that perspective, they weren't doing too badly. Why was it that the more you have, the more you seem to need?

Karen stopped briefly to adjust the load in her arms. A cold wind rustled the protective plastic bag encasing her clothes. With her free hand, she pushed it out of her face and started walking again. The car wasn't far away, she could see it, but her load was getting heavy and it was slowing her down. Footsteps broke the silence that filled the empty parking lot. Karen stopped and looked behind her. It must be a co-worker, she thought. Had she forgotten something? The footsteps stopped when she stopped. Karen saw no one behind her. The lot was nothing but shadows and cars under a dusting of snow. Karen's eyes followed her boot tracks as far as they could, which admittedly, wasn't very far. Hers were the only tracks. There was no one else's. The cold wind curled around her ears in a nasty whisper. The skin on her body broke out in gooseflesh under her winter clothes. She began to sweat. Karen listened past the wind and heard no footsteps but she knew someone was there. She could feel eyes locked on her. She felt her chest tighten and her heart race. Something just wasn't right. She felt uncomfortably exposed as if in the sights of a gun or being watched with infrared goggles. Humans had managed to beat down most of their animal instincts, but the survival instincts—sex, sleep, hunger, and sensing danger— remained. She shuddered. Karen knew that this was the same feeling that shook through the muscled body of a zebra upon the approach of the lion. She felt like prey. It was that chemical sense of predation. The zebra didn't see the lion—it didn't have to—it just knew. Karen just knew.

Karen started walking again, this time at a quicker pace. The other footsteps, the heavier footsteps, started again. They matched her step for step in a terrifying echo. Without stopping, she looked around and still saw no one. She tried to twist her head up and over the clothes in her arm, but she couldn't. Plastic wrap blew into her face creating a blind spot on her right-hand side. The parking lot was lit with the same antique lampposts that lit the rest of the town. They looked pretty, but they didn't have much of a range. It was a dark night. There were a lot of shadows. Karen's breathing was laboured. Her forehead was cold and sweaty. She got to the car, threw her clothes on the roof, and whipped around to face her would-be assailant.

There was no one. The parking lot was empty. In the distance, she could see The Shore Line Hotel, decorated with Christmas lights—red, yellow, green, and blue electric fireflies humming around every doorframe and every archway. A warm glow emanated from every window. The lampposts in the lot were strung with the same boughs of greenery and multi-coloured lights that decorated all of Edgartown Village. There was no stalker. There was no big burly, axe-wielding, knife-swinging psychopath running up behind her. Karen snorted in disgust. She felt foolish. She fished in her purse for her car keys, found them, and turned to unlock her door. The driver's side door swung open without a sound. She took her dry-cleaning from the roof and stuffed it in the backseat. Karen paused. She turned and looked around the parking lot one more time. Still nothing. Still no one. She was sure that she had heard footsteps. *Was she that overtired? Was she that hungry?* A gentle snow began to fall again, the same large flakes as earlier that day. It was actually a very pretty night. Stepping away from the open car door, Karen cautiously walked from the car, heading back the way she had come. She looked up one lane of the parking lot, and

85

then turned her head to look in the opposite direction. Now that her arms weren't burdened with her newly pressed work uniforms, she could get a full view of the lot. There was still no one. She walked a little further until she was between two cars parked side by side. She peered deeper into the lot—giving it one last sweep—still no one. The soles of her boots scraped along the ground. The asphalt under her feet felt gravelly and hard. Wet, but not covered in the soft layer of snow covering the rest of the lot. She looked down where she stood. Boot prints considerably larger than her own had scuffed up most of the snow. She looked back at her own tracks and they were side by side with the larger prints. The larger prints stopped here, exactly where Karen stood now, and headed further down the parking lot. Karen felt nauseous. Once again, she began to sweat. She was sweating from every pore. Karen was not alone. She ran toward her car as fast as she could. She looked in the direction of the tracks— they crossed the lot just three vehicles down on the right from her car and disappeared behind a station wagon. Beyond the station wagon was the end of the lot. It was just woods. Thick trees and bush that lined the far side of the lot. The same woods that were directly in front of her own car. Grateful that her door was open—grateful that she would not have to take the time to fumble for her keys or even for the door handle—Karen slid into her seat, pulled the door closed behind her, and locked it. Karen put the key in the ignition and turned it over. With a little too much force, she slammed the gearshift into reverse. The car jerked out of its parking spot narrowly missing the car behind it. She braked.

"Calm down!" Karen scolded herself. "You're fine! You're in your car. You're okay." Karen shifted the gearshift of the automatic transmission. "Just get home," she told herself in a reassuring tone. "Just get home." Karen pressed her foot gently onto the gas and the car eased slowly out of the parking lot.

8

"Do you have it?" Virginia asked.

"Yes," said Mike. Instinctively, he reached down to the right-hand, front pocket of his jeans and felt for the small square box.

"Show me!" Virginia demanded. Her face was glowing.

"No! She'll be back any second. Calm down, would ya? You're getting too excited. She's going to suspect something." Mike's tone betrayed just how nervous he was. He had managed to keep himself together this long, but now, sitting with Virginia...

"I can't help it! This is so exciting!" Virginia bounced up and down in her seat and clapped her hands.

"Jeez! Virginia if you ruin this for me—I swear, I will never forgive you," Mike glared at her. He was too nervous. His face was starting to burn up.

Virginia looked at him and sunk into her chair. "You're turning red! I'm sorry—you're right. I'm getting too wound up." Turning her focus to the table in front of them, Virginia slid one glass of ice water toward Mike and picked one up for herself. "Here...drink that. You'll feel better."

"Good call," said Mike. He took a deep gulp of the cold water and felt his face returning to its natural temperature and, he hoped, its natural colour as well.

"She's coming," Virginia said.

Mike turned and watched Trish as she slowly wiggled her way through the crowded pub. The Newes From America was a very popular spot. It had been fairly busy when Mike and Trish had sat down with Virginia and the crowd had steadily increased. Trish had a difficult time excusing herself past one person and then another. The room was long and narrow. It's width only allowed for two tables of four, one on each side of the room and now, with the tables full, the room was difficult to manage. People from the front bar had worked their way into the back bar to stand around the tables and talk to their friends. The waitresses had all but given up trying to give table service, opting to assist at the bars instead. Eventually, Trish made it to their table and plopped down in her seat. She exhaled with relief.

"Good lord!" she exclaimed. "That was not easy!" Trish laughed in spite of herself. "I think next time, I'll just pee in a cup!"

"Was there a line-up in the washroom?" asked Virginia.

"Surprisingly, no, which is a very good thing, because by the time I got there, I really had to go!" Trish picked up her wine and took a sip. She looked at the glass, which was almost empty, and finished it. "Are you guys almost ready to go? I don't want to miss the lighting of the lighthouse!"

"Me neither! This Christmas is like a storybook," said Mike. "I feel like a big kid!" He grinned sheepishly.

Trish leaned over and tilted her head up. She kissed him. "You are a big kid."

Virginia rolled her eyes. "Oh, please. Come on you two. You're melting the ice in my wine!"

Trish laughed at her friend. "Serves you right for being so white trash. Who puts ice in their wine? Classy."

"I'll have you know that I have a lot of class...it's just all low!" Virginia laughed at her own weak joke. "I think I might be drunk."

Trish laughed. "Well, you're not alone. I've definitely got a buzz on."

"That ties it. You ladies need some fresh air. Let's get out of here." Mike stood and picked up Trish's coat from the back of her chair. He held it out so that she could slip into it.

90

Trish stood up and looked back at Mike with the warmest of smiles. She put one arm into her coat, then the other. She shrugged it onto her body and took his hand. "You're so cool," she said.

Mike looked at Virginia and grinned. "No comment, Virginia?"

Virginia shook her head and smiled. "No...that was pretty cool."

*   *   *

From the bay window, William Singleton watched what he could still see of the distant flames. The windows whistled and William rubbed his arms for warmth through his long-sleeved shirt. This part of the room was a good fifteen degrees cooler than in his chair by the hearth. Certainly, some of that was because of the chair's proximity to the fire, but the cold winter wind rattling the antique window lights, in their mullions and muntins, played a big part. The two hundred year old rental property was beautiful. Its old-world charm was exactly what William had been looking for, but the house needed a lot of work. He was glad that the house wasn't his. It would cost a fortune to fix everything that needed fixing. Perhaps, he could see putting in his time with some manual work in the future—idle hands and all of that. If he could do it, William thought he just might enjoy it. He had found pleasure in that sort of work in the very distant past, but now... He tightened his grip on his coffee mug and looked down at his misshapen fingers. His dark brown skin was tight on his swollen knuckles. The heat of the mug slowly penetrated each one. It felt good. His hands had been quite idle of late, a lot more than he would have liked. William supposed that he should be grateful that the arthritis had come to him so late in life. Still, on cold days like today, when his knuckles felt like they were full of sand, and his fingers refused to straighten, it was hard to always focus on the bright side. William returned his gaze to the window, and the distant fire. He wished he had seen the flames earlier, but the tree line was so high in West Tisbury, early detection would have been impossible. There was such a distance between houses on this side of the island. Perhaps an islander would have noticed circumstances out of the ordinary a little more expeditiously, but someone visiting for the first time didn't have a chance. He hoped no one had been injured. At their peak, the flames had been so out of control, he doubted anyone had been home, but William was afraid that might be wishful thinking. The fire fighters had responded very quickly. William had been impressed. The fire station couldn't be far away.

The flames couldn't be seen at all now. There was nothing but a dull glow in the woods, and that was possibly just light from the fire trucks. William made his way back to his wingback chair. He sat down slowly, so as not to spill his coffee. Placing his mug on an oak table,

92

that looked as old as the house, he arranged the throw-cushions behind him and settled in. It felt like the chair had been plugged in. The fireplace had kept it warm. William's body soaked up the comforting heat. The miracle, William thought, was that he had stood from this chair, and noticed the fire outside at all. Earlier that day, he had discovered a copy of Charles Dickens' *Bleak House* in the library. He had been reading it when he got up to stretch and noticed the fire. He'd read *Bleak House* before, it was his favourite Dickens novel, but it had been a while. He remembered that the omniscient *Esther Summerson* told the story of *Jarndyce and Jarndyce* bleeding everyone dry. He remembered it only in a very general way. In actual fact, he remembered very little. Lately, he had been revisiting a lot of things that he used to enjoy, but one by one had given up over the years. Reading fiction was definitely one of those things. There had been a time when William had revelled in the rich prose of a good book. He had read voraciously. Yet reading, like so many of his creature comforts, had fallen by the wayside only to be replaced by work. One by one, he had let everything go.

As an investment banker, he had been at his desk before 7:00am every morning and would, more often than not, still be there at 1:00am. If he wasn't at his desk, he was entertaining clients. All the best restaurants, all of the sporting events, bars, anywhere the client wanted to go, William took them. He had never married or had children. Many of his co-workers had, and now they were all paying alimony and child support. William knew his limitations. If he couldn't be good at something, he wasn't going to do it. When he was sizing up potential clients, he always assessed the R.O.I., the return on investment. If it wasn't going to pay off, he wouldn't pursue it. Who would? It was the same with pursuing family life. He knew that he didn't have anywhere near the time for a successful relationship, so he didn't invest in one. It was that simple. William's mother had trained him that way. Raised him to be a success. Whitney Singleton had grown up poor and worked hard to become a nurse. A single mother, she had raised William and his brother to study and study hard. Their only playtime growing up had been school sports teams. Sports teams had the potential to pay-off in scholarships. Playing outside with friends did not. William's brother, Thomas, was a good football player, but he met the wrong boys. Thomas got mixed up with steroids. He got kicked off the team. That had lead to drugs and eventually, prison. William's grades had been excellent and he had received an education that had historically been reserved for privileged, white boys. At Harvard Business, William had definitely felt like a raisin in the mayonnaise at first, but he had done well, made friends, made connections. Whitney had been a hard mother—strict—but there was no way that her little boy was going to grow up like she did. It had paid off, for William at least. William Singleton was sitting in a $4000/week rental property on Martha's Vineyard. He had achieved what very few people did—white or black. Now, William was retired. He placed the book on his lap and returned his gaze to the snowy December night. Snowflakes caught the front porch lights as they danced their way to the ground. William picked up his coffee mug again, more seeking the warmth for his hands than the beverage inside.

William was alone. More than that, William felt alone. Loneliness was a foreign concept to William. He had never given it much thought, if any thought at all. He had always been too busy and surrounded by people. It's amazing just how friendly everyone is while you're making them money, he thought; however, William wasn't making anyone money anymore, including himself. One by one, everyone had moved on. Oh, he still had money. He had a lot of money. He had all the money that he had spent his entire life earning. That had been his sole focus. The money. He remembered how good he had felt with the closing of each deal. The charge of adrenaline that surged through him with the accepting of each cheque, each transfer of funds. William found it quite ironic, how successful he had felt making it, but now that he was just sitting around having it, he didn't feel very successful at all. He just felt alone. William hoped, with all of his heart, this trip to Martha's Vineyard would change that.

*   *   *

The slam of the car door in the driveway was loud enough to stir Sam Jones. He was half-asleep in front of the television. He hadn't meant to fall asleep at all, only sit down long enough to get the football highlights, but out he went. It seemed almost instant these days. As soon as his ass found the couch, it flicked a switch in his brain, and it was lights out. He rubbed his palms into his eyes as he sat up, and shook his head like a dog getting out of the bath. Sam stood up. The kitchen door opened and slammed shut. Eyes still half-closed, Sam followed the noise and padded his way to the back of the house.

"Hey honey," Sam's eyes widened at the sight of Karen, standing on the mat just inside the kitchen door. Her face was wild. Even under her heavy winter coat, he could see her trembling. "Jesus! What's the matter?"

Karen ran into Sam's arms and she started to cry.

Sam held her tightly and stroked her hair. "Are you okay? Are you hurt?" Karen didn't answer. Sam tried to keep the panic out of his voice, but he could feel it rising in his throat like a bad meal. He swallowed. "Karen?" He reached for her head with both hands and put one on either side of her face. Gently, he pushed her far enough away from him that he could tilt her face toward his own. "Honey? Are you hurt?"

Karen shook her head and wiped her nose on her sleeve. "No, I'm not hurt. I'm okay. I'm sorry. I'm just really freaked out." Karen took a breath. "There was a man in the hotel parking lot. He chased me to my car—at least I think he did. I know I heard footsteps, Sam—I know I did!"

"A man attacked you?" Sam exclaimed. He felt his blood race through his veins and his face started to burn. His temper was flaring. Sam's instinct was to grab a baseball bat and go find the son-of-a-bitch who could do this. He pictured himself driving down to the hotel and finding the bastard. But then he pictured Karen. He knew that would only upset her more. He could see her screaming and yelling for him to stop. She would ask him what would that solve and she would be right—just like she was always right.

Sam remembered he had read that the best thing to do in a situation like this was to remain calm. If he got upset, Karen would stay upset. The best thing for him to do was to stay quiet and collected. If he did that, subconsciously, Karen would follow suit. Sam had no idea where he got this information, probably one of the O Magazines that Karen was always bringing home from the hotel. He pulled Karen in tight and hugged her.

"No," Karen said. "No one attacked me."

"Okay, that's good," Sam tried to sound as soothing as he could. "You're not hurt and you're home now. I've got you. That's all that matters. Right?"

Pressed against Sam's chest, Karen nodded as best she could.

"No one's going to mess with you while I'm around," Sam said. "I can promise you that. Do you want some tea?

I could put on the kettle and make you some of that Sleepytime Tea that you like so much. What do you say?"

Karen nodded again.

"Alright, then. I'm going to make some tea. Why don't you take off your coat and your uniform. You'll feel better in some sweats."

"Okay," Karen said. "I feel a little stupid. I mean, I didn't even see the guy, but I know he was there. I could hear his footsteps booming behind me and then I saw his footprints! They were huge! They were at least the same size as yours!"

"I'm a size thirteen. That's pretty big alright," said Sam. "But you didn't even see him?"

Karen shook her head. "I had my hands full of my dry cleaning—oh crap!" she yelled.

"*What?*" asked Sam, alarmed.

"I left my dry cleaning in the car," Karen moaned.

Sam gave a sigh of relief. "Don't worry about it. I'll go get it. Is the car locked?"

Karen shook her head again. "No." She started pulling off her winter coat. "I just slammed the door and ran into the house."

Sam smiled at her. He could tell that she was settling down to her usual self. Now that she was feeling better, he felt better. Karen had never been an alarmist, but she had really been shaken up. He didn't like it. "Go upstairs and get changed, maybe even have a quick shower?"

"That's a good idea," said Karen. "Is there any food?"

"Macaroni, cheese, and tomato!" Sam said. "Made it myself! It's hot... it's tasty... *and it's cheap!*"

Karen laughed. "Is it any wonder why I love you?"

"Not to me, it's not." Sam winked at her. "I'm pretty goddamn lovable. Go have your shower. I'll dish up your dinner and get your clothes out of the car."

"I don't deserve you," said Karen.

"Probably not, but no one else does either. So, you might as well have me." Sam grinned.

Karen shrugged and kissed him. "Guess so." She turned and walked out of the kitchen and up the stairs.

Sam sighed as he watched her go. He felt the smile leave his face. In a whisper that was barely audible, even to him, Sam said, "I think you got that backwards, honey."

Sam had really disliked seeing Karen upset. Especially, these days when they were already dealing with so much. He tried to make a joke out of the fact that the macaroni, cheese, and tomato was cheap, but the fact of the matter was—*it was cheap*. It had cost him about five dollars to make the entire thing and they would be able to eat it for the next couple of days. Sam hated having to take things like that into consideration. Some goddamn provider he turned out to be. Karen put on a pretty good front, but he knew that she wanted things to be different, especially at Christmas. Last Christmas had been wonderful. They had entertained, decorated, spent lavishly, and gone to lots of parties. That was how the holidays were supposed to be. You were supposed to forget the bills and enjoy yourself. Make sure your friends enjoyed themselves too. Well, Sam was not enjoying himself. Christmas was in a couple of weeks, he was unemployed, and he was making his girlfriend eat five-dollar mac-and-cheese for two days at least. No, Sam was not enjoying himself at all.

Slipping on a pair of holiday oven mitts, a gift from his mother a couple of years back, Sam opened up the oven and pulled out the casserole. He set it down on the stove and shut the oven. It did smell good. Cheese and pasta, streaked with red stewed tomatoes, bubbled in the glass casserole dish. It may be cheap to make, but it was comfort food. That was something. Sam heard Karen turn on the shower upstairs. Sam set the casserole dish down on the burners to cool and pulled off the oven mitts. He had to get her dry cleaning out of the car.

The snow on the ground was minimal, and there was none on the gravel driveway. Deciding that he could go outside in his slippers, Sam pulled open the heavy kitchen door, and then pushed open the aluminium screen door. It was cold out. His breath came out in visible, white, puffs. The first time Sam saw those every winter, he remembered using them to mimic smoking when he was a kid. He smiled. One day, he hoped that he and Karen would have kids. Sam wondered if they would do that too.

The small, stained-wood stoop was two steps off the ground. Sam jumped over them and ran around to the side of the house. He stopped abruptly. The car door was open on the driver's side. *Had Karen been in such a hurry to get into the house that she had left the car door open? She must have been freaked out. That was not like her at all,* thought Sam. He leaned into the car, picked up the dry cleaning in one arm, and slammed the car door behind him. He turned and made his way toward the back of the house and the kitchen door. The kitchen light shone through the screen door. Sam pulled it open and it gave a faint metallic protest. He closed the wood door behind him and locked it. Sam listened. The shower was still going. He chuckled. *Nice, quick shower,* he thought. With the dry cleaning hooked on one finger, Sam walked through the house and hung the clothes in the front closet. The front door was wide open. *"What the hell?"* Sam said out loud. He closed the door and locked it.

Sam walked down the hall, passing photos of Karen and him, laughing and smiling on Lucy Vincent Beach, to the stairs that led up to the bathroom and two small bedrooms. "Karen? Honey? Dinner's ready!" There was no response. "Karen?" He listened briefly before going up the stairs two at a time. He could feel his heart beating in his chest. It was beating harder than it had been in the kitchen, harder than when Karen came home. Something wasn't right. Dampness was spreading in his armpits. His forehead glistened.

The bathroom was the first door at the top of the stairs. Sam knocked out of courtesy. "Honey?" He took the knob in his hand and turned it. The white wood door swung open easily and Sam was enveloped in a cloak of steam. His pulse raced. He was breathing through his mouth. Sam pulled back the shower curtain. The shower was empty. Sam reached into the tub and turned off the taps. He felt queasy. The skin crawled on his neck like a team of cockroaches. He turned toward their bedroom. *"Karen?"* He took two steps into the dimly lit room. The light on Karen's side of the bed, the side closest to the bathroom, was on. Her discarded uniform lay rumpled on the bedspread. Karen's panties and bra were on top of her uniform along with a pair of tights that wouldn't make it through another day. Sam checked the other bedroom. He couldn't think of a single reason as to why she would be in there, but he checked it anyway. Nothing. Empty. Just a spare bed, a desk, and a lot of boxes. *"Karen!"* he shouted. His words hung in the air momentarily then there was silence.

9

Overlooking Vineyard Sound, Edie sat on one of the over-stuffed burlap chairs in Laurie and Charles' den. Bubbas the cat snuggled in her lap, in a deep sleep. East Chop had always been one of her favourite places. It calmed her soul. On a sunny morning, Edie would drive to The ArtCliff Diner, have breakfast, and walk from Vineyard Haven out to East Chop. There was a bench at the base of East Chop Light with her name on it, or so she liked to think. Listening to the waves of the Atlantic roll into the base of the cliff, watching the early morning sun dance gold and diamonds across the water was as meditative a moment as she was likely to find. There were a lot of spots like that on Martha's Vineyard but this spot was near and dear to her heart.

Tonight was different. Edie sat staring out the window at the darkness. A black ocean met a black sky on a horizon far out of range of the naked eye. She could hear the waves gently lick the island's lip. The tide was out. Somewhere in the distance, a buoy clanged. Edie raised her large glass of Kim Crawford Sauvignon Blanc. She took a sip and the rich liquid rolled around her tongue before gliding down the back of her throat. There was something about wine. The sole purpose of each mouthful seemed to be to clear a path for the next. Edie drank again.

She could live at The Edgartown Inn for now. She would have to turn the water and the electricity back on, but that wouldn't be a problem. She had stayed there on numerous occasions when she had to work extremely late and be in the next morning. On those nights, she had stayed in one of the two guest rooms in the carriage house. Staying out there, across the garden, gave her some distance on a psychological level. This time, she wouldn't be able to do that. She'd stay in the main house. The Charles Sumner room—named for the nineteenth century, republican senator from Massachusetts known for his tireless work to free the slaves—was her go-to when she had to stay in the main house of the inn. It was roomy, bright, and on the main floor. The inn did have everything she would need, but her clothes were gone, her photos, her things. Sure, they were just things, but they were *her things*. Or at least, they had been her things. Now, they were her ashes, her dust. She supposed she still had her car. She didn't know how badly the fire had damaged it—if at all. Edie thought she had better start making a list of things that she needed to ask the fire department and a list of things that she would need. She turned away from the window to find Charles and Laurie sitting on the couch together, quietly, watching her. Edie forced a smile. "You look worried," she said.

"You deserve a little concern," Laurie said. "Don't you think?"

"I'll be fine. Your car was stolen tonight," Edie said. "Take care of your own crap."

Laurie winced.

Edie sighed. "I'm sorry. That was mean. It's not what I meant—exactly." She took a heavier gulp of wine than usual. "I'm not really good at pity." She stroked Bubbas on the head and the cat began to purr.

"Have you ever looked up 'pity' in the dictionary?" asked Charles. Both women stared at him, mute. "I have."

"Of course you have," said Laurie.

"Well, people are always talking about pity with such a negative connotation. Turns out, 'pity' means 'sympathy and compassion'. So, if you're going to accuse us of pity then have at it. I will never be ashamed of showing either sympathy or compassion. For my friends, I have an endless supply." Charles took a mouthful of his own glass of Kim Crawford. When that didn't make him feel any better, he emptied it and stood up. "Anyone else for more wine?"

Both women emptied their glasses and handed them to Charles.

Edie felt sheepish. "Sorry, you guys. I'm having a difficult time processing all of this." Edie rubbed her face. "I guess I can move into the inn. I'll have everything I need there. I'll have to turn the water and the heat back on."

"You'll do no such thing," said Laurie. "You'll stay here with us."

Edie smiled a genuine smile at her friend. "That's very sweet, but I am going to be homeless for quite some time—Christ, I'm homeless. It's weird hearing that out loud. I can't stay here indefinitely."

"Well, no. I suppose that's not practical," said Laurie.

Charles returned from the kitchen with three full glasses of wine. "You will stay for a month," he said. "That will give you enough time to process the larger issues that are coming your way. None of us even know what those issues are going to be yet. It will be better if you're not alone when things come up. Dealing with insurance is going to be a pain in the ass. Once your affairs are in order, you've got a new wardrobe, and the holidays are over," Charles winked at Edie. "We'll kick you out."

"Happily!" Laurie winked.

Edie chuckled at her friend. She looked from Laurie to Charles and held out her hands. Charles and Laurie reached out and took her hands in theirs. "Thank you," Edie said. They returned her smile.

Charles broke away first and picked up his wine. "To friendship!"

The women picked up their glasses. "To friendship!"

Fenway The Beagle leapt up from his bed on the kitchen floor and began to bark. He ran toward the front door. The doorbell rang and the door opened. Voices were muffled by the excited barks. Charles and Laurie looked at each other. Charles called out, "Hello?"

"Hey!" called a familiar voice. A moment later Chris and Jeff entered the back den with their arms full and Fenway in tow. "We brought wine and pizzas from Offshore!" said Chris.

"The wine isn't from Offshore," said Jeff from behind three, large, flat pizza boxes.

"Oh, shut up, Jeff," Chris said.

*   *   *

Using the side door that led from the driveway to the kitchen, Victor walked into the house weighed down with grocery bags from Cronig's Market. With no effort at all, he hoisted them onto the counter. Once free of his load, he turned around, closed the door, and turned on the overhead lights.

The kitchen was a simple, New England, country kitchen. It was bright—white tile and marble. It looked expensive, and in fact the materials had been, but Victor had renovated it himself. It had been his project last winter. That was the only way that they had been able to afford it. Violet was disgusted—she had been very vocal about it—but Victor was very proud of his work. Violet was never happy with anything Victor did. She saw nothing but embarrassment in having her husband doing the work around the house. Violet always wanted to hire the hottest decorator on-island, or better yet, call one in from America. There was no way Victor was letting that happen. Victor read the same magazines that Violet did. He saw what she wanted and went out and bought the same materials that any other contractor would buy. Victor was good with his hands—always had been. It ran in the family. His ancestors had built the house they lived in. There was no way that he was going to pay someone else's over-inflated labour costs. There was a direct correlation between labour costs and ego. It had nothing to do with the quality of work. Oh, there were excellent workmen on the island, Victor knew a lot of them. Good, hard working guys, whom Victor had known since boyhood. Those weren't the guys that Violet wanted to hire though. She looked down on them almost as much as she looked down on her own husband. Violet only wanted to hire the Patrick Ahearns of the island for bragging rights. She wouldn't know good craftsmanship from bad. It was foolish. Victor knew that he could do just as good a job. If his business was slow during the winter, why shouldn't he do the work himself?

Victor opened the refrigerator door and started putting away the perishable food. He had tried to keep his shopping on the healthy side. He bought some vegetables, both fresh and frozen, and some ground turkey. It looked like any cooking that was going to be done, was going to be done by him. Victor figured that he could make a big pot of chilli and portion it out for his lunches and dinners. That would save him some time.

The television still boomed in the other room. Real Housewives of god-knows-where were screaming at each other about something. Victor doubted Violet had moved from her spot in her chair. She was probably asleep. Well, passed out. As he put away the carton of orange juice that he had just purchased, he noticed that there was one less bottle of wine than there had been earlier. It knotted his stomach. He didn't know how to feel about her ever-growing alcohol consumption. It made him sad. She hadn't always been like this. They hadn't always been like this. They used to have a really good time together. In the beginning, they had laughed a lot, but not now. Now, she was angry and bitter all the time. He wasn't even sure why. When had their life become something that she despised so intensely? Before they had married, they hadn't been the type to dream of making millions. They hadn't planned to move to a mansion in the Hamptons or even to one of those enormous homes that were popping up all over the coast of Chappaquiddick and Martha's Vineyard. Victor remembered some of Violet's friends in

109

school having those aspirations, but not Violet. Before they were married, they had talked about living in Victor's family home—the home they lived in now—and raising a family. By anyone's standards, it was a good sized home and it was on a big piece of property. It impressed a lot of islanders. Generations of Shaws had lived there before him. Living in his family home had always been his plan. He had never made a secret of it. His parents had lived with them briefly in the beginning, that had been a bit tough, but now they lived in Florida. Violet had been happy about the idea then. She had been happy after Joey was born too, but not now. Now, she was hard, ugly. She used to be so pretty. It wasn't until Violet became so hateful that Victor came to realise just how much a person's looks rely on their disposition. A smiling, warm, inviting face is a good-looking face. A mean face is not. Violet's once bright eyes were now angry and dark. Her once broad, seemingly constant, smile was now tight, thin lipped and twisted. She was always on the attack. When he would ask her why, she always came back spitting insults. They hadn't made love in years. Violet mocked him for that too. But how could he? Why would he? He didn't even think that she really wanted to, not the way she treated him all day. He was sure the only reason she feigned interest was so she could mock him when he turned her down. It was just another way to get at him, needle him. Victor spent as much time as he could away from the house. Violet drank. His feelings over her

110

increasing consumption of alcohol were complicated. He didn't think that he could hold the alcohol entirely responsible for the change in Violet; he believed that alcohol fuelled a fire, it didn't ignite one. In the alcohol, her venom, her hatred found encouragement to grow, a healthy layer of compost and manure in one drained bottle after another, but the other side of that struck Victor as even darker. He tried not to acknowledge it as it riddled him with a sickening guilt—coming home to discover more than one bottle of wine had been consumed also meant peace and quiet...if only temporarily. Coming home to empty bottles, filled Victor with relief.

Victor left out all of the ingredients for chili out on the counter. He opened one of the cupboards below the counter and pulled out their largest, stockpot. He put it on the stove and turned on the burner. Victor poured what seemed like an appropriate amount of olive oil in the pot and added a spoonful of diced garlic. He peeled a large onion. Taking a butcher knife from the knife block and a cutting board out from under the sink, he began to chop.

*   *   *

Laurie's phone rang and she looked at the screen. "It's the station. Excuse me guys." She stood up and walked into the kitchen.

Edie picked up a slice of veggie pizza. Jeff and Chris had brought a veggie pizza, a pepperoni pizza, and

Charles' own creation "The Salty Canuck"—Italian sausage, sundried tomato, pepperoni, onion, green olives, and anchovies—which had become a group favourite. Between mouthfuls, Edie talked over the details of her insurance with Jeff and Chris. The ones she could remember anyway. She had left a message for her lawyer on his machine. She would go and see him in the morning. He had her policy and would help her settle everything. The whole experience had made her think about just how lucky she was—how lucky they all were. They all had such an incredible network of friends. Edie, who in the eyes of some, had just lost everything, was doing her best to stay positive. She had been thinking about selling the house in the very near future anyway. The belongings she had lost in the fire were just things. In fact, a lot of her sentimental belongings were in storage. She had been meaning to go through her storage unit and throw things out. Now, she was going to have to go through it a lot sooner than she had planned but for very different reasons. There were favourite dolls in there from her childhood, photos from her family, blankets, furniture, and mementos from her marriage to Mark. They were remembrances that would make her feel whole again. The smell and feel of her past. Photos, books, and clothing that would bring her back to a specific time and place and make her smile. In the end, Edie realised that even they were just things. They didn't mean anything. The past was gone. She was who she was right now, at this moment, and that was a very lucky woman, surrounded by friends.

Laurie walked back into the den, but she didn't sit down. Everyone stopped talking and looked up at her.

"What's up, Laurie?" asked Edie.

Laurie smiled at her and looked at Jeff. "I have a possible missing person in Edgartown. At the very least, I have an hysterical boyfriend."

"Who is it?" asked Jeff.

"Karen Malone," said Laurie.

"From The Shore Line Hotel? I know her. Nice girl," said Jeff. "She's missing? For how long?"

"Well, I'm not sure," Laurie ran her fingers through her long hair. "Her boyfriend, Sam, said she was home and then she wasn't. It was like she just disappeared. That's what Jack told me anyway. He wasn't making a whole lot of sense, frankly. I'm heading out there now. Jack's at the station." Laurie looked at Charles. "You want to come with me? Deputy?"

Charles stood up. "Sure."

"Okay," said Laurie. "I'll just have to change quickly."

Edie popped the last piece of pizza into her mouth. "It's turning into a busy night."

*　　*　　*

"You're cooking? That's a fucking joke."

113

Victor turned around to see Joey standing in the archway between the kitchen and the living room. Victor couldn't remember the last time that he had been happy to see his son. He scanned Joey quickly from head to toe. As usual, he was filthy. His jeans and shirt hadn't been washed or changed for days. His dark, oily, hair was matted to his forehead. Behind a sneer that matched his mother's, Victor could see yellow teeth embedded with plaque. Victor looked almost indifferently at his son. He had loved him at one time, when he was a boy. Then felt nothing but contempt. Now, he felt nothing at all. Just blank. Empty. That was the worst of it—feeling absolutely nothing for his child. Victor was sure that it was a defence mechanism. Turning off a switch. Victor was protecting himself from having to acknowledge what his son had become. It was just too painful. He knew as much as he wanted to know on a very superficial level. His son or not, Joey was mean. He was not a nice person. He had been a bully in school and it had eventually led to his expulsion. The overprotection and denial of his mother hadn't helped. She wouldn't accept the need for counselling. As a team, Victor believed they could have done something to help him, but on his own against the two of them, Victor had been powerless. The stories around town had eventually made they're way back to him—fights, theft, drugs. Victor told himself that some people were just bad, and Joey was one of them.

114

"Where have you been?" asked Victor. Not that he gave a shit, but he felt obligated to say something and that was the best he could come up with on such short notice.

"Out," said Joey.

The answer was ridiculous; it said nothing. It was also as much information as Victor wanted to hear. Victor turned back to his onions. He picked up the diced pieces and threw them into the oil and garlic. They sizzled when they hit the bottom of the pot. He opened the drawer in front of him and pulled out a can opener. He started opening a can of tomato paste. Victor could feel Joey's eyes boring into his back. The hair stood up on Victor's neck. His scalp got sticky with sweat and he felt his chest tighten. He didn't think that Joey would actually hurt him, but he had never been entirely sure, especially lately. Victor dumped a package of sliced, white mushrooms into the pot with the oil, garlic, and onion. He turned around to face his son, but Joey was gone.

Victor turned on the hot water and rinsed his hands under the running water. Satisfied, he turned it off and reached for a hand towel. He walked out of the kitchen just in time to see Joey walking slowly, methodically, up the stairs. He was carrying his mother across his arms like one of the monsters from a classic Universal Picture carried a fainted maiden. Frankenstein, Wolfman, Creature From The Black Lagoon, they had all carried their limp, almost lifeless women in front of them, slung over both arms—pathetic attempts at romance by a

115

misunderstood creature. Joey and Violet mimicked those creatures in an uncomfortable, familial farce. Violet's head lolled on her neck like that of a lifeless baby. Ignoring the presence of his father, Joey kept walking until they were out of sight. Victor heard Joey kick the bedroom door closed behind them. The hallway was dark and quiet. Victor went back to the kitchen and his cooking.

10

One look through the sliding glass doors, and the receptionist was on the phone, announcing a 'code blue' over the internal public address system. The hospital came alive. The doors slid open, and a doctor and a team of emergency workers ran toward Corey as he carried Tina into the hospital. Corey winced involuntarily at the hospital's stark white gleam—a drastic contrast to the dark Vineyard night. At first, a guttural, "Help!" was all that he could manage. Corey took a deep breath. "My girlfriend's been shot," Corey finally managed. His voice was weak. "She's pregnant. She's pregnant and she's been shot." Saying those words out loud took all of his energy. Two male nurses reached for Tina. Corey felt her weight lift from him as she was moved onto a gurney. His arms were cold, numb, and gelatinous. They felt like they had just been jiggled free of one of those copper jelly moulds from the sixties. He half-expected to look down at them and see fruit suspended in his biceps. Like jellied salads, his arms held their shape, but essentially, they were useless.

Stress raced behind Corey's eyes. His thoughts were becoming confusion. Corey tried to focus on the walls, on the reception desk, on anything, but he was finding it a challenge. He could hear blood pumping in his ears. Corey was out of his element. Getting Tina here, to this point, was the best he could do. He was still trying to sort out how this had become his life—Tina's life. This was not what their trip to Martha's Vineyard was supposed to be. This wasn't how it was supposed to go.

The gurney was under Tina, and she was being pulled away. A blood pressure cuff was on her arm, and an elastic strap held a clear, plastic mask over her nose and mouth. A nurse began cutting through her dress with those funny bent scissors they always had in hospitals. *"They must be so sharp,"* Thought Corey. *"Hey, that's Tina's favourite dress!"* Corey was being led in one direction and Tina was being taken away. The last he saw of her was her exposed, bloodied belly as her dress was pulled away by the nurse's gloved hand. Corey could feel his lips moving, but he wasn't sure if he was making any noise. Tina was gone. What did he do now? Protest? Chase her? There was nothing he could do for her. Corey felt like the second he had stepped through the hospital doors, his brain and his body had hit their limits. It had been all he

118

could do to make sure that he got them to that point. Now, he was shutting down—first his brain, then his body. Reaching forward to step with his left leg, his foot folded in as it hit the ground. He felt his ankle hit the linoleum with a sharp crack. His right knee buckled...then his left. Corey felt strong hands grab him under each arm. The hospital faded into a white blaze of light...

Corey knocked when he got to Cameron's office. The wood door was ajar, but closed enough that Corey didn't feel right just walking in.

"Come in!" called Cameron from behind the door.

Corey pushed the door open with his elbow, still wiping soapy water from his hands with paper towels. "You wanted to see me, Cam?"

"Yeah, man. I did. I was hoping that we could do each other a favour," said Cam.

"Sure," said Corey. "What do you need?"

"I can take care of those last two cars we need done before week's end, but I still have to deliver some Christmas packages before the end of the year too." Cam looked up at Corey from behind a cheap metal desk.

"What do you want me to do?" asked Corey.

"I was hoping you would make the deliveries for me. They're going out to friends and family which I realise kinda makes me sound like a dick." Cam stated matter-of-factly. "But if I go, it will take forever. People will be forcing me to come in for drinks and meals and I'll never get the hell out of there. I'll be stuck on that goddamned island for a week!"

"Island?"

"Oh, yeah, I didn't mention that. The deliveries are all on Martha's Vineyard. Have you ever been?" asked Cam.

Corey shook his head.

"What about Tina?"

"I'm not sure. I don't think so," Corey knew that she had never been, but he didn't want to tell Cameron. He wanted it to sound like there was a possibility that Tina had walked the beaches of the famous island—that it was certainly feasible that she had sailed its blue seas. The reality was that there wasn't a fart's chance in a hurricane that Tina or Corey had been on "The Vineyard". He just didn't want Cameron to know that.

"Well! This will be kinda cool then! This weekend is the Vineyard's 'Christmas In Edgartown' celebration! You'll have a blast. Really!" Cam stood up from behind the desk and walked across the room. He lifted a box from a shelf and set it on the desk in front of Corey. "All the presents are in here. It will take you less than a couple of hours to drop them all off. Then, the rest of the time is all yours. For your trouble, I'll pay you a thousand bucks. Consider it a Christmas bonus. You've been doing really good work around here—we did a lot of business this year because of you—you've earned it...and you'll be doing me a huge favour. What do you say?"

Corey couldn't believe his ears. "Absolutely, Cam. No problem at all. I really wanted to take Tina somewhere before the baby came, but I didn't think we were going to be

120

able to swing it." By 'swing it' he meant afford it, but he was hoping it sounded like they were too pressed for time. "This will be just enough to feel like a little getaway. It's their Christmas thing, you said? Tina really loves Christmas."

"It sure is. You're going to feel like you're walking around in Charlie Brown's fucking Christmas—no joke." Cam laughed. "Book a night somewhere if you can find a room and bring me the receipt."

Corey picked up the box. It was lighter than he imagined. "What's the present?"

"There's a few different parcels for a few people. When you get to the Vineyard, open the box and you'll see what I mean. They're all wrapped and addressed," Cam said. "They're just little token thank you gifts, mostly—pain in my fucking ass is what they are. Well, now they're a pain in you're ass!" Cam laughed at his own joke. "Alright. Go home and talk to Tina. You'll have some driving to do. Have fun, man! Just go to the island, get these out of the way, and then enjoy your weekend."

Corey picked up the box, and walked out of the garage to the car. Wrapping his left arm over the box, with his right, he took his keys out of his pocket, stuck one in the lock, and turned it. The heavy door of his 1970 Firebird swung open with the resentful purpose of an old man standing up from his favourite chair. Corey slid into the drivers seat. Dropping the box onto the passenger seat, Corey put on his seat belt, and closed the door. He drove off *the garage lot in, what he was sure was, record time. He couldn't wait to get home and tell Tina the good news.*

*   *   *

Mike, Trish, and Virginia walked up North Water Street toward The Shore Line Hotel and the Edgartown Lighthouse. Even though the snowfall had increased, the cloud cover was now intermittent. Bursts of blue moonlight filtered the night sky, illuminating the wintery scene around them. Skeletal shadows of leafless trees clawed their way across the snowy street. Yellow, green, and red Christmas lights were strung around each lamppost, their glow fending off the shadows of the night.

"This is amazing!" Mike exclaimed with child-like excitement. "It's like a movie! If *It's A Wonderful Life* had been in colour, it would have looked like this." Mike laughed with pure joy.

"Totally," said Virginia.

"I forget how pretty it is sometimes. I feel like islanders tend to take it all for granted," said Trish. "I love seeing it through your eyes, babe." She gave Mike's arm a squeeze. "I kinda feel like I'm seeing it for the first time. It's so beautiful."

"Hey!" Mike exclaimed. "Do you hear that?"

They all stopped talking and listened through the snowfall to the rise of voices up ahead.

"It's the carollers!" said Virginia.

"Christmas music is so happy! I love it!" said Trish.

"Did you all tell me there were going to be carollers?" asked Mike. "I don't think I knew that."

"Oh, there totally is! There's lots of things—carollers and everyone sings along, there's hot cider, and fresh baked cookies, eggnog. Then the lighting of the lighthouse!" said Virginia.

"I don't know how I lasted this long without Christmas In Edgartown," said Mike. "Has this been going on since back-in-the-day?"

"Not really," said Trish. "I think the first one was in, like, 1981."

"What did everyone do before that?" Mike asked.

"The same thing everyone does at Christmas," said Virginia. "They drank." The three friends laughed and made their way toward the sound of the carollers.

As North Water Street curved around the harbour, the glow of the Shore Line Hotel brightened the night. The hotel's American Colonial architecture, so prevalent throughout New England, was twinkling with holiday cheer, strung with white lights across every windowpane, every gable. Lights, boughs of garland, and red ribbon, trimmed the length of the picket fence and the crowded wraparound porch. People huddled together under the heat lamps. Each one of them, almost uniformly, holding a hot toddy with mittened hands. Their faces rosy from the night air, everyone laughed and caught up with friends whom they hadn't seen in the off-season.

Through the front doors of the hotel, Mike could see a warm, and inviting glow emanating from the crowded restaurant. Inside, people lined up at the bar. It was also where the carollers were. For the most part, people had herded themselves outside, braving the elements to secure a spot for the lighting of the Edgartown Lighthouse.

Mike led the girls along the crowded walk, up the stairs, and in the front doors of the hotel. The bar was off to the right and through what was usually a more than ample passageway, double doors clogged with excited Christmas partygoers. Mike turned around, reached out for the two women trailing behind him. With both arms, he corralled them out of the on-coming traffic. "Why don't you two wait here? I'll go get us drinks and come back for you."

"That works for me," said Virginia.

"Me too," agreed Trish. "I'm drowning in coats! I'm too short!"

Mike laughed. "We can't have that! I'll be right back, ladies." He turned back toward the bar and began to fight his way through the crowd.

As crowded as it was, Mike loved it. It really was the most Christmas-y experience of his life. Coming from Austin, Texas, his Christmas was a far cry from the traditional fairy tale holiday. He had always loved Christmas as a boy, and still did with his family back home. Austin went full out with the Christmas lights, and he loved the Armadillo Christmas Bazaar. He went skating on the Whole Foods roof, but skating in the sun when it

124

was seventy degrees just didn't scream Christmas to him. Especially, as a kid, when he would go home and watch Rudolph The Red-Nosed Reindeer, Frosty The Snowman, and Miracle On 34th Street. Even when he would watch White Christmas with his grandmother, the characters weren't happy until it snowed. There was Christmas magic in that snowfall—they knew it and he knew it. Mike found his place in line at The Shore Line Hotel Bar, and patiently waited his turn. He surveyed the crowd. The room was full of happy people. There was something about the island, thought Mike. People seemed to put a lot more effort into festivities. They enjoyed the simple pleasures in life a lot more than in the larger cities he had visited. It seemed to him that the islanders were less jaded—maybe because there were fewer options. People in bigger cities took a lot of their luxuries for granted. In the big cities, there were always several events going on every day and every night. Comparisons became inevitable. Attitudes were negative and nothing was ever as good as the first time or even the last time. What was the saying, "Familiarity breeds contempt"? Here, special occasions were just that— special. Islanders were excited about their events. Maybe because so many islanders put a lot of work into making them happen. Also, the islanders who didn't participate in the set-up always had friends or family who did. Vacationers were excited about being on holiday; that lent to the happy atmosphere too. It all made a big difference. Mike could see it. The positive energy was palpable.

Mike reached into his coat and pulled out the small, black velvet, box that had been burning a hole in his pocket all day. Gingerly, he opened it and looked inside. Its occupant picked up the light immediately and shone like he had plugged it in.

The ring was Mike's great-grandmother's ring. Mike had thought about buying a brand new ring for Trish, but somehow, antique just suited her better. Trish was an old soul. Something about the way she had gravitated toward living in one of the gingerbread cottages in Oak Bluffs, the way she tended to dress in long skirts and flat shoes. Trish was so knowledgeable beyond her years; Mike was always amazed at how smart she was. The way she wore her hair loose, barely wore any make-up, and was still so incredibly beautiful. His grandmother's ring was perfect. The centre stone was a quarter-carat flanked by a .20 diamond on either side, not too big to be considered splashy, but not so small that it wouldn't make an impression either. Its clarity was excellent—at least, that's what his mother said. Mike had to admit that he didn't know much about these things. What Mike loved about this ring was the setting. The setting was a raised floral lattice, delicate, feminine, and strong. The metal was 18-karat white gold but its rhodium plating gave it the lustre and strength of platinum. The European cuts on the stone, and the antique claw of the setting, gave the stones a warm and colourful glow that Mike hadn't seen in colder, modern rings. The ring embodied so many qualities that Mike

126

loved about Trish—her youthful energy, her old soul, her feminine gentleness and strength, and the fact that she was like no one she had ever met. When Mike had asked his mother for the ring, she had hesitated, but she could see by looking at him that Trish was the one. She gave it to him with her blessing.

"Excuse me, sir? What can I get you?"

Mike looked up to find himself face-to-face with the bartender, a young dark-haired girl with a big smile. Mike had been lost in thought. "Oh! I'm sorry!" Mike closed and lowered the ring box. "May I have two glasses of wine and a pint of Bad Martha's please?"

"You got it!"

"Thank you!" Mike barely got the words out when he was slammed from behind by a large man passing the bar. Mike's ribcage hit the bar rail hard. It felt like someone had swung a baseball bat into him. He gasped for air, the wind knocked out of him. Mike had reached out quickly to brace himself, but he still hit hard. He turned around just in time to catch the back of the huge, grubby man plough his way through the crowd.

The bartender came back and set down his wine in front of him. "Sir, are you okay? That guy really nailed you!"

Mike inhaled deeply before looking at the bartender. He grinned sheepishly. "Oh yeah, I've been in worse rodeos than this one and I ain't been bucked yet!"

The bartender laughed. "I'm not sure—is that a good thing?"

Mike grinned, still trying to fill his lungs with air. "Yes, I'm fine. Thank you though." Again, he inhaled as much air as he could. "I'm good."

"I'll be right back with that beer," she said.

"Actually, can you make it a club soda with lime? I think that would suit me fine."

"You got it." The bartender disappeared once more.

Mike rubbed his stomach. It hurt. He almost felt like he bruised a rib. He'd certainly done that in a rodeo.

"Here you go," The bartender said. "The drinks are on the house."

"Aw, thanks so much! That's really kind of you!" Mike smiled. "What do I owe you for the wine?"

"Nothing," said the bartender. She winked at him. "We're good."

Mike walked back over to Virginia and Trish with a broad smile. He handed the girls their drinks.

"What's with the grin?" asked Virginia.

"The bartender didn't charge me for the drinks!" exclaimed Mike.

"Wow! That's cool!" said Trish. "Who is it?"

"I don't know her name. I should have introduced myself, I guess."

Trish strained to catch a glimpse of the busy woman behind the bar. "I want to see who's making a pass at my man!" She winked playfully at Mike.

128

"Ha! No. It was nothing like that at all. Some linebacker went barrelling through and just about ran me over. She felt bad for me is all." Mike rubbed his stomach. "He really got me good." The memory of the incident made Mike wince reflexively.

"Jeez! Are you alright, hon?" Trish looked at him with genuine concern.

"Oh yeah," said Mike. "Like I told the bartender, I've been through worse rodeos."

Virginia laughed, "Of course, you have." Virginia looked at her iPhone. "Let's go outside and find a spot by the heaters. It's almost lighthouse time!"

11

When Laurie and Charles drove up the driveway, they found Sam Jones waiting for them in front of the house. Despite the cold, Sam was not wearing a coat or shoes. He was standing in his sock feet, with his arms wrapped around his chest, shivering on the front porch. As soon as Laurie put the car into park, Charles swung open the passenger door. He exploded out of the car, jumped over the front stairs, and landed on the porch with a heavy thud. He grabbed Sam by the shoulders. "Get inside, Sam! You're going to make yourself sick."

"I thought maybe I'd see Karen," Sam sputtered. Charles could feel Sam shaking in his grip. When he spoke, he stuttered like a frozen cartoon character.

"Even if you did see her, you're not going to be any good to her with hypothermia!" Charles opened the front door, pushed Sam inside, and followed him in. Laurie came in behind them and closed the heavy wood door, shutting out the cold night air.

"Is he okay?" she asked.

"I don't know—I think so," said Charles. Charles moved Sam gently toward Laurie, and Laurie took him by the shoulders. "Do you want to get him sorted on the couch with a blanket? I'll go see if I can find some coffee, or tea, anything hot."

Laurie nodded. "Sure."

Charles walked through the living room, back into the kitchen. There was already tea in a pot on the counter, and a kettle with a little water in it. Charles felt the pot of tea—it was still hot. He poured a mug for Sam. Before returning to the living room, Charles looked around the room. The back door was closed. He tried to open it—it was bolted. There were wet footprints on the floor. Karen's winter coat was hanging on the coat rack—or at least, a woman's coat was on the rack. He assumed it was Karen's. There was a casserole, macaroni and cheese—and maybe tomato—on the stove, but no one had eaten any of it yet. Charles spread his hand out just above the dish—it was still hot. Charles went back into the living room with the tea.

"This was already made. I hope that's okay." Charles passed it to Sam. "Drink this, Sam. It will help warm you up."

Sam reached his hands out from under the throw blanket in which he had been wrapped, and took the mug. "I made it for Karen."

Charles looked at Laurie. He sat back and let her do the talking.

Laurie looked at Sam with a kind but firm face. Her eyes were soft to draw him out, but her jaw was set and the muscles in her face were taut. "Tell me what happened, starting with Karen coming home from work, Sam. Take your time. The more you remember the better it is. Let me decide what's relevant. Okay?"

Sam nodded. "I was in here. I had fallen asleep on the couch. I didn't mean to, I just wanted to see the football highlights, ya know? Never fails, I always fall asleep. I shouldn't have sat down at all. Anyway, Karen came in through the Kitchen. She slammed the door, and it woke me up. She was screaming and yelling that some guy was chasing her! I thought that she meant a guy attacked her, but no one attacked her—turns out she didn't even see the guy. But she was sure convinced that there was someone there. I've never seen Karen so shaken up. She said, she saw really big footprints and everything. She said, she heard him running behind her, you know— in the parking lot at work—at the hotel. *Jesus, she was upset!* I told her to go and have a shower and change before supper. I thought it would calm her down, you know? That's why I made her this tea. It's got Chamomile in it. It's supposed to be soothing." Sam looked down at the mug of tea in his hands and took a sip. He swallowed, cleared his throat, and continued. "Then, when she went upstairs to take her shower, I went outside to get the dry-cleaning that she had forgotten out in the car. She was really wound up. I mean, she must have been, because when I went outside, the car door was open! She hadn't even closed it! I got the clothes, and closed, and locked the car. When I came inside, she was gone."

"Back up a bit, Sam," said Laurie. "We need to walk through that last part. You didn't step foot inside the house and realise that she was gone. What did you see, Sam? You came back inside the door with an arm load of clothes, and then what?" said Laurie.

Sam nodded and thought for a moment. He sipped more tea. Then he looked at Laurie with earnest eyes. "Right—sorry. I came back inside and took the dry-cleaning to the front hall. It's her uniforms for work, you know? That's where we keep them. She should be able to just leave them at the hotel but she's not allowed to—it's stupid. Anyway, I took them to the front hall—oh yeah—the front door was open! I thought it was weird at the time too. It was so cold—it is so cold out, you know? It's not like the door was open all night when I was home and Karen came in the back door and—aw Christ!"

"What, Sam?" asked Laurie.

"There were wet footprints on the floor—big ones too—just like Karen said she saw in the parking lot."

"There are wet footprints in the kitchen too," said Charles.

"Those could be mine from getting the cleaning," said Sam. "Then, I went upstairs and the shower was still running. I went into the bathroom and it was empty. Karen's uniform was still on our bed. She was just gone. She disappeared."

"Sam, has Karen mentioned any problems with any co-workers? Any unwanted attention from a man or anything like that?" asked Laurie.

Sam shook his head. "No, nothing!"

"I'm sorry, Sam. I have to ask you this—are you getting along? Was Karen happy with you?"

"You mean, do I think she was cheating? No, not at all. Karen and I love each other. I am always wondering what she sees in me, especially now because I don't even have a job or anything, but when it all comes down to it, we're happy, Chief... Really, we are."

"Do you have a recent photo of her that we could have? I'm sure most people, on-island, know who she is, but I'd like one anyway. Okay? There are a lot of tourists on the island right now. Maybe someone has seen her. I'm going to send forensics over here to see what they can find too. Okay?"

Sam nodded.

"Do your folks still live in West Tisbury?" asked Laurie.

"Yeah," said Sam.

134

"Can you stay with them for a couple of days?"

Sam nodded again. "Sure."

"Great," said Laurie. She stood up and walked across the room to place a phone call. When she was finished, she walked back over to the couch, Charles, and Sam.

"Tell her what you just told me, Sam," said Charles.

"Chief, I just remembered—it wasn't the kitchen door that woke me. It was Karen slamming the car door shut! I heard that crunch. You know? That car door sound?"

"Are you sure?" asked Laurie.

"Positive," said Sam. "I was already standing up, and walking toward the kitchen, when I heard her come in the back door."

"So, Karen slammed the car door hard enough to wake you up, in here, on the couch," said Laurie, "but the door was wide open when you went out to get the dry-cleaning."

"Yes," Sam said.

*   *   *

Karen woke up slowly. Her joints were stiff and her head felt heavy. She could hear her own blood coursing in her ears. She didn't want to move, or open her eyes. There was a slow and shallow pace in each breath. Karen could feel air flowing in and out of her nostrils. The air was cold.

135

She was cold. Her nostrils were hard and dry, not moist and supple. Her nose hairs were frozen hard and motionless. Their usefulness gone, they prickled as the night air wound its way around them. Karen could still smell though. In the icy air, there was a rich and heavy smell. It was sweet, and earthy, but with an undertone of oil or grease, she wasn't sure—something mechanical, maybe? Was she at a farm? It smelled like she was at a farm. Karen bought a lot of her produce at the farms on-island. The co-op farms like Ghost Island Farms were her favourites. The vegetables were much fresher than buying them at the grocery store.

Karen listened. She could hear something not so far away. *Swish, thunk, swish, thunk, swish, thunk*—it was steady, regular, rhythmic. The sound wasn't entirely unfamiliar, but she couldn't quite place it. Was it a machine? It had pace and rhythm like a machine, and that would explain the greasy smell.

Swish, thunk, swish, thunk, swish, thunk...

What was that sound?

Karen tried to move her toes, but discovered that she couldn't feel anything below her knees. She could feel her breathing, her chest rising and falling. Her breasts were sore from the cold. Her nipples rigid and aching. She shifted her hips slightly—found they were there—and they groaned as she forced them to function. She felt pain in her butt as it was pulled from its resting position. It stung, felt like her skin was tearing in little fissures. She was

136

lying on metal. Her skin had adhered to it in the cold. When Karen was a little girl, her mother had warned her about sticking her tongue to anything metal in the cold, because it would stick. Wasn't that why the schools turned off the outdoor water fountains in the winter? The cold would tear the skin off her tongue. That had terrified Karen as a little girl and now, her whole right side was frozen to a metal sheet or slab. As far as she could feel anyway. As her mind moved down, her legs faded from her awareness. There was no mind and body connection. Her legs just stopped—like they had been amputated at the knee a long time ago—the wound already stitched, and healed. Stumps. The feeling made her nauseous.

Swish, thunk, swish, thunk, swish, thunk...

Karen's shoulders shivered, and she felt her stomach flip-flop. The movement of her shoulders made her upper arms twitch, but they too, just faded away. Her hands weren't there. Karen tried to make a fist but her brain could not find the switch to flip in order to make her hands complete the command. Her mind was blank. Dark. Her fingers were not there to clench. Karen was telling her body to function. She could feel the strain, and pull, of sinew and muscle wrapping around her elbow, her upper right arm had also adhered to the cold metal beneath her, but then nothing. No pain. Just gone. Erased. Look ma...no hands.

Swish, thunk, swish, thunk, swish, thunk...

Karen knew that she had to open her eyes. The thought terrified her. Once her eyes were open, that was it. She would see what was going on, what was happening to her, and she would never unsee it. What if she didn't want to know? The last thing that she remembered was turning on the shower, going into the bedroom, and taking off her uniform. She remembered throwing it on the bed...

Swish, thunk, swish, thunk, swish, thunk...

Karen pushed her tongue out of her mouth to lick her lips. Her lips cracked, and tore, as she pulled them apart. She tasted the faint coppery warmth of blood. The sharp serrated slicing of the opening of her lips caused a chain reaction across her face. Small cold blades carved at her skin as muscles tried to fight her frozen flesh. Cold scalpel slices glided from her mouth, across her cheeks, and eyes. Every movement caused a chain reaction. She squinted reflexively at the pain then began to open her eyes. Her lids peeled back over dry eyes. Her vision was cloudy. There wasn't a lot of light—that didn't help. Where was she? As her vision cleared, Karen focussed straight ahead of her in the dark. Resting in front of her face were a pair of hands. Was there someone else here? The thought that she might not be alone gave her selfish comfort. They were tied together. Were her hands tied too? Is that why she couldn't feel them? Had they gone numb from being tied too tight? Karen tried to look past the hands in the dark, to see more of the company she kept. The fingers were limp—flaccid. There was no sign of

138

muscle tension, the kind of firmness that signifies life. The firmness created by blood coursing through veins. The skin on the hands was grey and blue. The fingernails were dark. The hands looked like they had been pricked with thousands of little needles. Karen swallowed with dread. Her throat was dry and thick. *That's how my face feels,* she thought. Karen held her breath, and felt her heart skip. *Those are my hands.*

Swish, thunk, swish, thunk, swish, thunk...clang!

That noise. Karen recognised it now. The rhythmic sound had stopped, and it had been followed by a clang—a definite clang. It was the clang of someone dropping a shovel. It was distinct. The noise she had been hearing was digging. The slice of a shovel into earth—*swish*—and the dropping of soil—*thunk*—but the digging stopped. The shovel had been thrown down. Whoever was digging, whatever they were digging, had finished.

Karen gave a hoarse grunt as she was yanked down the metal bed of the pick-up truck like a sack of grain. Skin that had adhered to the truck bed tore off like phyllo pastry. Hair pulled from her scalp. Scalp lifted from her skull. Karen felt a strong hand grab at her side and roll her over. An arm grabbed her roughly under her breasts, across her rib cage, and hauled her up. Karen's head lolled uselessly. She was overcome, first with dizziness, then nausea. She vomited. The warm spatter ran down her chest and stomach. She felt her bladder release. The warmth running down her legs felt nice. The man carrying her either did not notice or simply didn't care. Karen's vision was still weak. She tried to lift her head—to control it—anything she could do to see where she was going. She could hear the man breathing heavily in her right ear, but she could not see him. She could feel the bulk of him pressed against her back. He was walking slowly and with a heavy step. Karen couldn't kick, she couldn't claw. She tried to scream but could find no voice. The involuntary grunt in the flatbed had left her throat raw and sore. The man stopped walking. Karen hung in the man's arm, motionless. Numbness was creeping up her limbs now. Karen felt the hold of the man's arm release, and she fell. Karen's head spun in the air like that of a marionette. Her arms swung above her head in a black comedy. She hit the ground hard—first her knees, then her hips, back, and her head. Karen tried to focus but she couldn't see. It was too dark. Then, she heard it again.

Swish, thunk, swish, thunk, swish, thunk...

This time, she felt the cold earth hit her on the stomach, on the neck. Karen felt pebbles hit her cheeks. She got sand in her eyes, but did nothing about it. She did not even blink. Karen felt a shovel full of earth fall on her forehead. A faintly audible breath of air escaped her lips. It wasn't long before Karen stopped feeling entirely. Karen was dead.

* * *

Corey woke up in Martha's Vineyard Hospital. It was night and his room was dimly lit. Low light cast a murky yellow light across the green walls. He lifted his head slowly to look around. Pain unwound—fast and hot, across his skull like tendrils of a jellyfish. As he craned his neck, thin strips of fire rolled out from the base of his neck. They pulled through his flesh, pulled under his skin, they demanded his return to the support of the bed beneath him. Finally, his vision went white, and he dropped his head. Corey just lay there. His skin now glistening with beads of sweat. He waited for his breathing to regulate. With his right hand, he groped for the bed controls. He found it and raised it into his line of vision and tried to make sense of the symbols and buttons. Tentatively, he pressed a toggle switch, and slowly the head of his bed began to elevate. He could see three other beds. Two of them were occupied and one was empty. Both of his roommates were asleep, at least they looked like they were asleep. Corey lowered his bed back to its original, horizontal position. As the muscles in his neck relaxed, the pain in his head subsided, but a dull residual throb remained. Corey wasn't sure if he was crying or not, but he could feel tears leaking out of the corners of his eyes, and running toward the pale green pillow case...

When Corey got home, the door wasn't locked. He blew into the living room with considerably more energy than usual after a long day at the garage. He flung the door open, knocking over a coat rack that was always close to

141

toppling under the weight of too many coats. Tina jumped up from her place on the couch, and immediately clutched at her swollen belly with both hands.

"Holy crap, Corey! What are you trying to do—make me shoot this baby across the room? Right here? Right now? I'm about to pop as it is!" Tina took a deep breath. "You scared the bejeezus out of me!" Another deep breath and Tina turned to make her way slowly toward the kitchen. It was more of a kitchenette, really. The fridge and stove bookended a short counter top that had a sink carved in the centre.

Tina and Corey lived in a one bedroom apartment, but the living room, dining room, kitchen, was all one room. When the landlord had shown them the apartment, he had referred to it as "the great room". Corey and Tina both remembered having to cover their faces to choke back a laugh at this description. A multi-purpose room, like this, was a "great room" if you were a Kardashian, and you needed a golf cart to get from one side to the other. If you were an unemployed, pregnant woman with a boyfriend who worked in a garage, and you lived in a one bedroom walk-up over a Korean restaurant—there was nothing 'great' about it. Still, they did like their apartment. It was cosy. There was more than enough room for the two of them, but they weren't sure what they were going to do when the baby came. They figured that the three of them would share the room for a while until they figured something out.

"Sorry, babe! I've got a big surprise for you though!" Corey said as he righted the coat rack. He turned and beamed at Tina. He was bursting at the seams. He had been excited when Cam had given him the news in the office, but his excitement had grown with every mile home. Now, every cell in his body felt alive. It had been a long time since he had been able to bring home news like this. It seemed that ever since the good news of the baby, everything had been stressful.

A smile spread across her face as she watched the excitement in his eyes grow. Finally, she asked, "Okay, what is it?"

"Maybe you should sit down first," Corey said.

"Oh for crying out loud," Tina laughed. "Just tell me."

"Cameron has some deliveries to make, but he's too busy to do them himself. They have to be done before Christmas. So, he's asked me to do them!" Corey was still beaming.

Tina's smile was replaced by a quizzical grimace. "Did I miss something? Your surprise is that you are going to work overtime?"

"Not exactly..." Corey said smugly. "He has asked me to make the deliveries for him this weekend and you are coming with me! He's paying for the whole trip! It's sort of a 'Christmas bonus' for all of the good work that I've done this year. We can make a little trip out of it!"

"Oh, Corey." Tina's shoulders drooped a little. She looked down rubbed her belly again before continuing. "I'm

143

really happy for you, honey, but I'm tired. I'm not sure if I'm up for a road trip. Long days in a car?" Tina reached out for him. She put her hands around his neck and kissed him. "I don't want to rain on your parade, but I don't know if I can do it, hon."

Corey smiled and turned away from her. "I understand. The car ride, the ferry ride—it would be tough, I guess." He said.

"Really?" Tina asked. "You're not mad?"

"No, not at all," he shrugged. "I'll just go to Martha's Vineyard by myself. It's okay…"

"Martha's Vineyard!" Tina exclaimed.

"Oh yeah, didn't I mention that part? We're going to the Christmas In Edgartown celebration on Martha's Vineyard! Well, I guess, I am. I'll buy you a present though. Maybe they have a nice little lighthouse, or a mug, or something. Would you like a mug?" Corey's smiled mischievously. His eyes twinkled.

"We're going to Martha's Vineyard?" Tina kissed Corey hard.

"Well, I don't know, babe. I wouldn't want you to over-exert yourself. What with you being in such a delicate way and all…" Corey laughed at his own joke.

"Corey Johnson! What am I going to do with you?" Tina kissed him again. "I've always wanted to go to Martha's Vineyard. It sounds so romantic! And we're going to go at Christmas!"

"Yes, we are," Corey looked Tina square in the eyes, and held her face gently with both hands. She kissed him. It was a long and gentle kiss.

"I love you, ya big goof," said Tina.

"I love you too, sweet girl."

* * *

As they stepped outside, the crowd started counting down, "Ten!...Nine!...Eight!..." Opting to leave the masses under the porch heaters behind, Mike led Trish and Virginia down to the lawn. The three of them stood staring out into the darkness. Across the street there was a barrier of wild bush, and then nothing but black. Out in the darkness there was the ocean, Edgartown Harbor, and the Edgartown Lighthouse, but nothing could be seen. The three of them wrapped arms around each other. Mike felt the broadest of smiles stretch across his face.

"Five!...Four!...Three..."

The three of them joined in the count. Mike looked at the girls and saw the happiness on their faces. "Two!...ONE!"

The Edgartown Lighthouse burst into a multi-coloured spectacle. All of a sudden there was life where there hadn't been just a moment ago. The red, green, blue, and yellow lights outlined the black and white metal of the door, windows, catwalk, and lantern. Lights trimmed the wreath that hung festively in the centre of the tower. The sand of Lighthouse Beach was now awash with a warm holiday cheer. The black waves of Edgartown Harbor now sparkled with reflective multi-coloured light. Christmas In Edgartown was official. The festivities had begun.

Mike looked quickly at Virginia and nodded. Virginia giggled and took out her phone. Mike could feel his heart racing. His palms began to sweat in his gloves. He was surprised. Up until now, he hadn't been nervous at all. He didn't think that he was going to get nervous. Mike had begun to think that maybe only other guys got nervous when they proposed. He knew that he loved Trish and he knew that she loved him, so what was the big deal? The big deal was *that it was a big deal*. Mike was excited about the life that they were going to share. He was excited about all of the decisions they were going to make together— decisions about their lives, about their children's lives. He was excited about not having to face whatever was headed his way alone.

"Trish?" Mike turned toward her and felt his eyes well up with tears of emotion.

Trish turned to face him. She was smiling, almost laughing with joy. Happiness was written all over her face. Her cheeks were rosy from the cold. She saw the tears in his eyes and she sobered immediately. "Mike?"

"Trish, I knew, from the moment I first laid eyes on you in Pretty Vineyard Girls, that you were the one for me. Even before I heard you speak, I knew. I was so grateful when you agreed to go out with me. After that first date, I

146

was willing to do anything to keep you in my life, because I knew that I never wanted you to leave it." Mike got down on one knee.

Trish gasped and brought one mittened hand up to cover her gaping mouth. She began to cry. "Oh my god," was all she said.

"Oh, honey don't cry!" Mike said. His sober tone cracked into a smile, but only for a moment. He regained his composure and continued. "Trish, I would like nothing more than to have the honour of being your husband. Trish McKenzie, will you marry me?"

Trish wept openly. With his left hand, Mike reached for her right, and gently, slipped off her mitten. Still holding her hand, he kissed it. Mike reached into his pocket with his right hand. He reached deeper. Mike began to fish frantically. Mike began to sweat again. He stood up.

Virginia, who had been recording the event with her iPhone, paused and looked at Mike. "What's going on, Mike?" Tears streamed her face. Her voice had a serious tone.

"My ring!" Mike said with alarm. "The ring is gone!"

12

William Singleton stepped out of his gold and white, 1975 Chevy Blazer onto the, near-deserted, parking lot of Menemsha Harbor. There were two trucks—besides his—and one car, in the lot. It was early morning and the tracks that each vehicle had made in the snow were still fresh. The snowfall had increased overnight and everything was covered in about two inches of fluffy, big flakes. Sure, it was off-season, but fishermen still worked the boats all year. There weren't as many of them, but they were there. Some of them were working at maintenance and some were still fishing. The larger boats were all tied to the docks in the inner harbour, each of them with a corresponding shack, cottage, or home. The homes were above the harbour at the top of long, wooden staircases. The moorings in the outer harbour stood empty. In the

148

summer they were all leashed to brightly coloured, pleasure boats of all shapes and sizes. Now, they were just twisted, grey, wood poles that stuck out of the sea, their colour darkening where they broke the ocean's surface.

In the winter, Menemsha was grey and cold. The ocean was still. The fishing shacks were cedar, greyed by the elements and the salt air. The ground was frozen, almost entirely devoid of colour, and hard. The soil lacked the subtle give that it conceded under the warming influence of the summer sun. Popular Menemsha eateries like The Galley and The Home Port were boarded up, shut down for the season. The bright colours of their signage and A-frames were temporarily out of sight. All that remained were their grey winter façades. Menemsha Blues and their fun summer clothes were all locked up, their blinds drawn. The rich green foliage had made its escape too. The Menemsha Hills were brown and ashy. Leaves had blanched, or browned, died, and fallen—swept away by autumnal storms like much-used parchment paper. Branches were lonely and bare. Everything was dead.

Even though they were gloved, William plunged his hands deep into his coat pockets. He buried his chin into his scarf and collar. On the far side of the harbour, he spotted a fisherman loading the flatbed of his pick-up truck with tools and carry-alls. William headed in his direction.

He could see the beauty in Menemsha. Even in this, it's darkest, least popular season, William could see its beauty. There was a calming and a restorative quality about Menemsha. He wasn't able to pinpoint it. He doubted that it was one single characteristic that made Menemsha so magnetic, but rather a combination. People didn't flock to this port because of the mournful clang of the buoys in the harbour; they didn't come just to watch the fishing boat traffic that seemed so foreign and romantic to those who lived the big city life. People didn't come just for the amazingly, fresh seafood although, William suspected, that was as big a part of it as anything. It never ceased to amaze William how far out of their way people would go for good food. Any business that promised people either the best food, or the best sex, of their lives was a money-maker. His years in investments had taught him that.

At the thought of seafood, William looked up and saw that Menemsha Fish Market was open. He made a mental note to pick up some fresh fish for supper that night.

The caw of the seagulls, the ripple of the ocean, the tangy scent of fish, lobster, and salt water that sat in the back of your throat and didn't go away, the beach, and sunset in summer—all of it—it all blended together into the perfect detoxifier. Somehow, this entirely accidental combination cleansed the soul with a child-like happiness that no wall of adult cynicism could deny, and even in winter, William could still feel it. It was sleepy, but it was there. It was cold, and it was sharp, and it was grey, but it

150

was still there. Somehow, even the cold wind had a faint and friendly laugh.

"Good morning!" William Singleton's usually strong baritone came out muddled and croaky in that way the first words of morning sometimes do. Perhaps, he thought, it was nerves. He cleared his throat and tried again. "Good morning!"

The white-haired fisherman heaved a large plastic container onto the flatbed and turned in the direction of William's voice. His eyes twinkled iceberg blue, and his face was pink from the cold. His strong hands were red and chapped, but he either didn't notice or didn't care. "Bonjour!"

"You're French?" asked William. He felt foolish right after he said it, but the man's response had surprised him.

"I am," the fisherman smiled mischievously. "But if you walked all the way over here to tell me that, you've wasted your time. I already knew." He picked up another container, the same as the first one, and let it drop on the trunk with a loud, *bam.* "The wife finally broke it to me last Christmas. It was hard to take at first, but I've learned to accept it."

"I'm Sorry—you surprised me. I haven't heard anything but a Massachusetts accent since I got here," William explained. He wasn't used to feeling foolish and he didn't like it. He could feel himself burning up beneath his scarf.

The fisherman laughed. "Ça ne fait rien! No worries. I'm just pulling the line off your spool." He brushed off his hands and extended one to William. "Captain Keith Hurtubise."

"William Singleton," William shook his hand. "A pleasure."

"What can I do for you, Mr Singleton?" asked Keith.

"Please, call me William," said William.

"What can I do for you, William?" Keith asked again. "The folks here tend to call me Captain Keith."

"Have you been here a long time, Captain Keith?"

"I suppose that depends on your definition of a 'long time'. I've been here longer than most but not as long as a couple—here and there." Keith narrowed his eyes at William.

"Would you say that you knew everyone around here then?" asked William. William saw Captain Keith furrow his brow.

"William, I'm going to be straight up with you now. I don't think that you're the FBI. Even if you were, I may still have a Quebecois accent, and I might throw in a French word or saying now and again—mostly just to prove to my old brain that I can—but I emigrated from Canada a long time ago, and my papers are in order." Captain Keith stood a little taller and puffed up slightly.

William thought he looked like a silverback gorilla that was about to beat his chest in threat. He stepped back a bit. "I'm sorry, I don't follow you."

152

"Well, that's my point—I don't follow you either. Mon Dieu! Stop with the interrogation, and ask me what you want to know. No one around here is going to go for that either. They'll just clam right up. That's friendly advice. Now, let's try this again, mon ami. *What can I do for you, William?*" Keith relaxed in his stance, but only a little.

"I'm looking for someone," said William. "He's a fisherman around here."

"Well, now we're getting somewhere, if he's a fisherman around these parts, I surely know him. What's his name?" The twinkle was starting to return to Captain Keith's eye.

"Mark Sparks," William said.

Keith's shoulders went lax. Every last bit of breath left his body in a rumbling exhale. His eyes dulled, and for the first time since they started talking, Keith really stared at William. "Tabarnac," he said.

*   *   *

Edie woke up in Charles' and Laurie's guest room after a long sleep, but not feeling particularly well rested. Her sleep had been shallow and fitful. There were too many things on her mind for her to lose herself in a proper sleep. She was still dealing with the mechanics of it all. The emotional attachment to the whole experience was still buried deep underneath a growing "to do" list.

The first thing she was going to have to do was go to the bank. Her purse and wallet had gone up in the fire. She didn't have any identification, and more importantly at present, she didn't have a bankcard or any credit cards. She would have to reapply for all of them, which was a real pain in the ass. She was also going to have to take out a fair bit of cash. There were a few things that she needed immediately. She was going to have to buy some clothes, for starters. Little things like toiletries, she had at the inn. She even had a couple of spare toothbrushes there. She could stop and pick up what she needed. She was also going to have to figure out where her car was. It must still be back at the house—what was the house. Edie still thought, on some level, that she should be staying at the inn, but Charles and Laurie wouldn't hear of it, at least not right away. Maybe they were right. Maybe it was important to be around loved ones right now. She could hear herself saying the exact same thing to them, if the roles were reversed. Edie wondered, why was it so difficult for people to take their own advice?

Edie sat up in bed and looked around. It was a pretty room. The floor was dark wood, the same that ran throughout the house. A large, pale sisal, area rug covered most of it. Laurie had painted the walls a soothing, beach grass green, and the trim was white. Whitewashed wood made up the bones of the furniture. The comforter, curtains, accent vases, frames, and knick-knacks, were sea glass turquoise. Throw cushions were butter yellow.

154

Like all of the rooms in Laurie and Charles' home, this one was light, warm, and comfortable. Laurie had worked very hard to draw the beach into every corner of the house. She had succeeded. Laurie had good taste for a cop.

Edie's eyes focussed on the turquoise, wingback chair that stood beside the window, facing the ocean. Draped over it was a white robe with a piece of paper sticking out of the pocket. Edie pushed back the covers, and stepped down onto the coarse texture of the sisal rug. She walked across the room, and ran her hand over the robe. It was soft. The full, rich terrycloth felt comforting on her hand. Edie pulled the piece of paper out of the pocket of the robe. It was a note. She recognised Charles' handwriting right away.

'Dear Edie,

We hope you slept well. Here is a robe for you to wear around the house. We have put your clothes in the wash. They might be dry by the time you wake up. Under the robe are a few things that Laurie thinks will fit you just in case. She had to go to work and I have gone with her. I will be back this afternoon. If you will be here, call me, and I will bring home some lunch.

Love,

Charles.

P.S. I took photos of you while you were sleeping. I will be selling them on Craigslist to make up for the enormous expense, and emotional burden, of having you here. XO'

Edie laughed out loud. "Asshole," was all she said. Attached to the note, with a paperclip, were three twenty-dollar bills. On one of the bills was a sticky note that read, *'Cab Money'*. Edie felt the tears begin to well up on her lower lids.

*   *   *

As he pulled over onto the side of the road, in front of Edie's property, Victor strained his neck to get a better look out his windshield. Where was Edie's house? *What the hell had happened here?* Victor put the truck into park, unbuckled his seatbelt, and stepped out beside the stonewall he had been building, all without taking his eyes off of the still-smoking debris on the top of the hill. With an absent-minded swing, he gently pushed the door closed. The door swung with the complaint of metal on metal, barely gaining enough momentum to click shut. Instead of inspecting and returning to his work at the wall, Victor made his way up the long drive.

The second storey of Edie's beautiful home was gone. There wasn't even a support beam standing. From what Victor could see, it had collapsed into what remained of the first floor. The first floor windows were gone and the walls were black. Edie's home had been a log home. There were no sharp, charred stalactites of wood jutting toward the sky. All of the logs had been horizontal. The fire had made a fast meal the chinking leaving long gaping holes;

156

flames had eaten away window frames and left black maws in silent screams. The heavy stench of wood smoke hung thick in the air, but not the rich pleasant scent of a fireplace. Mixed with the stench of burnt rubber and charred metal, the black scent quickly coated Victor's sinuses. He gagged. Victor cleared his throat and spit up as much phlegm as he could gather—it didn't help. Halfway up the drive, a large man held up a hand so big that it could have held a basketball.

"I'm afraid I can't let you go up there, bud," the large man said. He wasn't a fat man—just big. He was tall and broad. Large features were centred on a face framed by white hair.

"What the hell happened? Where's Edie? Is she okay?" Victor was embarrassed that Edie's well being hadn't occurred to him until that very moment. He had been so overwhelmed by the sight in front of him, that he hadn't had time to think through any of the potential consequences.

"May I ask who you are?" The large man said. "I'm Fire Chief Peter Jefferies—retired. What's your business here?"

"I'm building a stonewall for Edie." Victor turned back toward the wall. He narrowed his eyes. From this angle on the hill, it looked cock-eyed. He'd have to fix that. The last thing he needed was someone else mucking about with his work. "At least, I *was* building a stonewall for

Edie." Victor turned back toward Chief Jefferies. "I doubt that I am anymore. Did you say that she was okay?"

"Yes, yes, Edie's fine. She was down at the bottom of the drive when the fire really caught," Chief Peter Jefferies said. "What did you say your name was?"

Victor extended his hand. "Sorry, Victor—Victor Helm. I'm a mason. I live here in West Tisbury."

"Victor Helm. I think I knew your father. He was a mason too. That must be your old man, right? There can't be two masons named Victor Helm on this island by sheer coincidence."

"Yes sir, that was my Dad," Victor said with pride.

"Nice man," said Chief Jefferies. "You living up in his place?"

"Yes, we are," said Victor. The pride slipped slightly at the mention of his family. He hoped that the questions would either stop, or take a different tack altogether.

"That's a nice house—real nice house. I was up there with my wife a long time ago. I don't remember what for—my boy was just young—probably something my wife and your mother set up. You know how the women are," Chief Jefferies paused.

The Chief's friendly expression disappeared, and just for a moment, he looked pained. He winced like a man does when he gets blood taken at the doctor's office, thought Victor. That was exactly it. The Chief looked as if he had tapped an unpleasant memory, and it was bleeding out.

158

Regaining his composure, he looked around, and grinned. "I guess we're not supposed to say things like that anymore."

"I won't tell," smiled Victor.

"Anyway, nice house is all I'm saying." The Chief extended his enormous hand toward Victor once more, but this time in a handshake. "Edie have your number?"

Victor shook the man's hand. Even though Victor was by no means a small man, he watched in disbelief as his own hand disappeared into the Chief's paw. "Oh yes."

"Why don't you give me your card just in case?" said the Chief. "The boys here say that she lost everything except the clothes on her back. Her phone was probably in the house too."

Victor handed over a card and watched as the Chief put it into his breast pocket.

"I'll give it to her personally. You have a good day, now, Mr Helm." The Chief smiled. It was a friendly smile, but it also told Victor, in no uncertain terms, that he was done here.

Victor walked down the drive to his truck. The orange tarp that he had left covering his progress on the wall had blown back, exposing his work. Victor secured it once again with stones. He debated on rolling it up and taking it with him. If he was done, he was done—although he did want to come back and straighten that one end. The soil at the end of the wall was slightly higher than the surrounding area. It would have to be smoothed out.

Snow, fire trucks, police cars, it had been busy here last night. Lord knows what they had stirred up. If Victor hadn't covered the wall with a brightly coloured tarp, he'd be starting again from scratch—that, he knew for sure. Victor leaned in and gave the earth a pounding. He looked at the wall from the end and eyeballed it. Victor decided that everything was fine, at least for now. He also decided to leave the tarp where it was. Better wait and talk to Edie first, he thought. Maybe her insurance would come through and she would want an even better wall. Stranger things have happened. He got into his truck and drove toward The Black Dog Tavern. It was a little late, but he wanted a cup of coffee and a good breakfast.

*　　*　　*

"Mark Sparks is a name I haven't heard in a long time," said Captain Keith. He ran a hand through his snowy hair. "What brings you around asking about Mark? Why now?"

William looked carefully at the Keith. He tried to analyse what he was thinking behind his pale blue eyes. The Captain's face was expressionless. "Mark is my brother—half-brother. So, you know him?"

"I'm sorry, William. You're brother is dead."

13

Mike thought he was going to be sick. *He'd lost his great-grandmother's ring!* How was he going to explain that to his mother? Worse than that—how was he ever going to be able to look at another ring in Trish's finger without feeling nauseous? Without being haunted with the knowledge of the ring that was supposed to be there. No matter how beautiful the replacement ring was, it would be exactly that—the replacement ring. It would be a constant reminder that his great-grandmother's ring was gone. It would be like that for the rest of their lives. It was gone! Mike pressed the heels of his hands into his eyes and rubbed them. When his eyes could no longer stand the pressure, he ran his fingers roughly through his hair. It was wet. He hadn't stopped sweating since the proposal. They had searched, but how were they supposed to find anything at night, in a swarm of people, at The Shore Line Hotel? They had tried to search the beach—the dirt path down to the beach was walled on both sides with thick beach grass—that had been impossible. And there were just too many people on the path and on the beach. The hotel was the same. Mike left a description of the ring with the manager, Mr Nelson. And while his expression had been sympathetic, he wasn't very reassuring.

Finally, the two girls had talked Mike into leaving. If they hadn't, he would still be there now, sifting through the sand at the base of the Edgartown Lighthouse with his bare hands. The three of them had walked back to the car in silence. It was still in the lot by The Newes. Virginia had taken her leave there. She headed to the Edgartown Police Station to meet Jack. She promised to tell him what happened in case anyone turned it in.

Mike sat on the edge of the bed in Trish's house. He could barely look at Trish. She sat quietly on her side of the bed, drinking tea. He looked at her once and could see the worry in her face. She wasn't worried about the ring—he knew it. Trish was worried about him. That made everything worse. Shame, anger, sadness, all tied his stomach into knots. This was as close as Mike had ever come to crying as an adult. He still wasn't ruling it out.

For Christ's sake—he had it in the truck. He had it at the Newes! He knew that he had the ring at the hotel bar too. He had taken it out, and looked at it, when he was in line for drinks! Mike slowed his train of thought down to

162

a crawl. He went through every second. He must have put the ring back in his pocket. In fact, he *knew* he put it back in his pocket. *Guaranteed.* He could still hear the ring box snap shut. He could feel the snap of the lid reverberate through his fingers. He could feel the felt box on his fingertips. He remembered feeling his keys stab the back of his hand, when he put the ring back in his pocket. So, what happened? Had someone seen the ring over his shoulder and lifted it? That's the only explanation. That must be what happened. But how could someone lift that ring box out of his pocket without his knowing?

Mike's eyes widened with realisation. It was that guy—the linebacker. The one who had slammed him into the bar when he walked by—why hadn't he thought of it before! What an idiot! Of course, it was him!

"I know what happened to the ring," Mike almost mumbled it, like he was afraid to say the words out loud. Like he was afraid that saying them out loud might make them untrue.

Trish set her tea down on her nightstand and leaned forward. "What did you say, babe?"

Mike turned to face her. "I know what happened to the ring—I mean, at least, I think I know what happened to the ring."

"What?" Trish asked.

"That guy! That guy who slammed me into the bar— he picked my pocket! He freaking mugged me!" Mike exclaimed.

"Are you sure?" asked Trish.

"Well, no I suppose I'm not sure. I don't have any proof, but think about it. He was a huge guy, and I watched him walk away through the crowd and not hit anyone else. There was no one yelling before he hit me either, so he wasn't causing a commotion, bullying his way through the entire room. I was the only one he slammed like a locomotive hitting a steer on tracks! Why? I had just been looking at the ring while I was waiting for our drinks. I had it out! He must have seen the ring—or at least the ring box—in my hand, watched me put it in my coat pocket and come right at me!"

"Did you see his face?" asked Trish. "Would you recognise him if you saw him again?"

Mike slumped a little. He shook his head. "I didn't see his face." He looked at Trish blankly for a moment, but then brightened. "But he was a really big guy, and he kinda stood out. I think I'd know him again. He looked pretty rough. I don't think he changed his clothes very often, and he smelled like a skunk that had been beaten to death with a salmon!"

Trish shook her head. "Well that's a start. We need to call Jack."

*   *   *

Corey drove through Falmouth on Woods Hole Road. The sky was clear, blue, and virtually cloudless. The

164

warmth of the sun heated the car. If it wasn't for the brown and bare trees all around them, Corey could almost believe that it was spring. The road curved to the right and the Atlantic Ocean appeared in front of them on the left. Tina couldn't conceal her excitement. Planting her hands on either side of her, she pushed her nine-month-pregnant body up as far as she could, out of her seat, and across Corey. Atlantic blue smiled up at them with licks of silver peaking every wave. Tina didn't want to miss a moment of it. At the sudden movement, Corey glanced quickly in Tina's direction, only to see her coming almost directly at him. Corey jerked back with a start. When he saw the smile stretched across her face, he couldn't help but laugh.

"Jesus! Be careful honey!" He chuckled. "I don't want to run us off the road just because you can't wait to see the freaking ocean! We'll be on the boat soon enough!" Tina settled back into the passenger seat, but her smile did not fade.

Corey turned his attention from the road just long enough to look out over the harbour. He couldn't see the ferry. As the trees that lined the highway flew past the window, Corey caught glimpses of a small bay punctuated by cedar shingled homes, each with their own deepwater dock. There were still a couple of sailboats tied to their moorings. Corey wondered if they stayed there all year. He hadn't thought that was possible, but what did he know? Corey really didn't know anything about boats. He was an inner-city boy—cars were his thing. When he was a kid, he

165

and his friends used to steal them. He got caught, he straightened himself out, and now, he fixed them, but he was still all about cars. Being on the ocean was a new experience for him. It was beautiful, there was no doubt about that—still no ferry though. As long as he was driving along the water, he knew he wasn't lost. In fact, they had passed green signs with white ferry symbols and 'Martha's Vineyard' written in big white lettering, so he knew he was in the right place. That thought had just crossed his mind when they passed another large green sign. This one read, 'Martha's Vineyard Next Left'.

Tina clapped her hands and squeaked with delight. "Corey, honey, did you see the sign? We're here! We're here!"

"Yes! I saw it!" Corey laughed again at her excitement. A warmth spread across his chest and down into his stomach. It had been a long time since he had seen Tina this happy. Oh sure, they were both happy, generally speaking, but how long had it been since something really excited either one of them? They had both been happy when they found out that Tina was pregnant, but pregnancy came with strings attached. A baby meant financial stress. Corey loved the idea of having a little boy or girl running around; he saw summer fun in the park and tobogganing in the winter, but he would have to be a complete moron to not see the expenses that came along with every single aspect of having a kid. He knew that Tina did too. They both knew that everything would work out fine, just like it did for everyone

166

else. There were plenty of people out there raising kids who were a lot worse off than they were. Yet, the stress was always back there, shadowing every thought that he had, until today. This weekend Corey couldn't think about anything except making Tina happy, and so far he was hitting it out of the park.

"Corey! There it is! There's the ferry!"

They came to a fork in the road. Woods Hole Road veered off to the right and the road to the terminal branched off to the left. Directly in front of them, docking in the distance was the ferry.

The ferry was huge—certainly, larger than Corey had expected. Corey hadn't really known what to expect. He hadn't really thought that much about it. He had given plenty of thought to the trip itself. He had thought about romantic walks surrounded by Captain's houses decked out in Christmas lights. He had thought about eating his weight in clam chowder—it was a personal favourite. But he hadn't thought about the ferry itself. It only made sense that it would be enormous—it didn't just hold people, it held cars for crying out loud, although he had no idea how many—but it wasn't until he saw it with his own eyes, that the boat's size really registered.

The ferry was gleaming steel, painted white with black trim. Corey thought it was pretty slick looking. There was a large black band about halfway up on both the starboard and port sides. Each stripe ran from the bow to the stern. If it was on a Camaro or a Mustang, it would be called a racing stripe, thought Corey. He didn't have a clue what it was called on a ferry. Corey imagined racing ferries and chuckled inwardly.

"It's huge! Isn't it Corey?" Tina asked rhetorically.

He nodded. "It sure is."

"It's like a cruise ship!"

Corey drove through the metal gate and stopped at the small, shingled booth. He rolled down his window and blinked reflexively at the rush of cold air. The man in the booth opened his window and turned to face Corey.

"Good morning," the man said. "What boat are you on?"

"We're on the 10:45 to Vineyard Haven, sir." Corey reached out his hand with a print out of his reservation, but the man in the booth ignored it.

"Last name?" the man asked.

"Johnson, Corey Johnson," Corey said.

Without looking Corey in the eye, the man in the booth pointed to a row of cars. "This is your boat coming in. Go get in line behind those cars there. They'll board you once everyone disembarks. Enjoy."

Corey steered the Firebird around the parking lot and took his place behind the rest of the cars waiting for the boat. There weren't many. Corey guessed there were about twenty vehicles in total. He should have asked the guy how many cars would fit on the boat. He really wanted to know. Corey put the car in park and turned off the engine. He smiled at Tina. "Do you want to get out and stretch your legs a bit?" Corey nodded toward the single storey building on the other side of the parking lot. "There's probably a bathroom in that building over there."

Tina followed Corey's gaze. "I do need to pee, but what if we start boarding?"

"The boat isn't even in dock yet. Then the cars and the people have to disembark before we can board. I'll bet you have ten, maybe fifteen minutes. Go, if you have to go," he said.

"Okay," Tina unbuckled her seatbelt and opened her door. "I'll hurry." She got out and closed the door behind her.

Corey chuckled. Tina hadn't really hurried anywhere in the last three months, but he thought it was cute that she thought she did.

Corey reached behind him and grabbed his backpack. He unzipped the front pocket and pulled out his reservation confirmation for The Ashley Inn and the map he had printed out that showed how to get there from the ferry. It looked easy enough. The place was right on Main Street in Edgartown. There had been a few cheaper places in Vineyard Haven, but this place looked really nice—just the kind of place that Tina would like—and it was right in Edgartown. Tina really couldn't walk as far as she used to, and Corey didn't like to push it. The last thing he wanted to do was cause Tina stress, and have her go into labour on Martha's Vineyard. He hadn't shown The Ashley Inn website to her. When she had asked him where they were

169

staying, he claimed he couldn't remember the name of the place, and that it was just a generic hotel room, nothing special. Then, he reminded her that they were on a budget. While parts of that story were certainly true, 'generic hotel room' was definitely a bold-faced lie. The Ashley Inn was a beautiful country inn—exactly the kind of place Corey imagined staying in on Martha's Vineyard. Tina was going to flip when she saw it. Of all of the places that he saw to stay on Martha's Vineyard, The Ashley Inn was definitely Corey's favourite—and it included breakfast too!

Corey looked up ahead of him. The boat had docked and its enormous bow doors had slid open, exposing its cavernous interior. Cars were pouring out, one by one, and people were being herded down the gangplank. None of them looked very happy. Corey took that to be a good sign. If people didn't look happy to leave, it must be a cool place. He had a great feeling about Martha's Vineyard. Corey and Tina were going to be talking about this trip for the rest of their lives—he was sure of it.

The passenger door opened and Tina plonked back into her seat. "Is it time?"

Corey watched as the Steamship Authority employees started waving cars forward and one-by-one the drivers in front of him started their engines. When the car in front of him roared to life, Corey followed suit. "Here we go!" he said.

*   *   *

The day was bright and cold. Snow fluttered toward the ground in large flakes, adding to the layer that had accrued overnight. The black Edgartown Police cruiser pulled up in front of The Shore Line Hotel, and parked at the mouth of the path that led down to The Edgartown Lighthouse. Charles and Laurie stepped out into the fresh cold of the winter air, and looked up at the old hotel. Like a lot of the houses in Edgartown Village, The Shore Line Hotel gave the impression that it had always been there. Additions had been built over the years, but the original structure, the main building, had been in place for three hundred years. White wood with green shingled roofs, turrets, and gables, wooden shutters that had been painted a deep forest green, the hotel was classic New England. The grounds were enclosed by a short, white, picket fence that looked almost comical against the grandeur of the building. Laurie and Charles gave each other a quick glance of acknowledgement, and headed toward the main entrance. The break in the picket fence opened onto a slate path, which ended at the front stairs of the hotel's wrap-around veranda. The heaters on the porch were blowing full force, but there was no one outside to take advantage of them. Boughs of pine, strung across every archway, sparkled with Christmas lights, but the lights had considerably less effect than they did at night. The daylight bleached out most of their seasonal, multi-coloured flicker, but not all of it. Fresh snow added a soft

171

and ethereal glow to each and every bulb. It was a look that Charles only identified with Christmas, and the sparkle of the lights was strong enough to make him smile as he followed Laurie into the hotel.

The hotel foyer was inviting. There was a Christmas tree in the corner, between the bay window and the fireplace that looked like Norman Rockwell himself decorated it. There were more boughs of pine on the fireplace, although these were not trimmed with Christmas lights. Nutcrackers in an assortment of sizes stood guard on the mantle, and a fire filled the room with crackles, pops, and welcoming warmth.

Laurie walked directly to the front desk of the hotel, but Charles took his time, absorbing every detail that he could. There was a large staircase in the centre of the room that led to the second floor. Glass paned doors beside the entrance led into the bar, or at the very least, one of the restaurants. Beside the staircase was a desk and computer. Sitting at the desk was a middle-aged woman, with bleached blonde hair, wearing a hotel uniform. Charles guessed that neither the hair colour nor the uniform had fit the woman properly for at least a decade. She was slouched low over the computer. The frayed mop that was the colour and consistency of dried hay hid her face. Charles also guessed from the positioning of the desk that the woman was the front desk manager, or at the very least, she was sitting at the manager's desk.

There was no one at the front desk when Laurie arrived, so she tapped the bell. A sharp *ping* pierced through the calm of the foyer, and the bleached-blonde looked up with a start. Her feet which had been splayed out underneath her chair, scrambled for purchase on the shiny wood floor. Finally, she grabbed at her desk with both hands, and forced herself up.

Charles watched the woman struggle to stand. She looked up in their direction and, for the first time, Charles got a good look at her. The woman's face was puffy and tired. Her eye makeup consisted of heavy black eyeliner and mascara. The contrast was alarming against the complete lack of colour anywhere else on her person. Surrounded by the Christmas décor, Charles couldn't help but think that the woman looked like a snowman, white and bulky, with straw hair, and coal eyes, except there was no child-like whimsy in her smile, just a sycophantic leer. "Chief Knickles!" the woman shouted across the room a little louder than what was necessary.

Barely audible, Charles heard Laurie mumble, "*Christ,*" under her breath. Clearly, Laurie knew the woman. Charles did not.

"Well, this is an honour!" the woman said. As she walked across the room, she ran her hands over her white uniform shirt and navy skirt in a vain attempt to straighten herself out. "Can I get you some coffee—or maybe something to eat? The danishes are just out of the oven!"

"No, thank you, Violet. Is Barry here?" asked Laurie.

"Mr Nelson? Yes, he's here. Shall I tell him what it's about?" asked Violet.

"That's okay, Violet. I'll tell him. Don't worry about it," said Laurie. She looked at Charles long enough to convey her thoughts and turned back to Violet. The lack of information left Violet's face awash with disappointment.

"Oh, I don't mind," said Violet. "Police business is it? I hope everything is okay. If I can be of any help at all..."

"Thank you Violet, we appreciate that," Laurie inhaled deeply and then exhaled. "If you could just tell Barry we're here..."

Violet turned toward Charles. She stuck out her hand, determined not to leave the conversation without gaining some information that might tell her what the Chief's visit was about. "I'm Violet Helm. I'm the front desk manager here at The Shore Line Hotel."

Charles shook her hand. "Hi Violet. I'm Charles." Charles pulled his hand away. It was sticky. Clearly, Violet had been dipping into the fresh pastries herself. He watched as Violet's stare became more intense. Her smile broadened revealing teeth caked with dough and lipstick. Charles knew that she was waiting for him to continue, but he just smiled pleasantly.

"Violet..." Laurie said. "Are you going to tell Barry that I'm here or shall I head back to his office myself?" Her tone told everyone in the room that the conversation was over.

174

Violet scurried out of the room like a rat being hosed off the street. She disappeared behind a wooden door and a sign that read, *Employees Only*.

When she was safely out of earshot, Laurie said to Charles, "I have no patience for that woman."

Charles chuckled. "Really? You hid it so well!" Charles grabbed a couple of tissues out of a box on the front desk and wiped his hand as best he could. "You don't see any Purell around here do you?" Charles peeked behind the front desk.

Laurie grinned and shook her head. "She thinks everything is her business. How she ended up manager at such a lovely hotel is beyond me."

"How did she end up here?" asked Charles. Upon finding a pump bottle of the hand sanitizer, Charles squirted a sufficient dollop into his palm, and rubbed his hands together. He waved his hands in the air, encouraging the alcohol to evaporate.

"I really have no idea. It all happened long before I got here. Slim pickings in the hotel industry that year, I guess." Laurie turned toward the employee door as it swung open and Violet returned to the lobby.

"I'll take you back now, Chief Knickles," Violet said with the same grin.

"That's fine, Violet," said Laurie. "Violet, I can't help but notice that you are the only one at the desk. I don't want to take you away from your duties. You are far too important out here to worry about me. Thank you for announcing me—I know the way." Laurie smiled as sweetly.

Charles watched Violet. It was clear that she was trying to figure out a way to get back to the office without disagreeing with the Police Chief's statement of her importance to the hotel. Violet's posture slumped with defeat.

"Thank you Chief," Violet said begrudgingly. "I appreciate that." She stepped aside as the two visitors headed back to the offices. She added quickly, "If there's anything I can do—"

"Thank you!" Laurie cut her off without turning around.

Barry Ullman's office, and the other employee areas from what Charles could see, was a striking contrast to the guest areas. The guest areas had been updated in seaside colours that, while still classic, were considerably more contemporary than the back of house. The General Manager's office was painted in a shade of terracotta and the wood trim was dark. The desk was also heavy, dark wood and the chairs facing it were rich brown leather. The whole effect told Charles that the back offices hadn't been decorated since the early or mid-seventies. There was nothing wrong with the décor, the furniture was in good repair, and from what Charles could see, the rooms were very clean. They were just dated. Employee offices really didn't need to be anything but clean and functional. It made sense to Charles that The Shore Line Hotel would have other priorities.

When they entered the room, Barry Nelson stood up, smiled, and reached a welcoming hand across his desk. "Chief Knickles! It's so good to see you. Am I mistaken or is this your husband? Charles, I think? Yes?"

Charles took the man's hand and shook it. Barry Nelson had a firm and pleasant handshake. "Yes, Charles. Nice to meet you, Barry. You have a beautiful hotel."

"Thank you! You and the Chief here should come and spend a night as our guests—sort of a 'stay-cation', if you will. On the house, of course." Barry Nelson's smile was certainly that of a practiced professional, but it came across as genuine.

"That's very generous of you, Barry, but we can't accept," said Laurie. "Optics. It wouldn't look right."

Barry paused for a moment in thought, and then brightened. "What if I gave you a weekend's free stay to put into a raffle for everyone at The Edgartown Police Department? It would make a great door prize. I'd like to be able to do something to show our thanks for your officers—all your hard work."

Laurie smiled. "That we can do. Thank you, Barry. I really appreciate that."

"Oh, that's good. That makes me feel better—a good way to start the day. Now, why are you really here, Chief?" Barry put his elbows on his desk and folded his hands in front of his chin. His smile never left his face.

"We're here about Karen Malone," said Laurie.

"Karen worked last night," said Barry. "We love Karen."

Laurie nodded. "Yes, and she disappeared last night right after her shift."

Barry stopped smiling. "She never made it home? You were talking to...oh, what is his name...Sam? Her boyfriend, Sam Jones?"

"Well, she did make it home actually. It looks like Karen was taken from inside her home," said Laurie.

"Oh my God," said Barry. He swallowed. "That's awful! It's scary, actually."

"Before she disappeared, Karen told Sam that she believed that she was being followed here in your parking lot, after her shift."

"Oh, lord," said Barry. The broad smile that had seemed screwed onto his face was gone. His eyes were wide and he grimaced as if he were being forced to smell something foul.

"Were you here last night?" asked Laurie.

Barry nodded. "Yes, it was the lighting of the Edgartown Lighthouse last night. It's one of our busiest nights of the year. I spent most of the evening in the restaurant and the kitchen. We never have enough hands on deck for nights like that."

"Do you remember seeing anyone suspicious? Do you remember anyone showing an unusual amount of attention to Karen, for example?" asked Laurie.

178

Barry shook his head slowly. "I don't, but as I said, I was really busy and I was on the other side of the hotel. Karen was over here at the desk. She stayed until the night auditor came in. She came in early too."

"Is the same girl working tonight?" asked Laurie.

"Yes, she'll be in at eleven tonight," said Barry. "Her name is Becky Wood. Do you know her?"

Laurie shook her head. "Islander?"

"Yes, nice girl. I can get you her phone number and home address, if you like," Barry offered.

"That would be great. Thank you." Laurie smiled.

"Chief, I hadn't really given this much thought except for the irritation that it caused my staff and me—young girls tend to be unreliable from time to time—but now that you're here about Karen, I'm worried," said Barry. He ran his hand through his dirty blonde hair and then took a mouthful of coffee.

"What is it?" Laurie asked.

"As I said, it's probably nothing...at least, I hope it's nothing," Barry paused. He winced as if the words he was about to say were going to cause him physical pain. "Karen stayed late last night because her co-worker, Amelia Davis, didn't show up to relieve her last night. Karen covered the first half of Amelia's shift, and Becky Wood, our night auditor, came in early to cover the back half."

"Has Amelia not shown up for work before?" asked Laurie.

"No, never. We even sent her home once because she came in sick, and she should have been in bed," said Barry. "Young girls can be unreliable, but really when I think about it, not Amelia."

"Have you heard from her?" asked Laurie.

"No, and she didn't show up for work this morning either."

14

Victor sat at one of the window side, wooden tables of the Black Dog Tavern. He had ordered 'The Loretta' breakfast when he arrived, and eaten most of it. The over-easy eggs were gone, as were the crisp pieces of bacon, and his white toast. He wasn't hungry anymore but the potatoes were salty and tasty, and he found himself picking at them piece by piece.

"Can I warm up your coffee?"

Victor turned his attention from the window and looked up at the waitress. She was smiling and pleasant looking.

"More coffee?" she repeated.

"Oh, yes! Sorry about that," Victor said. He held out his mug. "My mind was somewhere else."

"No problem," the waitress said. She topped up his mug and looked down at his plate. "Are you finished with that?"

Victor looked down at his potatoes. Absent-mindedly, he had mauled them rather violently with his fork. Vaguely warm, red and yellow, milky lumps stared up at him from his plate like a freshly beaten body. Victor grimaced. "Definitely. Thank you." He put down his fork and leaned back. The waitress swiped up his plate with her one free hand, and headed back to the kitchen. Victor took a sip of his newly poured coffee and turned his attention back to the view outside his window.

The restaurant was right on the beach. As far as vacation experiences went, it was hard to beat The Black Dog Tavern. The food was good, reasonably priced, and people could sit all day and watch the goings-on of Vineyard Haven Harbor. Victor was facing west which meant that he had the view of the ferries coming and going. Even being an islander, Victor never tired of watching the ferries or any of the boats. Violet hated it. Violet thought it was boring. If it had been up to her, as soon as she realised that this was all that island life was going to offer her, they would have moved to New York City or Miami or any of the big cities. She said that there would be more opportunities for the both of them in a big city. She said that it would be less of a financial burden if Victor found a good job in a good company and worked his way up the corporate ladder. Victor knew all too well what the opportunities would be for Violet.

Violet would have a better opportunity of finding herself a man who made a lot of money. Then she could tell Victor where to go and leave him. Sometimes, Victor wished that she would leave him. Sometimes, he wished that she would leave and take Joey with her. He imagined coming home to a house that wasn't heavy with anger and resentment. Victor thought of dating again. He fantasised about meeting someone who loved him for who he was and what he had to offer. It must be so nice to come home to a house like that. He knew that other people did it. He knew that other people didn't come home to people who hated him. People who resented him for who he was and what they felt he had turned him into. That was the real reason, wasn't it? Violet hated Victor because she saw what she had become. Violet saw who she was—who she was now—when she looked in the mirror and she *loathed* Victor for it. She blamed him for every extra pound, every wrinkle, and every fold. She heard herself when she grovelled to the guests at the hotel, she saw herself sitting eating dinner with the only man who would spend time with her—her son, and she hated Victor for every word she uttered, every glass of wine she drank, and every time she screamed at him for not being a man in their home and for not being a man in their bed. Victor stared hard at the ferry and tried to push out the memories of being in bed with Violet. He tried to focus on the waves hitting the shore but the

183

memories of Violet were washing their way in. Violet was slapping him on his back and on his head. She was hitting him hard enough to leave a mark and screaming, *"Why doesn't that fucking noodle dick ever work in our bedroom, Victor? Other men are dying to fuck me. I meet handsome men at the hotel every day! Maybe I should let them!"* Victor could see her picking up one of her pink and sloppy breasts and stroking it like a pet cat. *"I could just go up to their hotel room with towels or room service. Do you ever wonder if I do that Victor? Do you picture me sucking their cocks in their rooms?"* Victor could see Violet smiling at him. Her teeth looked sharp in the dim light, pointed. Her eyes so full of hate that he could barely look at her. *"Although I don't know what I'd do with a dick that worked!"* That's when Victor had left the last time. He left the room and he left the house. He didn't go back for three days. He hadn't answered his phone either. Sometimes he wondered why he had gone back at all. He should have taken off and left. He could have left the entire island and started a new life. The house was even entirely in his name—he could call a realtor and sell it. But he didn't. He didn't and he knew why he didn't—guilt. He had gone back out of guilt. Victor had returned to the house, but he never returned to the bedroom.

Victor reached up reflexively to wipe his cheek. He was surprised to find it wet. He was crying.

Joey slammed his full body weight down onto the bench across the table from his father so hard that for a

184

moment, Victor thought the bench saw going to collapse underneath him.

"Can I order some breakfast?" Joey asked. Without waiting for a response, he turned his face toward the restaurant interior and called out, "Can we get some service over here?" Then without missing a beat, he looked at Victor and said, "I don't know why you always come here. The service is fucking brutal."

Victor stared at his son and debated on arguing the point. He thought about pointing out that Joey had just sat down and that the restaurant was busy, but he decided against it. There were no words that would turn him around. There was no scenario that would make Joey have a moment of clarity and realise the error of his ways. Instead he asked, "How did you know I was here?"

Joey shrugged and huffed mockingly. "This is where you always come for breakfast if you're not eating at home." Then Joey's tone changed and Victor knew what was coming. "Anyway, Dad, I was hoping you could do me a favour."

Here it comes, thought Victor. Joey only ever needed one favour—especially if he was calling him *Dad*. Mentally, Victor started going through his wallet. He couldn't remember how much money he had on him. "How much?" Victor saw the anger briefly flicker in Joey's eyes, but it extinguished quickly as Joey remembered that he still needed the money.

Joey tried to smile. His teeth looked like Indian corn. "Just a couple of hundred," he said.

"What happened to the money that I just gave you?" Victor asked calmly.

Joey's eyes flickered again. "I had to pay some people. I'll pay you back! I'm doing a couple of jobs for a couple of people; I just haven't been paid yet." Joey leaned in. "Can I have the money or not, Victor?"

Victor stared at Joey and tried to find even a hint of the little boy that he had been once. He couldn't see him. Impossibly, Joey's once sweet blue eyes were black and his blonde angel hair was dark and matted. Victor leaned onto one hip and pulled his wallet out of his back pocket. He thought his breakfast might come back up and it wasn't sure if it was because of the fact that he was enabling his son and he knew it, because of the guilt of wanting his son as far away from him as he could get, or just the smell of him. Victor prayed to god that it was the last one. "Joey, you could use a shower and some clean clothes."

"What's the point? All the girls on this fucking island are stuck-up sluts anyway."

"You might just feel better about yourself, Joe. You could get a girlfriend if you put a little effort into it." Even Victor could hear the insincerity dripping from that last statement.

"Don't worry—I get it when I need it."

Victor looked in his wallet. There were three twenties in it. "All I have is sixty bucks," said Victor.

186

Joey reached into the wallet and snatched the money out before Victor could argue. "Fine. You can owe me the rest." Joey stood from the table, nearly knocking it over, and walked out without saying good-bye or thank you.

Victor watched him leave. He sighed. He was shaking with relief. He was relieved that his only child was gone. Victor knew guilt wasn't far behind.

*　　*　　*

William watched as Captain Keith unscrewed the outer lid from his Thermos. He flipped it over and, after unscrewing the stopper, filled it halfway with coffee. Keith then handed it to William. William took off his gloves and took the cup. The warmth felt good. He brought it up to his face and took a sip. Captain Keith liked his coffee strong and so did William.

"Here, hold up there William," Keith said. He reached into the cupboard beside his chair and pulled out a bottle of Irish whiskey. "A wee dram for what ails ya."

William shrugged and extended his cup to the Captain, who poured him a generous 'wee dram'. William soaked in his surroundings. The two men were sitting in Captain Keith's shack on Menemsha Harbor. The Captain had been working in it for an hour before William came along—he had caught him packing up—so the heater had been on, although William didn't think it was all that much warmer inside than it was outside. They were out of the wind though. That was a big plus. The shack was nothing more than a clapboard box on a two by four frame. There was a door centred on the north wall with a window on either side. The windows were the shack's only light source, but cans of WD-40 and jars of screws, lined up on the window sills, meant that the room was mostly cast in shadow. Inside, there was a workbench and shelves that all looked older than the Captain himself. A small generator took up a low shelf in one corner of the floor and rope, line, fishing gear, and tools hung from hooks of every shape and size on the walls. Some of the hooks looked like they had been there for a hundred years—rusted until they were one with the wall on which they hung. Others were shiny and silver as if Captain Keith had screwed them to the wall that very morning. For all William knew, he had.

"You're Mark Spark's brother then?" asked Keith. He took a healthy gulp from his own mug of coffee and whiskey.

"Half," said William with a slow nod. "We had different fathers. Hence, the difference in our last names."

"Well, I'm sorry that you've come all this way for naught," said Keith. "Can I ask you why you never tried to contact Mark before now? I don't mean to pry; it's just that Mark has been gone a long time. He hasn't had any family come around asking about him. Not that I know of anyway, and I think that I would have heard about it. We

188

might not like other people coming around asking questions about our business, but fishermen are a gossipy bunch. Like a bunch of old grandmères when we're together."

William smiled pleasantly. "No. There would have been no one else. We had no other family—not that I know of anyway. We haven't spoken for decades. Look where that gets you. Take it from me, Captain—life is too short."

"Oui, mon ami. That is the truth," Keith raised his mug.

"You haven't told me what happened to him."

"Did you know that he was a lobster fisherman, here, on the island?" asked Keith.

William shook his head and looked away from the other man. He was embarrassed at how little he knew about his only sibling. "No. I didn't know much about him at all. I only found out that he moved to Martha's Vineyard from his old landlord in Sanibel."

"Well, that's what he was. He worked the lobster boats and he was good at it. Mark was well liked among the boys here. As far as I know, he was well liked across the island. He was a good man, William. Your brother, Mark, was a good man."

William smiled faintly. Not so much because it was a comfort to know that his only brother had been a pillar of society, but rather because he knew what Keith was trying to do, and he appreciated it. It had been a long time since someone had gone out of their way to show him that level

189

of kindness—taken his feelings into consideration. William had been nothing but business for so long, he had forgotten how good it felt to care for someone, or how good it felt to have someone care for him. Even a simple gesture by this man, a complete stranger, stood out. That was no way to live. It had taken him far too long to figure that out. That was why he had missed out on having a brother in his life. It was so much easier to turn the emotions off and push them out of his mind. But that hadn't earned him anything but a lot of money and the right to be completely and utterly alone.

"William?" Captain Keith leaned forward and turned in William's direction. "Are you alright?"

William looked up at Keith and cleared his throat. "Oh, I am sorry. Thank you Keith. That's nice of you to say. A lobster fisherman? Well, we didn't have that in common. Go on...please."

"There's not that much to tell you, really. Mark went out early that morning like he always did. The wind was there but it was a manageable twenty knots. They had fifteen lobster pots that they wanted to check on. I remember talking to Mark's captain about it the day before. He was a good man too. Working lobster traps is tough work—dangerous work. I remember the weather network showed that there was the possibility of storm activity coming in that afternoon, but there was nothing to worry about, or so we all thought. Other men went out. I didn't, as luck would have it. Then the sea got mean, really mean. It can happen you know—it can turn on you in a flash. On that same day, another boat No Limits went out and the ocean got a hold of her. One big wave crashed them into another. Their windows in the wheelhouse blew out, and they took on water fast. Three men went out on that boat and only one came back."

"And Mark's boat?"

Captain Keith was silent for a moment. When he did speak, his voice was quiet, almost a whisper. It was as if telling these stories was bad luck. As if he was afraid that the ocean would hear him. "The Ellen Jane?" Keith shook his head grimly. "She didn't come back at all."

The two men sat in silence for a long time. William couldn't think of anything else to say and Keith, it seemed, had spoken his piece. William could feel the cold seeping into his fingers once again. He looked down and the cup, that had once been warming them with hot coffee and whiskey, was empty. He handed it back to his host. Keith raised the Thermos in the unspoken offer of a refill, but William shook his head. He had definitely had enough. He just wanted to go back to his rental house, try and get a good night's sleep, and leave Martha's Vineyard for good in the morning. His original plan had been to stay significantly longer, but there didn't seem to be much point now. The fantasies he had allowed himself to entertain of dinners, and long restorative conversations, with his estranged brother—maybe even meeting his family—were gone. Martha's Vineyard had been a symbol of hope, but now, the whole place was starting to make William angry. It was completely irrational, but the island had just killed his brother—dead. The loneliness of his life metastasized onto every inch of his being with a malignancy that it had never had before. This had been it—his last chance at having a family. Dead. William stood up.

"Thank you for your time, Captain. It was greatly appreciated." William spoke in a robotic, business tone. It was the same one that he had heard himself use in hundreds of boardrooms over decades.

"I'm sorry that I didn't have better news for you, William," said Keith. "Why don't you come up to the house for supper tomorrow? The Missus is an excellent cook and she was a big fan of Mark's. I know she'd love to meet you."

"Thank you, no. I will probably be leaving in the morning. There doesn't seem to be much point in my staying any longer. I should go home." William headed toward the door of the shack and took the handle in his gloved hand. He started to open it, stopped, and looked at Keith. "Was there a service? Is there a stone laid for Mark?"

"I'm not sure if there's a stone, but there was a nice service. As I said, Mark was well liked. It was more of a celebration of life really. That's how his widow wanted it," Keith said.

"Widow?" asked William.

"Yes. Oh for Christ's sake! Tabarnac! Of course! You don't know that he was married. What is wrong with me?" Keith shook his head in frustration. "I almost let you leave without telling you Mark married. Nice lady, too. You should go and say hello! She is still here on the island. This is where they met! They got married in the same church that they had his service. Her name is Edie, Edie Sparks."

15

Mike and Trish walked into the Edgartown Police Station on Peases Point Way and found Sergeant Dan Thomas on the desk. The sergeant looked up as they walked in and gave them a familiar smile. He sat back in his swivel chair. "Hey guys!" he said. "What's up?"

"Hi Dan," said Trish. "Is Jack here?"

"Yeah, I think so. Hold on a sec.," Sergeant Thomas picked up the receiver on the desk phone. There was a pause, and then he spoke again. "Detective Burrell? Hi, Trish McKenzie and that Mike guy are here to see you." The sergeant hung up the phone and looked at Trish. "He'll be right out." He turned and gave Mike a perfunctory nod and smile.

"Thanks, Dan," Trish said. She paused for a moment and then she said, "Dan have you met my boyfriend, Mike

Walker?" The two men stared at each other awkwardly for a moment before Mike finally extended his hand.

"Mike Walker! Pleased to meet you officer," said Mike.

Sergeant Dan cleared his throat and shook Mike's hand. "Yes, I remember you from that business last year with Pretty Vineyard Girls and Donald Dunn. I don't think that we were ever formally introduced. Nice to meet you, Mike. Sounds like you're from Texas?"

"Yes sir! Austin, born and raised," Mike said. His chest puffed out and he stood a little taller at the mention of his hometown.

"That's a nice part of the country. I was down there with my family on vacation once when I was a lot younger. We loved Texas," said Sergeant Dan.

Trish felt the tension in the room melt away. *See,* she thought. *Was that so hard? That's a damn site better than 'that Mike guy'.* This was a shining example of why more women should be ruling the world. Trish chuckled.

The door to the back offices opened and Jack walked toward them, putting on the winter coat of his uniform as he came. "Hey guys! You want to go to Espresso Love with me? I only have a couple of minutes." He turned his attentions to Sergeant Dan. "Thanks Dan. Much appreciated. What can I get for you?"

Dan raised his eyebrows in thought. "Large regular? One of those blueberry scones?"

Jack smiled. "You got it."

The three friends walked down Peases Point Way toward Main Street, Edgartown. Snow was still falling, it had been all day, and Martha's Vineyard was truly looking like a winter wonderland.

"What's going on, guys? Mike man—I heard about your ring. That sucks. Virginia gave me a full description, but to be honest, with no leads, I wouldn't get my hopes up if I were you. We do get them turned in sometimes though."

"That's why we're here," Mike said. "I think I know when I lost it. I actually don't think I lost it at all—I think I was mugged."

"You think you were mugged?" Jack stopped short on the sidewalk and looked Mike directly in the eye. "When?"

"At the Lighthouse thing last night. Where you were supposed to meet us with Virginia!" exclaimed Mike.

"You think you were mugged at The Shore Line Hotel?" asked Jack.

Mike nodded.

"By who?" asked Jack. "Did you get a look at the guy?"

Mike looked sheepish. "Well, sorta. He was a big guy—dirty—and he smelled god-awful. His hair was kinda dark, but not real dark. Like a wet prairie dog, ya know?"

"No, not really," Jack said. "What makes you think this big guy mugged you?"

196

"I was in line for drinks at the hotel bar, and I had just been looking at the ring. When I put it back in my pocket, I got side swiped by that linebacker! He wasn't causing a commotion anywhere else in the room or I would have heard him coming—he only hit me and he got me good. Knocked the wind right out of me." Mike rubbed his ribs as he thought about it. "The girl at the bar felt so bad for me she gave me free drinks."

"If I gave you some mug shots to look at, would you be able to pick him out?" asked Jack.

Mike's cheeks reddened. "I didn't see his face."

"You didn't see his face?" asked Jack. He turned and looked at Trish. "Did you see him?"

Trish shook her head. "Virginia and I were waiting over by the door. It was really crowded. That's why Mike went for the drinks." Trish looked at Mike and then at Jack. Then she looked back at Mike and asked, "Do you think the bartender would have seen his face?"

Mike looked at her. Hope and possibility crept across his face. "Yeah, she probably did."

"Jack, do you think you could talk to her? Ask her a few questions? Just see if she saw him? We could start there couldn't we?" said Trish.

Jack sighed. "Sure. No problem. I'll get over there today. Did you get the name of the bartender?"

Mike shook his head. "No, but she had long, dark hair and a big smile. She was pretty as a penny."

"No problem. They'll have her on the schedule." Jack smiled. "We'll figure it out, bud."

"Thanks Jack," said Trish. "What's Virginia up to today? I haven't heard from her."

"She's working actually," Jack said.

"What? Working where? She's not at the store—Alice is."

Jack shook his head. "No, she's at The Shore Line— on the front desk. They're really short staffed over there for some reason. She used to work there a while back, so they asked her to cover a few shifts over the holiday weekend." Jack smiled. "I'm working mostly anyway, and she said she wanted some extra Christmas cash. So, that's cool. I told her that she had better not be buying me anything expensive for Christmas. Is she, Trish? Tell her not to, okay?"

"I'm not saying anything!" Trish winked with a playful smile. She looked up at Mike. He wasn't smiling. She couldn't blame him. All of a sudden she felt bad for laughing with Jack when he was still torn up inside over the ring—her ring. She nudged him and whispered, "Hey...you okay? Jack said he would go over today and ask about the guy who slammed into you. We'll sort it out. Okay?"

"You want me to go now?" asked Jack. "What the Hell, I'll go now."

"Really?" asked Mike.

"Sure."

198

The three of them had no sooner turned around when a squad car slowed down beside them. The passenger window slid down with an electronic hum, and Chief Laurie Knickles leaned forward from her position in the driver's seat. "Jack, I need you back at the station, right away. I've got a G.B.C. going out and I need you there for the debriefing. Hi Mike, Trish." Without waiting for a response, Laurie drove to the station. The three of them watched the squad car turn into the drive.

"Sorry guys," said Jack. "I'll have to do it later."

"No problem. We understand. We'll go get coffee at Espresso Love for everyone and bring it back," said Trish, but Jack was already jogging up the street to the station. Trish turned to continue walking toward Main Street, but Mike stopped her. "What?" she asked.

"Let's get the truck and head down to the hotel ourselves. We can get coffee for everyone on our way back," Mike started back toward the police station.

"You want to go and talk to the bartender ourselves?" asked Trish.

"Damn straight I do. I'm not going to be able to wait around. That was a real good idea you had. Let's go see if the bartender saw that guy's face. That way we'll know whether Jack will be wasting his time or not. That's all."

Trish looked at Mike and realised that there was no way he was going to do anything else until they had exhausted every avenue looking for that ring. "Alright...let's go."

*   *   *

Edie sat in the back of a cab and watched the world of West Tisbury go by. The layer of snow on the ground was thickening. Snow blanketed the split rail fences and the stone walls for which this part of the island was famous. Even the thinnest of branches, now barren of their summer foliage, was lined with a topping of white fluff. She should have been focussed on her plan for the future, her immediate future, but Edie couldn't help but be drawn into the Christmas scene going on outside her window. It was actually funny, she thought. How everyone associated Christmas with snow. The fact is that most places in the world never have snow at Christmas. Edie remembered reading that the real reason that everyone associated the white of snow with Christmas was because of Charles Dickens. Apparently there had been a few years in England that had been Charles Dickens' formative years as well as particularly snowy ones in England. For this reason, Dickens always fantasized about a white Christmas, and had done so when he wrote A Christmas Carol. Edie wasn't entirely sure how based in fact that story was, but she liked it. She liked the image of a young Dickens being mesmerised by all that snow. Edie found it mesmerising herself and she loved a white Christmas. Even the movie, White Christmas, was her favourite. She was supposed to watch it this season with Chris Johns,

Jeff's hockey player husband, but now she had more important things to get sorted. The first one was to get her car back. She only hoped it wasn't damaged in the fire. She couldn't, for the life of her, remember how close she had parked it to the house.

Edie's cab pulled into the mouth of her driveway and she asked him to stop there. She had no idea what, or who, was waiting for her at the top of the hill and she didn't know how she was going to react. The last thing that she wanted to find herself doing was crying on the shoulder of a cab driver that would probably keep her on the meter for his trouble.

Edie stepped out, took a deep breath, and looked up the drive. She should be able to see the top of the second floor—she couldn't. She took another deep breath. She jumped with a start as her cab began to roll away. She turned back to face her property. Out of the corner of her right eye, she caught a flutter of movement. Edie turned to see the rustle of the tarp that Victor had used to cover his wall.

"Get it together, Edie," she said. "It was just a house. It was only full of things. No one was hurt. You're okay— you'll build a new house and it will be beautiful. Now, just go up there and get your damn car!" One more deep breath and Edie started marching up the hill. Her movements were exaggerated like those of an angry five year old. The higher up the hill she climbed, the more damage was exposed.

Her house was gone. She had envisioned herself walking through the charred remains of her living room, a black kitchen with wires hanging from the ceiling, the entire mess dripping with water from the fire trucks, but that was not what she was going to be doing today or any other day. There wasn't enough house to walk through. She could maybe walk over it, but there was no roof left standing. There was no ceiling left of the main floor. The corners were the strongest parts of the walls remaining, but the entire house had been hollowed out. On some level, Edie thought it might be a little easier to take because the complete and utter ruination had left a heap that was entirely unrecognisable as her home. If she could see something that she loved, if she spotted something of sentimental value that was charred and disfigured, then she might not be able to take it. That might be the end of her. The thought of that happening sent a shock of fear through her gut. Edie knew that she had to get out of there before that did happen. She was just going to get her car and leave.

At the top of the hill, she was met with a friendly and familiar face. Edie smiled, "Peter!"

"Edie, honey, how are you doing old girl?" Peter Jefferies walked over and gave Edie a big hug.

Edie felt herself let go in the warmth and comfort of Peter's big arms. It felt so good to be held. She could feel emotion start to rise up in her and she forced it down and pushed herself out of Peter's embrace. "Watch where

202

you're throwing that 'old girl' stuff, Mr Jefferies. I remember your retirement party!" Edie smiled up at her friend. Edie was not a tall woman and it almost hurt her neck to look all the way up and find Peter's face at close proximity. "Which begs the question, what are you doing here? You retired!"

"I know, I know...I like to help the boys out from time to time. It gives me something to do and they're always happy to have an extra body who knows the routine and is willing to do the crappy stuff like deter the lookie-loos." Peter smiled. "We had a guy out here looking for you. I took his card..." Peter reached into his coat pocket and pulled out a white business card. "Ah, yeah, this is the guy—Victor Helm. Your wall guy?"

"Oh yes, Victor." Edie took the card, read it, and put it into her coat. "I guess I should call him too." She looked back at Peter. "I'll add him to my list...my ever-growing list."

"I imagine that you have your hands pretty full right about now. I've seen it before." Peter smiled warmly. "I know that it probably seems nearly impossible to believe right now, but you'll get through this. I promise."

Edie returned the smile. "I know...thanks." Edie looked around and spotted her PT Cruiser convertible. It looked okay from here. It was parked about thirty-five feet from the base of the house. Surely that had been far enough to save it. "How's my car?"

Peter followed her gaze. "I think it's fine," he said. "To be honest, I haven't really taken a good look at her. Let's go check it out."

They walked over to the car, approaching from the rear, and Peter kicked a couple of tires. He looked her keenly up and down, running a large hand over the convertible top and then the hood. "She seems great. I'm surprised that your soft top survived all of the sparks, but you can tell from the soot and burns on the ground that she was up wind. If the wind had been blowing the other way, she would have gone up for sure."

"Well, something had to go my way eventually," Edie smiled.

"You have your keys?" asked Peter.

"They're in it," Edie said grinning. Living out here, there never seemed to be much point in locking it up. Besides, if someone comes all the way out here to steal my car, they're going to have a way to do it without keys. Locks keep things safe from honest people."

Peter laughed. "So true." He opened up the driver's door. "Get in and turn her over."

Edie slipped into the driver's seat and turned her key in the ignition. The car roared to life like there was nothing wrong. Edie was almost shocked at how the sound of the familiar sound of her engine made everything seem so normal for a moment. "Maybe this is a sign that my luck is starting to change." Edie stepped back out of the car and gave her friend a hug. "I'm glad you were here, Pete. I didn't know how this was going to go."

A gold and white Chevy Blazer rolled up Edie's drive and stopped in front of the debris that had been her house. After sitting in neutral for a brief moment, the engine went silent and the driver's door opened. A tall, handsome, black man stepped out of the truck and closed the door behind him. He rubbed his hands together and turned to look at Peter and Edie. Without smiling, he walked toward them with formal steps.

Edie stiffened beside Peter Jefferies. She recognised the man right away. This was the last thing that she needed. *What the Christ was he doing here?* "So much for luck," she said to no one in particular.

16

Following people who all seemed to know where they were going, Corey and Tina walked up the metal steps to the passenger area of the ferry. Corey watched as people dispersed to seats that may as well have been reserved for them. No one looked around. No one seemed to feel the need to make a decision as to where to sit—they just knew. It was clear that the boat was full of seasoned Vineyard travellers. This windowed room of blue chairs, vinyl booths, and the occasional television was full of people who knew exactly what they were doing. After an awkward pause, Corey selected two window seats, past the snack bar, on the port side of the boat. Tina plopped down with an exaggerated exhalation and Corey stretched out beside her. He took in the room. The windows covered the port, bow, and starboard of the vessel on this level. It was an unusual mix

206

of industrial and hospitality. Corey wasn't sure that he had ever seen anything like it before. The centre hub of the room was the snack bar. It reminded him of a hospital cafeteria.

"Do you want something to eat? Drink?" asked Corey.

Tina surveyed their surroundings. "Where do you suppose the bathroom is?"

Spotting the sign hanging from the ceiling, Corey pointed down the corridor toward the stern. "That way," he said. "Why don't you go to the bathroom and I'll get us some snacks when you come back? I'd go now but I don't want to lose our seats." He looked around again at the quickly filling room. "I suppose we could just leave our coats here. I'm only going thirty feet away."

"I'm sure that will be cool. Can you get me a decaf coffee and a muffin? Blueberry if they have it," Tina smiled.

Corey returned the smile. "Sure."

Tina leaned toward him, and pressed her lips firmly against his. Without pulling away, she spoke in a muffled voice, "I love you Corey Johnson." She pulled away then and laughing, wiped her lipstick from his mouth. "You're the best time I ever had."

Corey beamed. He felt his cheeks redden. "Did you get that from a movie?"

Tina laughed again and shrugged. "I'm not sure—maybe." She stood up, took off her coat, and draped it over her seat. "Okay, I'll be back in a tick!"

Corey watched her go and felt his chest puff up instinctively. There was some inner biological reaction that

207

had him almost exploding with pride. Corey knew—even without looking around the room—that he was with the most beautiful woman on the boat. There was no question in his mind. At some point, each and every day, Corey looked at Tina and could not believe his luck. He looked at Tina and felt like he was punching way above his weight class. The crazy thing was—Tina said that she was the lucky one. Tina would hug him and kiss him and say, 'I don't know what I ever did to deserve you, but I am so grateful.' Other people would tell him that Tina was always saying that he, Corey, was 'wonderful' and 'inspiring'. Apparently, she talked about him all the time when she was out with her friends. While her girlfriends were complaining about their husbands and boyfriends, Tina was sweetly singing his praises. Whenever Corey heard this, it left him proud as punch but completely bewildered. Part of him lived in constant fear that one day, she was going to wake up from whatever stupor she was in, take a good look at him, and wonder what the hell she had been thinking! So far, though, so far, so good. Corey figured that was the secret to a healthy relationship. When both parties felt that against all odds in the universe, somehow, they had both lucked out and won first prize. Corey certainly felt that way.

Corey walked up to the snack bar and went directly to the cashier. "Good afternoon! Do I ask you for coffee or..." he trailed off.

"No," said the middle aged woman in the uniform. "The coffee is around the other side there." She motioned around the island in the middle of the room. "Behind that cash there."

"Oh, thank you. Can I pay now?" he asked.

"Certainly," she said. "Just a coffee? What size?" She poised a manicured finger over the till, ready to key in his order.

"Two large coffees, please, and—do you have blueberry muffins?" Corey looked around.

"Yes. Two coffees and a blueberry muffin?" The woman started punching at her keyboard and it beeped with every touch.

"Um, yes, and a clam chowder, please."

"Clam chowder," she repeated. "Anything else?"

Corey shook his head. "That's it. You take Visa?"

The woman passed him the handheld credit machine. "Go ahead."

Corey pushed his card into the heel of the machine and punched in his code. Once it cleared, he handed it back.

"Do you want your receipt?" the woman asked.

"No, that's fine," Corey said. A young man, who was also working behind the counter, brought him his chowder and his muffin. Corey thanked him and made his way over to the coffee area. He filled two cups with coffee, one with decaf and one with regular, and added milk to both. He stacked the muffin on top of the chowder and the two coffees on top of each other and carefully made his way back to their seats, dodging the other passengers as he went.

Back at their seats, he wedged a coffee into the holder fixed to each chair and sat down.

Tina came back and spotted the muffin right away. "Oh, they had blueberry muffins! Yum!" She sat down and took the muffin from Corey. "This is my coffee?" Tina broke a piece off of the top of the muffin and popped it into her mouth. "Mmmm! Good muffin! Really fresh. What did you get?"

"Chowder," said Corey.

"Of course you did!" Tina said. "You love your chowder!"

The ship's horn sounded and the boat began to rumble and vibrate with the revving of the engines.

"Here we go!" exclaimed Tina.

Corey had to admit, he was excited. He looked out the window at the shore of Woods Hole, at the small house on the cove and watched as they started to recede from his view. They were moving—heading out into the Atlantic Ocean. "This is pretty cool!" Corey said. Corey turned and looked at Tina. They both laughed with excitement.

*   *   *

William walked toward the only two people who were standing at the address that Captain Keith had given him. He was confused. This was the address of his brother's widow? He looked up at the remains of the home. Given where he was in West Tisbury, this must also be the fire

210

that he had called in. It couldn't be a coincidence. There couldn't have been two such immense conflagrations on the island last night, could there? There just couldn't. William continued to soak in the extent of the damage. He was sorry that he hadn't been able to call it in sooner. Perhaps he would have been able to save the home. He just prayed that there hadn't been any injuries. He hoped that everyone who lived here was safe.

The two people in front of him were a comedy of opposites. The man was huge and the woman was very small. William took them both to be about his age. They were both white. The man looked pleasant enough but the woman looked very angry. She also looked familiar. He couldn't quite get a good look at her behind all of her winter apparel. Still...

"Good afternoon, my name is William Singleton. I believe that this is the scene of a fire that I called in yesterday evening. Is everyone alright?" William turned to look at the house once again. "I certainly am sorry that I didn't call in it sooner, but I was reading and didn't see it until I got up to stretch my legs."

"You called this in?" spat Edie.

"Yes, I believe so," said William. That voice was familiar too. Who was this woman? "Please, tell me that there were no injuries. Please, say that we have that to be grateful for at the very least."

"No," said Edie. "There were no injuries. Everyone is fine."

211

"Madame—I'm sorry—you seem so familiar to me, but—" A switch flipped in William's brain. A light went on exposing a memory file that he hadn't been able to read until just now. The woman standing in front of him was the woman from the concert at The Old Whaling Church. "Of course! The concert!"

Edie glared at him. "Yes, the concert," she said. "If you were the one who called in the fire last night, I am grateful, but I'd appreciate it if you left now. I just don't care to be talking to you right now. Thank you, Mr Singleton."

William looked at the woman standing in front of him. She was going through a lot and he had not been very kind to her. He had been condescending and more than likely rude. Now, he was standing in front of her, only making matters worse. But the fire hadn't even been the real reason that he had come to this property at all. He had been looking for Mark's widow. He was still looking for her. Thoughts were starting to process through his mind at a rapid pace. The flashes of fantasies he had conjured up, sitting with his brother and his family, laughing, sharing meals, finding roots to call his own—now those thoughts were filled with this woman. This had to be her. This had to be Edie Sparks—his sister-in-law.

"Ma'am, I am not actually here about the fire. That is just a surprising and awful happenstance," William said.

Edie scrunched up her face in confusion. "You mean, you didn't call in the fire?"

"Oh no, I did! But that is just a coincidence. A man in Menemsha Harbor—Captain Keith, gave me this address. I believe he is a friend of yours?" asked William. He was speaking quickly like a reporter chasing an uncooperative witness. He knew that his time was short. This woman was close to asking her large friend to escort him off of her property.

"Keith?" Edie's face went lax. Even in the cold winter air, she paled. "I haven't seen him or Catherine for a very long time. I don't head down that way anymore."

Her voice had softened considerably, and William took this as a sign that he could continue. "I went down there looking for a man by the name of Mark Sparks." He paused. Edie stared at him, but her eyes were almost empty. The fight that was in her eyes when he arrived was gone. She was retreating. "Ma'am...are you Edie? Are you Edie Sparks?"

Edie continued to stare at William—through William. After a moment, she nodded and said, "Yes. I'm Edie Sparks."

"Mrs Sparks, I'm Mark's half-brother. Your brother-in-law," said William. He watched her face as he tried to gauge, which way this conversation was going to go. He didn't know whether she was going to explode and order him away or embrace him. Before he could figure it out, Edie fell forward landing on his stomach.

"Edie!" The big man who had been standing quietly by the car, ran forward.

William caught her slumped body as she slipped down the front of his coat. His arthritic hands burned under the strain. "She's fainted!" He said.

The two men lifted her into the car and turned on the heater. William also saw the big man press a button at the side of the seat that turned on the seat warmer.

"I'm going to call an ambulance," he said. "This girl has been through a lot. I think she's finally had enough." He extended his hand. "I'm Peter Jefferies. Captain in the Fire Department—retired. They'll get an ambulance out here wicked quick for me." He pulled out his phone and made the call.

William shook the man's hand while he spoke on the phone. Peter had strong, big hands, and his grip hurt William's joints. When he broke free, he rubbed his knuckles.

"Do you have a card, Mr Singleton?" asked Peter.

"Yes," said William. He reached into his pocket, found a card, and passed it to Peter.

"Thank you. We'll be in touch. Have a good day."

William had a lot of questions, but he could see that this was neither the time nor the place. He walked back to his car. Nothing on this trip was going as he had planned. In fact, he seemed to be making things worse everywhere he went on this god forsaken island; however, he couldn't leave now. He had actually found a family member. He had met his brother's widow. That was something. Even if she did hate his guts.

*   *   *

He dug his shovel into the cold ground. The soil was hard and rocky, but he was strong. When his shovel was completely buried, he pulled. He could feel all of the muscles in his back expand. He felt the sleeves of his coat tighten around his arms and shoulders. He pushed down with his right hand at the top of the shovel and pulled up with his left. The earth tore away and he threw it over his left shoulder. He didn't think about it. He just did it.

He dug. He sliced the shovel into the ground again and heaved it over his shoulder. He kept a pace. This was his third hole. He wasn't sure how many he would end up digging. At first he thought he would just need the one, but then he thought that something might go wrong and he needed a test run. Everything had gone so well that he thought he would dig another. He was building a plan, a kind of alibi. The more holes, the more confusing it would be. The more random the whole thing would seem. He was digging this hole now and then there would be at least one more. Probably just one. The second hole hadn't worked out so well. He hadn't planned that far ahead. He hadn't dug the hole before he was ready to fill it. That was bad. He had to dig and fill the second hole all at once, and that had been too much work. It had caused problems. He wasn't going to do that again. Although he had learned that he didn't need a box. He had readied a box for the first one and that had been a complete waste of time and energy. These were the benefits of digging more than one hole. These were the things that you learned along the way. Education is never a waste. So, he dug.

He dug. He sliced his shovel into the ground, and tossed the earth behind him. Soon, he would be down in the hole while he dug. He liked that part. He liked the smell of the earth. The sweet and final smell of it. It was final. He liked the idea of that final earthy smell. Actually, that meant, for the last hole, he was going to need a box after all. Not for this one though. It didn't matter about this hole. Too much work. But for the last hole, he was definitely going to need a box. These were the things you learned along the way. He pushed his shovel a little deeper into the ground. He flexed. He pulled. He hurled the earth over his shoulder.

He dug.

17

Chief Laurie Knickles sat behind her desk, typing on her computer. Charles stood at the back of the room, in order to give the other officers the chairs and other prime office real estate. As it turned out, he could have taken a seat because all of the officers, after they had filed in, remained standing.

"Gentlemen, I have just issued a General Broadcast. We have at the very least one missing person—possibly two. At the moment, the woman in question is Karen Malone. Every station, and every squad car on-island now has Karen's photo and personal details. There is very good reason to believe that Karen Malone was stalked in the parking lot after her shift was over at The Shore Line Hotel last night. She was then taken from inside her home. I have already spoken to her boyfriend, Sam Jones. They live together in West Tisbury."

"Where was he at the time of the abduction?" asked Detective Jack Burrell.

"He was home as well," said Laurie.

"He was home when she was abducted? Is he a suspect?" asked Sergeant Dan Thomas.

"Well, of course, anything is possible, but that's not the feeling that I got," said Laurie. "He seemed authentic to me."

"Has anyone spoken to the people at the hotel?" asked Jack.

"Yes, Charles and I were just there, but we're going to have to go back again," Laurie said. "I was down there this morning to talk to the General Manager, Barry Nelson. As we all know, last night, when Karen wrapped up her shift, it was a particularly busy night for The Shore Line. It was the lighting of the Edgartown Lighthouse. I don't suppose either of you were there last night?" she asked.

Dan shook his head. "I was here," he said.

"I was supposed to go, but ended up looking for your truck," said Jack.

"How's that going?" asked Laurie.

"Nothing yet," said Jack.

Laurie looked glum. "Well, keep an eye out. I had almost forgotten about it with Karen's disappearance, and Edie's house burning down. Christ, what a Christmas." She shook her head with disgust. "Oh, but before we get

218

too far off topic, while we were at The Shore Line this morning, we found out that Karen had to come in early for her shift last night to cover for a girl by the name of Amelia Davis. Does that name ring a bell?"

Jack nodded. "I know Amelia. She's a nice lady. Her family lives over on Chappaquiddick, although I don't think they're out there very often. I know the house."

"Well, Amelia didn't show up for her shift last night, or for her shift this morning. Can you go out to that house, when we're done here please Jack?" asked the Chief although everyone in the room knew that it wasn't really a question.

"Yeah, sure Chief," said Jack. Jack's forehead creased and he started chewing his lip. He turned to look at Charles and then back at the Chief across the desk. He turned to look at Charles again.

"What's the matter, Jack?" asked Charles.

"Well, do you guys think that there's a connection to the hotel and the girls' disappearances?"

"Technically, we don't even know if Amelia has disappeared. She could be in bed with the flu. You know how bad the cell service can be out there on Chappy, especially if the house is down toward Wasque. That's why I want you to go out there. But if it turns out there is reason to worry about Amelia as well, then I would say that the hotel is too big of a coincidence to overlook, wouldn't you?" said Laurie.

"Why?" asked Charles.

"Well, it's just that Virginia is working there now for the next couple of days, because they're short staffed on the desk. Now, that I now why, I don't know if I want her there at all!" exclaimed Jack.

Laurie and Charles looked at each other but didn't speak a word.

Finally, Sergeant Dan said, "Is she there now, man?"

Jack nodded. "Yeah."

"Well, it's daylight and the hotel is busy—she'll be okay. Go out to Chappy and check out Amelia's place. Then, find out when Virginia's done, pick her up, and drive her home yourself," Dan offered.

Jack nodded again. "Yeah, that's a good idea."

"Thanks Dan," Laurie smiled for the first time since they had entered the office. "Dan, will you look into Karen's social media, and see if there is anything on there that looks unusual? Any comments on Instagram or Facebook that are threatening or even just look a little off. Also, we're going to have to get a ping on her phone. Find out where it is. It's probably back at her house, now that I think about it. Karen had gone up for a shower when she disappeared. That's gotta be the one place people don't take their cell phones these days."

"Karen's purse was hanging on the hook with her coat in the kitchen. I saw it there. I imagine that her phone is in it," said Charles.

"That figures," said Laurie. "Okay, you two—Chappy and social media—let's get at it."

220

Laurie's cell phone rang as the two officers turned and walked out of the office. She started to greet the person on the other end, but she was cut off. After a pause, she said, "We'll be right there." She ended the call and shoved her phone into her pocket. Standing up from her desk, Laurie grabbed her coat.

"Where will we be?" asked Charles.

"Edie just passed out. She's at Martha's Vineyard Hospital."

*   *   *

Mike parked his truck at the end of North Water Street, across from The Shore Line Hotel, and at the mouth of the path that led to the Edgartown Lighthouse. The snow had not stopped falling, and the layer on the ground was quite thick. Everything was covered in pristine white. Evergreen trees and bushes, and boughs of pine, all had a multi-coloured glow, lit from within by unseen Christmas lights. Regardless of his stress about his missing ring, and the constant feeling of nausea in his stomach, Mike couldn't help but admire the beauty of it all. He opened the truck door and stepped out. His boots crunched on the fresh snow, packing it beneath him. He looked across the hood of the truck and his eyes followed the path down the hill to the lighthouse. The catwalk and the lantern room of the Edgartown Lighthouse were strung with multicoloured lights. A wreath hung halfway up the

221

tower, and was lit in the same colours. The door and window were trimmed as well. The falling snow and the surrounding ocean gave the entire scene an impossibly Hollywood feel. Up until a couple of days ago, Mike would have never believed that this kind of Christmas actually existed in the world. He still half-expected to hear someone yell, "Cut!" and the snow machine would stop blowing. The house lights would come on. A director would come down on a crane like in the old pictures he watched with his Nana. The background would shut off, and a crew would walk onto the set, take down the lighthouse—which was just painted plywood—and take it all away. But of course, none of this happened. This was what Christmas really looked like if you just happened to be on Martha's Vineyard.

Mike walked up to the archway in the white picket fence surrounding the hotel lawn, and stepped aside to allow Trish to go first.

Trish smiled up at him. "Thank you, kind sir."

He grinned, "Ma'am."

"I am all for women's lib," said Trish. "But I have to admit, I do love your southern chivalry."

Mike laughed. "Women's rights or no women's rights, my Mama would string me up by my man parts if she ever found out that I did not hold a door open for a lady."

Trish turned around, stretched up onto her tip-toes, and kissed Mike on the cheek. "Well, you'd better keep it up then...I'm quite fond of your 'man parts'."

Mike blushed. He reached down and found her hand with his, and they walked up to the hotel together. They climbed the stairs to the porch. Mike pulled the door open and, once again, stepped aside to allow Trish to go first.

The front room was a lot less busy than it had been on their last visit. It had seemed like the entire town was at the hotel the night before. Now, the traffic was steady, but not overwhelming.

"Look!" said Trish. "Virginia is working the front desk! You go and check out the restaurant, and I'm going to go and talk to Virginia. Okay?"

Mike thought about it. "Sounds good." He watched her walk toward the desk and their friend. He liked the idea of Virginia working at the desk. That could be a good thing for him. She'd be able to keep her ear to the ground in case anything came up about the ring. Mike turned around and walked through the glass doors that opened into the restaurant.

Just like the rest of the hotel, the restaurant was fully decked out for the holiday. The white pillars and tables and chairs were all trimmed with red and green velvet ribbon. The pillars looked like giant candy canes. Immediately to his left, there was a plate of gingerbread men cookies. Mike eyed them hungrily. He had been so distracted that he hadn't realised just how hungry he was.

In fact, he wasn't sure that he had eaten at all since dinner the night before at The Newes.

"Go ahead," a voice said. "Take one."

Mike looked up and saw the same pretty, dark haired bartender from the night before. "It's you!"

"I almost always am," she smiled at him. "Take two cookies if you want. They're really good."

Mike picked up two cookies and walked toward the bar.

"Would you like a coffee to go with those?" asked the bartender. She picked up a nondescript ceramic mug, filled it from a glass pot, and set it down in front of him before he had a chance to answer.

As soon as mike inhaled the rich scent rising from the steaming cup, coffee seemed like a great idea. "Thank you," he said.

"They're great if you dunk 'em," she said.

It took Mike a second before he caught on. "Oh! The cookies!" Mike looked at the two gingerbread men staring up at him from his hand and noticed, for the first time, that one of them was a gingerbread woman. Feeling almost silly, he brought the gingerbread woman up to his mouth and took a big bite, removing her legs and half of her skirt in one fell swoop. "Mmmm..." he said. "They are good."

"Told ya," said the bartender.

"Do you remember me?" asked Mike.

"I'm sorry handsome, you're going to have to do better than that. I see a lot of faces." The bartender picked

224

up a blue rag and started wiping down the bar's surface even though it already looked spotless to Mike.

"I was here last night."

"The whole island was here last night," she said.

"I got body-checked by a great big guy. He slammed me into the bar pretty good. You were there," Mike said eagerly.

"Oh damn!" The bartender put down her cloth and looked at Mike with narrower eyes, like she hadn't really looked at him at all since he walked in. "Of course! Yes, I remember you. You ordered a beer and two glasses of wine. Then that asshole slammed you, and I gave them to you on the house."

Mike smiled. "Yes! That was me! That was very kind of you too. You didn't have to do that, ma'am."

"I don't like people to have a bad experience in my bar. That asshole should have been banned from this bar—*from this hotel*—a long time ago, but that doesn't look like it's ever going to happen." She shook her head in disgust. "The Vineyard should do its own version of Survivor. That guy would be voted off this island right quick."

"So, you know who he is?" asked Mike.

"Unfortunately," said the bartender.

"Ma'am, I'd really appreciate it if you'd tell me his name," said Mike.

"I'd really appreciate it if you'd stop calling me ma'am," the bartender quipped. "Monica," she said. "My name is Monica."

Mike extended his hand. "It's a real pleasure, Monica. I'm Mike."

Monica shook his hand and then folded her arms across her chest. "That guy who body-checked you last night—his name is Joey Helm. His mother is the concierge here at the hotel. She's a piece of work. She's got a lot of people fooled, but mark my words, she's pure trash." Monica scowled as she spoke about the mother and son. "I suppose I shouldn't talk, I'm not exactly a Kennedy myself, but there is something about just being a good person, you know? Decent folk. Those two? They are not decent folk."

Mike nodded. "Well, I don't know the mother, but I believe you about the guy."

"So, why do you want to know about him now anyway?" asked Monica. "I don't think you can press charges. He sideswiped you, sure, but the room was really busy. Even with me as a witness, he'll just say that it was an accident."

"Did you notice that I was the only guy that he bumped into last night? He walked through the entire room and I was the only one that he hit, and hit hard," said Mike.

"That's true," said Monica. "That's kinda weird no that you say it like that. So, why did he hit you?"

Mike gave her an apologetic look. "I probably shouldn't say—especially if his Mom works here, but I promise you, I'm after him. And if this Joey guy is guilty like I think he is, he's going down."

"Well, I don't know what you think he did, but I'd be willing to put money on the fact that he did it," Monica topped up his coffee. "Good luck my friend. Keep me posted."

*   *   *

Corey drove down Main Street Edgartown and turned onto the red brick, circular driveway of The Ashley Inn. It was a two hundred year old home that had been converted into a country inn years ago. The inn was a three storey, white wooden home, with a small porch in front just big enough to stand on while you pulled the open the front door. Large windows were framed with green wooden shutters that matched the evergreen shrubs up front. A tall white fence with a latch gate sectioned off the backyard on the right hand side of the inn. There was a small area encased by the circular drive that Corey was sure was filled with flowers every season. Right now, like everything, it was layered with snow. The Ashley Inn was exactly what he had hoped it would be. He hoped it was what Tina was hoping for too.

"They must have a parking lot of something around back. I'll ask the guy when we go in," Corey said.

Tina leaned forward as much as her belly would allow, and looked through the windshield at the country inn. "This place is beautiful!" she said. "You told me not to get my hopes up! Corey Johnson are you fooling me or is it a dump inside? It doesn't look like it possibly could be."

"Why don't we go inside and check it out?" Corey smiled slyly at her.

Tina got out of the car and walked around to the steps that led up to the front door. She looked back at Corey who was retrieving their suitcase from the trunk. "It's so pretty, Corey!"

Corey closed the trunk and looked up at Tina. He smiled. "I'm glad you like it, honey. I thought it looked perfect when I booked it."

They walked up the stairs and Tina opened the heavy wood door.

They stepped into a parlour that greeted them with the rich scent of Christmas. There was a fire crackling in the hearth and a robust fraser fir decorated for the season in the front window. Corey and Tina inhaled the woody tones deeply.

The room was exactly as it had looked on the website, and Corey was relieved. White wood wainscoting covered the lower half of the walls and a warm, earth tone paint covered the top. Most of the wood trim in the room was white except for the cherry wood banister of the staircase, directly in front of them.

"Oh Corey, it's so lovely," said Tina. "and it smells so good in here too!"

"You can't beat the smell of a wood fire," said Corey.

"I smell baking too. Don't you?" asked Tina.

Corey shook his head.

"Maybe it's just me. I swear, ever since I've been pregnant, all I smell is food!" she said.

"No, it's not just you," said a voice from the other room. "I just took two loaves of bread out of the oven. They're for your breakfast tomorrow." A tall, young man with dark hair and a warm smile stepped out of the back room and walked toward them. "You must be Corey and Tina?" He offered his hand to Corey. "I'm Paul. We spoke on the phone."

"Nice to meet you Paul. I'm Corey and this is my girlfriend Tina."

"It's nice to meet you too. I'm glad you made it in before the snow got really bad. It's supposed to be a real blizzard tonight. I don't mind though. It makes everything really Christmas-y!" Paul looked down at their suitcase. "Is that your only bag?"

Tina nodded. "Yes."

Paul picked it up. "Why don't I take you to your room then and get you settled. Where did you park?"

"Just out front," Corey said.

"We have a parking lot out back. I'll show you how to get to it." Paul led them up to the second floor on stairs that creaked under his weight.

Tina giggled. "I love creaky stairs. They're so homey."

Once at the top, Paul turned to Tina. "You know, every once in a while, we get someone who complains about the noise of the stairs, and I tell myself that I should probably fix them, but I think I would actually miss the sound they make. I'm with you. It's a friendly sound." He smiled. "I think some people just like to complain." Paul continued down a short hall to a door with a wrought iron number six nailed at eye level, dead centre. "Here we are!" he said enthusiastically. "Number six." He slipped his key in the lock and turned the knob. The door swung open silently. He stepped back for his guests.

Tina gasped as she stepped in and absorbed the room's delicately flowered, blue and white, wallpaper and the caramel stained, wide plank, hardwood flooring. Two of the four windows in the room were set deep into the vaulted ceiling. The queen bed was centred in the room and upholstered with classic white embroidered bedspread and white linens. There was a small antique desk and chair, as well as two white club chairs. The whole room was cast in a warm glow emanating from the matching lamps on the nightstands. "Oh, Corey! It's exactly what I would have wanted in a Vineyard weekend!"

Corey looked at Paul, "It's a great room, Paul. Thank you."

"I'm glad you like it. The wi-fi password is here on the desk, along with a list of the goings-on this weekend for Christmas In Edgartown. There are extra blankets here in

230

this drawer, and if you really need to, you can adjust your thermostat here. There is a TV, if you should want one, but why anyone would come to Martha's Vineyard to watch TV is beyond me. I don't even watch it and I live here." Paul laughed at his own small joke. "If you have any other questions, please don't hesitate to ask. Oh," Paul turned to Corey. "If you want to come down with me, I'll show you where to put your car. Unless you're going out right away."

"I actually do have some errands to run that I would like to get out of the way. Then our weekend will be our own," Corey looked at Tina. "Did you want to have a nap while I ran those errands for Cam?"

Tina shook her head vigorously. "No way! I want to come with you! I want to soak up as much of Martha's Vineyard as I can!"

Corey looked at Paul. "Would it be okay if we left the car out front for maybe thirty minutes at most? Just long enough to freshen up before we head out?"

Paul smiled. "No problem at all." He held up two room keys and jingled them. "I'll leave your room keys here on the desk. Have fun guys." Paul left the room and closed the door behind him.

Tina threw her arms around Corey's neck. "This is turning out to be the best weekend ever!"

18

Jack sat in his patrol car and waited for the Chappy Ferry to return to the Edgartown side. In the off-season, there was only the one boat. Long gone were the line-ups of vacationers and fishermen. Line-ups so long that they required their own police officer to navigate the cars across North Water Street. Cars and trucks with semi-deflated tires, and windows covered with permit stickers of all colours, signifying that they were legally allowed to drive and fish on specific beaches, but not now. Right now, in December, no one was going over to Chappaquiddick. Even with the added attraction of the holidays, all of the action was in Edgartown Village. So, Jack sat beside the Old Sculpin Gallery alone.

When the ferry docked in Edgartown. The captain dropped the chain and walked to the edge of the boat.

With exaggerated swoops of his arm, he motioned for Jack to board. Jack put the cruiser into drive and slowed forward, following the ferry captain's hand signals until he was motioned to stop at which point, Jack shut off his engine. The captain put the chain back up and hopped onto his chair. Slowly, the ferry began its 527 foot journey from Edgartown to Chappaquiddick.

Despite the cold, Jack got out of the car. He always liked to stretch his legs, and watch the harbour go by when he took the ferry over. Especially on a snowy day. There was something kind of cool about watching snow fall into the ocean. Jack wasn't sure what it was, but he liked it.

"Quiet today, Ryan?" Jack almost had to yell to be heard over the ferry engine.

Ryan nodded from his perch in the captain's booth. He shouted back, "I've only taken one person over Chappy side today." He motioned with his thumb. "Just now."

"Who was it?" Jack asked more to make conversation than out of actual curiosity.

"That crazy blonde actress who has a place out Cape Poge way. She's out here quite a bit. Don't get me wrong, she's nice enough, but man, all she ever wants to talk about is erosion. She's all bent out of shape about it. I say if you're going to be that worried about erosion, don't buy a multimillion dollar beach house on top of a cliff on Chappaquiddick. You know what I mean?" Ryan shook his head and rolled his eyes.

"Fair point," said Jack. Almost at Chappy, Jack slipped back behind the wheel, and closed the door. With the press of a button, his window slid open.

"Oh well," said Ryan. "It's none of my business." Ryan steered the boat expertly into its slip, and once it was in place, put the ferry in neutral. He jumped down from his perch, and walked to the bow, securing it in place. He dropped the chain and motioned Jack forward.

"Thanks man," said Jack. "I won't be long. I'll see you in a few."

"Sounds good," said Ryan.

Jack drove up Chappaquiddick Road, past the Chappaquiddick Beach Club and Caleb Pond, and turned right onto Litchfield Road. He remembered being out at Amelia's family's place a few times for summer barbecues. He couldn't remember the address or even the name of the road she was on for the life of him, but he knew that he could find it. There was a lot of that on Martha's Vineyard. People really didn't know anyone's address. Not like people did in the big cities. Here, people just knew where everyone lived. Directions on the Vineyard consisted of instructions like "make a left at the fork and it's the bright red mailbox" or "it's the third house past the old Mayhew place". Islanders would rarely tell anyone that they lived at a specific, numerical, street address.

Jack leaned into the windshield and looked at the upcoming turn-off. Deciding that this was the place, he turned right, and drove slowly up the drive. He wasn't entirely sure that he was in the right spot. Being out here in the Chappy bush was a very different experience in the winter. Bare branches, layered with snow, set a very different stage than the full, leafy, greens of summer. He did remember thinking that the drive went on forever. Jack took another corner in the drive, and the house came into sight. This was the place alright.

While definitely built in the traditional New England style, the house was larger than most. It was two storey, grey shingled, with white trim. The front door was over-sized, and centred behind two white pillars. There was a peaked roof at either end of the house. Jack had seen larger homes on the island, but this one was still one of the bigger ones. He never did know what Amelia's family did to acquire their wealth, he just knew that Amelia worked at the hotel, and she was a very nice and down to earth kinda girl. He liked her.

Pulling into the circular drive, Jack parked, and stepped out of the car. He walked up to the front door, and slipped on one of the two front steps. They were still covered in snow. If anyone was home, they hadn't been outside since the snow started falling the night before. Jack thought that was odd. He knocked, then noticing the button on the right, rang the doorbell. It was loud. Jack stood there in silence. There were no birds, and there was no wind. The snow was still falling, although Jack was protected under the small overhang on the porch. Everything was so still. Jack leaned forward and peeked in the vertical window that ran along the side of the door frame. There was no movement inside either. He rang the doorbell again. An electronic version of the cliché *ding-dong* boomed through the house, and still there was no sign of life. Jack turned around. There were no cars here either. This wasn't the kind of place that you could walk to, well, you could, but it just wouldn't be practical not to have a vehicle. Jack walked around to the north-east end of the building. There were two large garage doors at that end of the drive, but the doors had no windows. It was impossible to tell if there was a car or truck inside. There were no tracks in the snow. Nothing gave the slightest hint as to whether or not anyone had been at the property since the summer. Was there another house on Martha's Vineyard that Jack didn't know about? It seemed unlikely. People like this always had more than one place, but if it was on-island, he would have heard about it.

Jack turned around and scanned the property. There wasn't much to see. At least, there wasn't much to see at this time of year. It was a thick, pristine blanket of white. That's it. The trees were old on this part of the island. They were tall and thick. Long branches reached out far from their trunks. There was about an even spread of coniferous and deciduous trees, or winter and summer trees as he had called them when he was a kid. The long limbs of the summer trees carried thin walls of snow stacked gently on even the thinnest of limbs, while the needles of the winter trees were weighted low to the

236

ground with their heavy, white burdens. So quiet, thought Jack. It was like a painting.

A long dark patch at the end of the stone wall caught Jack's eye. It was impossible to make out what it was; it was too far away. Jack stepped off of the snow covered, gravel driveway, and onto the equally, snow covered lawn. His steps were exaggerated in the snow and walking was tiring. As he got closer, the dark spot took shape. It was a pile of dirt. There was nothing odd about a pile of dirt out on Chappaquiddick. People were always planting and building something on their vast properties, but in the winter? In fact, the odd thing about this pile of dirt was that there wasn't anywhere near as much snow on it as there was on the rest of the land. As Jack got closer, he could see that between him and the pile of dirt was a hole—a big hole. The hole was a rectangle, at least five feet long, three feet wide, and maybe four feet deep. What the hell was someone digging out here for? Jack stopped at the side of the hole and shuddered. It looked like a grave, he thought. Wind picked up and there was a snap behind him. Jack jumped and turned around. He could see nothing. Just his own tracks in the snow, and bright white everywhere he could see. No movement. He looked back toward the squad car. He was maybe seventy-five feet away, he thought. Was it more? Jack felt mildly panicky for a moment at the thought of having to make a run for the car. He shook his head.

"You're being stupid," he said out loud.

Jack turned his focus back to the hole in front of him. There were large boot prints, and animal prints around the hole's perimeter. The paw prints were on top of the boot prints. Jack crouched down, took off his right glove and felt one of them. It was frozen. It was definitely a dog. A dog had been here a while ago, but it was there fairly soon after the person who dug the hole. The continued weight of the man on the snow and dirt had muddied up the frozen ground, but not for long. The dog was there soon enough after to leave prints of its own. Again, Jack turned around, he felt uncomfortable. He felt like he wasn't alone anymore.

Jack pulled a small flashlight off of a clip on his belt and turned it on. He shone it down to the bottom of the hole. More boot prints. He had expected that. The only way to dig a hole this deep was to get down in it. Jack remembered having to dig an outhouse at the cottage when he was a kid. Somehow, he didn't think that's what the owner of this place was doing.

Jack continued to scan the hole with the flashlight. There were dog prints down in the hole as well. Why would a dog go down in the hole? It wouldn't have been all that easy—especially to get out. There must have been a reason. He shone his light up the right hand side of the hole. It was one of the narrower ends of the rectangular hole. A couple of stones jutted out into the hole, but other than that, it was non-descript. He scanned the longer wall across from him with the light. Roots stuck out into the

238

hole. There were points where the shovel—Jack assumed it was a shovel—had broken larger roots.

Jack moved his light to the wall on the left—the other narrower wall. At the bottom of the wall, there were scratches, claw marks, whatever had drawn the dog down into the hole was there. Jack could see it now too. There was a lump in the dirt, like a larger root maybe, sticking out of the wall. Jack squinted but couldn't make it out. A dog wouldn't jump down into the hole for a root. There were plenty of roots sticking out of the pile of dirt and, from what Jack could see, the dog had entirely ignored that. He hadn't even peed on it. Jack knew that he was going to have to jump down into the hole if he wanted to see what the dog was clawing at. He looked around him again. He couldn't shake the feeling that he was not alone. He hadn't felt this way up at the house. Quite the contrary in fact, he hadn't felt anything but stillness and isolation on that front porch, but now, here, out at the end of the stone wall, and on the edge of the woods, he knew there was someone else there.

Jack turned back to the hole, and before he lost his nerve entirely, jumped down into it. He landed with a heavy thud. What had marginally resembled a grave before, completely felt like one now. Jack was overcome with dread. He was overwhelmed with the earthy smell of death. Every instinct told him to get out of that hole, and to get out now. He felt cold. Jack forced himself to kneel down toward the corner where the bottom of the hole met the left wall. He shone his light down closer. The dirt walls had been clawed repeatedly. The animal had dug a hole within the hole. It had created a dent in the wall about six inches across. It had found something. In the centre was a grey, blue lump. Jack reached out with his still gloved, left hand, and touched it. It yielded to his pressure and then snapped back into place. It was a hand.

*   *   *

Edie woke up in a pale green room that was slightly cooler than comfortable. Without lifting her head, she scanned what she could see, mostly ceiling, and figured out that she was in the hospital. She couldn't remember how she got there. She wasn't entirely sure what the last thing was that she could remember. She remembered waking up at Charles and Laurie's house. She remembered having coffee and toast in the den, and watching the ocean roll in on East Chop. Was she in a cab? Yes, she had taken a cab to her place to get her car. Peter Jefferies had been there, which had been a surprise—a good surprise. It was always nice to see Peter. He was at her house. Well, her property. She didn't have a house anymore. Edie wasn't sure exactly what she had been expecting, repairing a few rooms maybe? But she hadn't been expecting the entire house to be gone. That had been hard to take. At least no one had been hurt. Those words rang a bell. Someone else had said that too.
240

Whatever was left of the house would have to be bulldozed and a new house was going to have to be built. Edie tried to focus on that, tried to focus on the excitement of building a beautiful new home. She would keep it small and quaint—a cottage really—she didn't need a lot of room. It was just her. She had been alone since Mark was gone. Mark! That bell in her head rang again. Edie started to feel nauseous. Her head started to spin. Was this a panic attack? Is that what she was having? Her chest was tightening. It was that man. It was that man from the Whaling Church, he had told her something about Mark. Edie started to cry.

"Hey now, Edie? Edie look at me. You're alright," said a soft voice. "Look at me."

Edie turned her head down to see that Charles and Laurie were in the room. Laurie was now dabbing Edie's forehead with a cold cloth. Despite the cool temperature of the room, it felt good. "Yeah?" That was all Edie could figure out to say. She didn't even know what she meant by it. She looked at Charles who was setting down a tray of large coffee cups on her bedside table.

"We're here and nothing is going to happen to you," Laurie said. She leaned in and hugged her friend.

Edie hugged her back and the display of emotion was more than Edie could control. She began to weep openly. She cried hard. It was the first time that she had cried since she lost her house. The first time that she had really let herself feel her loss, feel the devastation that was going on in her life. Laurie's grip tightened as Edie's sobs increased. Edie felt her chest let go and her stomach unknot. She cried until she shook. Her hands and feet felt numb. She felt Laurie sit on the bed beside her and Edie snuggled into her warmth. She sniffled. "It's so freaking cold in these bloody rooms." Edie chuckled.

Charles stood up, took off his winter coat, and wrapped it around his friend.

"Thanks," Edie said. She smiled at her friend through red, swollen eyes.

Charles then handed her a small box of hospital tissues.

Edie blew her nose on a tissue, discarded it, and took two more from the box to wipe her eyes. She kept those tissues in her hands for future use. She sighed. "What the hell am I doing here?"

"We were going to ask you the same question," Charles said. "What *are* you doing here?"

"How did I get here?" asked Edie.

"Peter Jefferies called an ambulance," Laurie said. "We got the call at the station. You were out at your place. Apparently, you fainted."

"I don't faint," Edie mocked defensively.

"Well you do now," said Laurie.

"What do you remember?" Charles asked. Charles stood up and passed Laurie one of the paper cups from the tray he had been carrying. Laurie took it, then she pressed a button on the bed remote. The bed hummed, and shifted Edie smoothly into a seated position. Once she was comfortable, Charles handed her a cup as well.

"Coffee?" asked Edie anxiously.

"We have coffee; you have herbal tea," Laurie said. "Doctor's orders."

Edie frowned. "Well, at least it's hot."

"Apparently, you're not allowed to have any caffeine until they decide whether or not you are having panic attacks," Laurie said.

"I don't have panic attacks either," Edie said indignantly.

Charles and Laurie chuckled. "God, you're a pain in the ass," Charles said.

All three of the friends laughed at that.

"Edie, what do you remember?" Charles asked again.

Edie sobered. "I remember going to my place in a cab and I remember that Peter Jefferies was there. I went to get my car. I remember that it worked. My car worked. That made me happy. Then that man showed up, Charles. That man from the Minnesingers' concert. The one who upset me. Remember?"

Charles nodded.

"Well, he showed up in this old yellow and white truck," she said. "He told me that he was the one who called in the fire. He was the one who called the fire department."

Laurie opened the plastic lid on her coffee and took a sip. "That was good of him. You must have been grateful, but I can't see that as being enough to make you pass out."

Edie looked from one friend to the other. She wasn't sure why she found this next part so difficult to say but she did. She could feel it lodged in her throat like cork waiting to pop. Edie knew that as soon as she said it, that was it, there would be no going back. It would be real. "That wasn't all that he said," Edie looked down at her chest. All of a sudden felt very vulnerable in her thin hospital gown and Charles' coat. She sipped her tea. It was terrible. "He said that he was my brother-in-law. He said that he was Mark's brother."

*   *   *

"I'm glad you called, Peter," said Chris, lacing up his skates.

"I figured it was about time, I did," Peter stood up. He was already a big man and on skates, he was enormous. "How many guys can say they have an NHL player for a son-in-law? We might not be able to shoot a puck today, but at least, we can get out and have a skate!"

Chris stood. "It's funny that I never do it anymore. I miss it," said Chris.

"My son never was one for athletics," Peter shook his head. "Whenever he was forced into it at school, he was pretty good. He's just never been all that interested."

"It's hard enough for me to get him to the gym," Chris laughed. "I'll never get him skating."

The two men lumbered toward the gate in the boards surrounding the rink. The interior of The Martha's Vineyard Ice Arena was white and purple. A white gabled roof with purple metal beams gleamed high overhead. White walls lined with sponsors' advertisements ran the length of the ice on both sides, and a large American and Canadian flag hung on either side of the scoreboard behind the net.

Chris glided onto the ice like he had been born in skates. He felt a tingle in his body that he hadn't felt in a very long time. Adrenaline sent an undercurrent through him, almost as if his muscle memory was prepping for a game. He spun with unconscious ease to face Peter.

Peter's size was working against him. "Alright, alright, you don't have to show the old man up that badly," Peter's tone was only half-joking.

"What are you talking about? I haven't done anything!" Chris said defensively. "All I did was get on the ice!"

"I know," said Peter. "That's what worries me."

Chris looked around. "It's a nice arena."

Peter found his footing and started skating. "It is," he said. "They did a real nice job."

Chris glided alongside his father-in-law effortlessly.

"Is this bugging you?" Peter asked.

"Is what bugging me?" asked Chris.

"Skating so slowly with me. You probably want to haul off and tear up the ice."

Chris laughed. "No, not really. It might have when I was younger, but not now. I can appreciate it for what it is. I was thinking about joining one of the leagues they have here, or at the very least, show up for a pick-up game or two. See what it's like. I wonder if there are any other serious players on-island."

Peter shook his head. "Not that I've ever heard of. Certainly, not any ex-NHL players, that's for sure. Weekend warriors at best." Peter looked down at Chris's skates. "It really is amazing. It's almost like your skates don't even touch the ice. When did you start skating?"

"I started skating when I was three. I started playing hockey that same year," said Chris matter-of-factly. "I don't remember ever not being able to skate. And the first time in my entire life that I remember not being on a hockey team, was when I retired. Crazy, eh?"

Peter shook his head. "That is crazy," said Peter.

The two men skated in silence. The rink wasn't crowded. There was a young father teaching his son how to skate with a chair, and a young couple skating and holding hands, but mostly, they had the rink to themselves.

Chris loved the smell of an ice rink. It didn't matter where he was or what level of hockey he was playing, there was a scent that was particular to ice rinks. It felt like home to him. There were certainly big chunks of his life when he spent more time in a rink, on skates, than he did anywhere else. While his friends all partied and stayed out late, Chris was always in bed early, and up before dawn. More often than not, he was on the ice before dawn, doing skating drills with his team mates. He was never sure why his parents had put him into hockey, but they did. He had never questioned it. It was just something he did. Like a race horse, that was who he was. That was a long time ago. Now he worked out in the gym, cooked and baked a lot, and took care of Jeff. That was his life on Martha's Vineyard, and it was a good life.

"Peter..." said Chris.

"Here we go," said Peter.

"What?" asked Chris.

"You didn't ask me to come skating to tell me that you were thinking about playing pick-up hockey," Peter said. "You have something specific on your mind. You had something on your mind when I bumped into you and Jeff in Edgartown. I could tell."

"You're right," said Chris. "I did. We both did actually. Although I had been saying to Jeff that I would really like to see more of you. It's ridiculous that we three live on this island and we hardly see you. You have to promise me that we'll see you more often. We should start regular Sunday dinners or something."

"You'd better check with Jeff on that one," said Peter.

"And here we are," Chris said. "The reason why I asked you to come skating. What is the deal with you and Jeff? You two barely see each other, although now at Christmas I can barely get him to see anyone. He's always a bit of a grump from time to time, but at Christmas, he's unbearable. I spend most of the holidays threatening him—*and I like Christmas!*" exclaimed Chris. "If you can explain that one, I'll owe you big time!"

Peter didn't say anything. Chris watched Peter's face as the two of them skated. Peter pursed his lips and furrowed his brow. Then he squinted up at Chris as if the sun was behind him.

"Have you asked Jeff about all of this?" asked Peter.

"Yes," said Chris. "Several times. I just get the standard *"I'm fine"* or *"I don't want to talk about it"*. I don't care if you're his father or not, I don't mind telling ya, it makes me want to punch him upside the head!"

Peter chuckled quietly. "That's alright. There have been plenty of times that I wanted to punch him upside the head too...and I think the feeling was mutual." Peter frowned. "Look, I don't want to skate anymore. Let's go talk somewhere else." He turned and crossed toward the door in the wooden boards.

19

Police Chief Jeff Jefferies walked into Edie's hospital room to find that it was standing room only. He smiled broadly at his three friends. "So this is where the party moved to!" he said.

Charles grinned. "What are you doing here?"

"I have a gunshot wound downstairs. Pregnant girl. It doesn't look good either," he said grimly. "Helluva Christmas present."

"Do you know what happened?" asked Laurie.

"Not exactly," said Jeff. "It looks like domestic violence. Both the girl and the boyfriend are still out of it. We won't know what happened to them until at least one of them wakes up. He walked her into the emergency last night."

"How are you doing, old girl?" Jeff asked Edie.

Edie glared at him. "Listen you, I'll almost take that 'old girl' crap from your father, but I'll be damned if I'm going to take it from you!"

"Sounds like you're fine," Jeff grinned. Charles, Laurie, and Jeff all laughed.

"Oh, go to hell the lot of ya!" Edie said before giving in and laughing with them.

"I'm glad you sound good. I was worried," Jeff said with a more serious tone. He grabbed at her foot through the thin hospital blanket and shook it.

"No need to worry, big guy. I'm like fake fruit—I don't bruise that easy," Edie winked.

"Did you see my Dad?" asked Jeff. "I heard he called in the ambulance.

Edie nodded. "He was at my place when I went to go and get my car."

"Ah. I suppose that makes sense." Jeff shook his head. "The smartest thing that fire department ever did was make that man retire."

"Why?" asked Laurie. "He was an excellent fire-fighter."

"They knew damned well that he'd keep on working even after they stopped paying him," Jeff said.

Laurie chuckled, "Fair point."

"Try being a volunteer deputy with the police department!" said Charles.

Laurie raised an eyebrow. "Nobody's twisting your arm."

The four friends laughed again.

Laurie's phone rang and she reached into her pocket and answered it. She said nothing and then hung up. She looked at Jeff. "Can you stay here with Edie for a while?"

"I don't need a babysitter," Edie said.

Jeff ignored her. "Yeah, sure. Why? What's up?"

"That was Jack. He just found a body buried out on Chappaquiddick," she said.

"Jesus!" he said. "I don't remember this island ever having a Christmas like this. Go! We'll be fine."

Charles took his coat back from Edie and put it on. "You going to be okay?" he asked.

Edie nodded. "I'll be fine. Thank you for coming by. You guys really did me a world of good."

"We'll be back as soon as we can," said Laurie.

"I'm glad at least that you got your truck back," said Jeff. "That's some good news."

Laurie stopped and stared at him. "I didn't get my truck back."

"I don't understand," said Jeff. "Your truck—it's down in the parking lot. I just saw it when I came in."

*   *   *

Victor sat in the shed behind his family home, cleaning a pair of hedge clippers. They didn't really need cleaning, but he liked to find things to do out in the shed. Violet and Joey were both home and he would do anything

251

he could to leave them to their own devices. As soon as he went inside, one of them would pounce, and it wouldn't take long for the other one to jump in. Neither of them had any use for the shed though. The shed seemed to be his territory, at least for the time being. Victor did notice three gas cans and a few rags in the corner that hadn't been there before. They weren't his. They must be Joe's. The cans were worn, dented, and dirty. There's no way that Violet would even touch them, let alone have a use for them. Joe had a truck. He would have use for gas, but it seemed out of character for him to spend money on something practical like back up gas for his vehicle. Joey wasn't the Boy Scout type—he was never prepared. Victor supposed that he could ask Joey about them, but the idea made his head hurt. There were any number of responses that an inquiry like that might solicit, but the simplest and most probable, was *'mind your own fuckin' business!'* So, Victor decided to do just that and save them all the headache.

Victor decided that the garden shears were clean enough and returned them to the hook on the wall. He picked up the shovel by the door and started wiping it down with the same rag that he had used on the shears. The shovel actually was dirty. At least, cleaning the shovel made Victor feel more productive. He could tell himself that there was a reason for being out in the shed instead of hiding from his family. For a short while, he could lie to himself and believe that he had a normal and loving home life. He could believe that he had the kind of family that he used to have. The kind they had when Joe was little. Victor rubbed at the blade of the shovel, cleaning off dirt and twigs, bits of roots. He looked into his vague reflection in the clean blade, and saw Joey running barefoot through the campground—a little boy in nothing but a red bathing suit, his blonde hair fluttering in the breeze like a kite. He was laughing. Victor couldn't remember the last time he had seen Joe laugh. At least not with pure joy. He had seen Joe laugh with cruelty, laugh at someone he was bullying, but Joe never laughed anymore with delight. That boy running through the campground on Illumination Night, marvelling at the coloured lanterns, clapping his hands because he didn't know how else to express his happiness was long gone—that light extinguished.

How did that happen? Where had they failed him as parents? Violet had become bitter over the years. She had been happy in the beginning too. She had chased Joe through the campground on Illumination Night right along with Victor. It had been a family game. They had been a family back then. A real family. Victor wasn't sure when Violet had changed, really changed. She hadn't turned over night. He remembered trying to work more, because she had started to want nicer things. They needed more money. He liked working, he didn't mind it at first, but then she seemed to get angry at him because he worked too much and she had to raise Joey all by herself, and she wasn't having any fun. She wasn't getting enough attention. Had she taken it out on the boy when he wasn't around? There was no way of knowing now. Joey had certainly been exposed to more than his share of fighting. That had been the beginning of the end. He realised that now, but at the time, he hadn't. At the time, he had told himself that every family goes through their tough patches. Violet started lashing out with ridiculous spending. That meant that he had to take more, and more, jobs to pay off the credit cards. Eventually, they were living almost entirely separate lives. Then the accusations started. Victor was too tired to make love to her, and she accused him of being unfaithful. '*Are you fucking the rich bitches that are hiring you! What services are they really hiring you for Victor? Cause I'm certainly not getting any servicing at home!*' He would try, but the fatigue, the yelling, it had all been too much for him. He would lie on top of her with his flaccid penis in hand, trying to shovel it into her, but it wasn't happening. It just lay there between her clammy thighs like an uncooked sausage on raw turkey breasts. She had glared up at him and said, '*Get off of me, you loser.*'

Victor avoided them both as much as he could now. He knew the end was coming soon. The time was coming when he would not, could not, take it anymore. He needed some peace.

His stomach rumbled. He was hungry. Victor looked at his watch and realised that it was past lunchtime.

Breakfast at The Black Dog had been a long time ago. It had worn off. There was chili in the freezer. He would go into the house and get some. If he stayed in the kitchen, he might be alright.

Victor hung the shovel on the wall, and opened the shed door. The snow was still falling and the sky was dark. He walked across the backyard, but ducked back when he saw movement in the kitchen. Silently, he crept up to the window and peeked in. Joe was in the kitchen. Victor watched. He noticed that Joey still hadn't changed his clothing. He was filthy. There was a bottle of wine on the counter in front of him. Catering to his mother as usual, thought Victor. What struck Victor as odd was the fact that there was only one glass. It wasn't like Joey to let someone drink alone. Victor watched as Joey pulled a small bottle out of his shirt. He unscrewed the lid and poured a clear liquid into the wine bottle. Replacing the lid, he returned the bottle to his shirt, picked up the wine and the glass, and walked out to the living room. Joey turned the light out behind him.

Victor stepped away from the window and walked around to the side door of the house. His stomach was really growling now. He definitely needed some food. The snow that had fallen on the side porch had been pushed aside by the opening of the screen door. Far be it for Violet or Joey to shovel it. Victor picked up a broom that was leaning against the house, and swept off the remainder. "Was that so hard?" he asked in a hushed voice. He returned the broom to where he found it, and opened the screen door and then the wooden door. Victor removed his boots in the covered porch and then walked, sock-footed, into the kitchen. He closed the door quietly behind him. The TV was on in the den, loud like it always was. For this, Victor was grateful. Neither Violet nor Joey seemed to have heard him come in. If he stayed quiet, maybe he would be able to eat his meal in peace. He opened the freezer and pulled out one of the portions of chili that he had scooped into Tupperware the night before. It wasn't that he thought the chili would go bad before he had the chance to eat it, but he knew that if he didn't freeze it, Violet and Joey would eat it without even considering leaving him any. If he froze it, it was too much work—they wouldn't touch it.

Victor turned on the stove and dumped the frozen chili into a non-stick pot. He decided that the whir and beep of the microwave would strike up too much curiosity from the other room. The stove would be quieter. Victor padded over to the end of the counter and pulled a wooden spoon out of the ceramic utensil jar. He walked back over to the stove, and moved the frozen lump of chili around in the pot as it began to melt.

Heavy footsteps thudded, and creaked on the stairs leading up to the second floor. Victor recognised them as Joey's footsteps. He looked at his watch. It was far too early for Joey to go to bed. Victor stopped stirring and listened. The footsteps stopped at the top of the stairs, and then a door slammed shut. Victor jumped at the sound. It echoed through the house. Victor took the pot off the heat and quietly made his way into the hallway toward the den. The TV was still on, but the room was empty. The wine bottle that Victor had seen Joey bring in, was still on the table beside Violet's chair. There was no sign of Violet. Had Joey been drinking alone? That was certainly possible, but Violet had been home at one point, that afternoon. Her car had been in the driveway when Victor returned. He walked over to the window and looked outside. Violet's car was still there. All three vehicles were there—Joey's truck, Victor's truck, and Violet's car. Victor walked back over to the foot of the stairs. He just stood there. There was no way he was going upstairs. Victor stood there and his body started to tingle. He heard it once, then again. Then slowly, it picked up speed, the unmistakeable sound of a bed scraping on a hardwood floor. Groaning. A man groaning. Deep and animalistic. Panting and out of shape. The bed scraped louder. The guttural growls of the man permeated the house. Victor was frozen at the foot of the stairs. The headboard banged against the wall. Victor recognised that sound from a long time ago. It stirred deep memories of years past. Sweat broke out on Victor's forehead and he dropped the wooden spoon he had been holding. His knees buckled and that was enough to break the force that had been holding him in place. Victor ran through the kitchen and out onto the porch. His stocking feet slipped on the wet wood, and he fell onto the snow covered backyard. Victor heaved and rolled over onto all fours like a dog. On his hands and knees, he vomited.

*   *   *

Charles and Laurie crossed the parking lot of the Martha's Vineyard Hospital looking for Laurie's truck. It didn't take them long to find it. Jeff was right. It was just sitting there. There weren't even any cars around it.

"Hiding in plain site," Charles said.

"No kidding," said Laurie. She walked around to the driver's side and pulled on the door handle. It opened. She leaned in and pulled back immediately. "Jesus! What is that smell?"

Charles opened the passenger side door. "There's a lot of blood on this side. Not just blood though. I think your truck is how Jeff's domestic violence case got to the hospital. Didn't he say the girl was pregnant?"

"Yeah," said Laurie. She closed the driver's door and walked around to the passenger side.

"I think her water broke in the truck," said Charles.

Laurie peered into the truck and looked at the stain on the seat and the floor. "I think you're right." She stepped back. "Can you call Jeff and tell him? He'll get some of his people out here to look at it. They can match the blood to the girl in the hospital. We don't have time for this. We have to get out to Chappaquiddick."

Charles nodded. "Sure, no problem."

258

"You always said that you liked the thrill of a mystery. This Christmas must be a real thrill for you," said Laurie only half-joking. "It sure isn't the Christmas that I had planned for you."

Charles hugged her. "This is only Christmas In Edgartown. Our real Christmas will be great. We'll have another chance at a traditional Christmas In Edgartown celebration next year."

"I know," said Laurie. She broke away from him, and walked around to the back of the truck. She opened the back hatch. "All your presents are still here," she feigned a smile. "That's something."

*   *   *

William sat at the desk in his front room, and pulled a greeting card out of a paper bag. He had drove into Vineyard Haven after leaving Edie's place and bought the card at Rainy Day on Main Street. He had considered buying a gift as well, but decided at this point, a gift would be overdoing it. The card was blank inside, but the front was a painting of the Edgartown Lighthouse in a snowy, holiday scene. Christmas lights adorned the lighthouse and there was a wreath hanging halfway up the tower, much like there was right now. It had been a long time since William had written in a card of any kind. Even when he sent them out to business associates, he had his assistant fill them out for him. Long before he retired,

William had realised that one of the advantages of having the same assistant work for you for a long time was eventually, they signed your name better than you did. William pulled open the centre drawer in the desk and pulled out a pen. He wished his assistant was here now. He didn't have a clue what to write.

William set down the pen, and reached with his right hand for his mug of tea. He took a sip and, as he always did, relished the warmth in his hands. Then, he set down the mug and pushed away the card. It was best, he thought, if he practiced on a piece of paper. Pulling a pad of paper from the same drawer in which he had found the pen, he began to write. *Dear Mrs Sparks...* He stopped. That looked ridiculous. Calling her by his brother's last name struck him as overwhelmingly obtuse. *'Dear Edie'* was far too familiar. Finally, he decided on *'Edie'*. Yes, that worked. William picked up his mug, took another sip of tea, and continued with his note.

Edie,

I came to this island with the purpose of finding my brother. We had become very estranged, obviously, and I wanted to mend that bridge. It was my every wish to connect with family. Family is something that I have never had. Mark was my half-brother, I'm not sure if you even knew I existed before today. Judging by your reaction, I'm thinking that you did not. I am very sorry to have startled you, especially on the heels of the tragic fire at your home. I would also like to apologise for my behaviour at the concert. I thought I was

260

being funny, but clearly, I was not. I am a man of business. Human relationships have never been my strong suit.

Edie, you owe me nothing. I know and appreciate that. I will understand if you want me to leave you in peace. I will never have a relationship with my brother, and now, I have no family left. If you can see your way clear to having supper with me, when you are well and at your convenience, I would love to hear any information that you would be willing to share about him.

Best,

William Singleton

William read and re-read his note. Satisfied, he transcribed it into the card, enclosed a business card, and slipped it into the accompanying envelope. On the envelope, he wrote, *Edie.*

20

Corey reached into the backseat and pulled the box that Cameron had given him up front. It wasn't heavy or particularly large. It was a generic cardboard box with four flaps on the top and bottom. The bottom had been taped shut with one of those industrial hot tape dispensers, but the top four flaps had just been folded over each other to keep the contents secure.

"Here hon," Corey passed the box to Tina in the passenger seat. "Have a look in here and see if you can't find a list of addresses or something to tell us where we're supposed to drop these things off. Cam said there was more than one in there."

Tina took the box and flipped open the cardboard flaps. "Ooh! They're pretty!" she said. "They're little Christmas presents!" She pulled one out to show Corey.

262

"Did Cam wrap these himself? He sure did a good job! I wish I could wrap like that."

Corey laughed. "Somehow, I doubt it. I can't see Cameron sitting down to wrap a bunch of presents for people he doesn't even want to see. You know what I mean? I'm guessing his wife did it, or somebody."

Tina smiled. "Yeah, I guess you're right." She fished around in the box with her left hand and pulled a piece of paper off of the bottom of the box. She scanned it quickly, "Here's the list!" she said.

"Great!" said Corey. "Where do we go first?"

"Well, there are two stops in Edgartown," Tina said. "Shall we start there? I mean we're in Edgartown now. Kinda makes sense, right?"

"Sure. Where's our first stop?"

"Well, I am not really sure. One is on South Summer Street and the other is on Cow Bay Road." Tina looked up at Corey. "I don't know where either of those is."

Corey typed one address into his phone and then the other. "Well, South Summer Street is back in town. It's not far from here. The other one, Cow Bay is on our way out of town to Oak Bluffs. Do we have to go to Oak Bluffs?"

Tina consulted their list. She nodded. "Yes, we do!"

"Okay, so we'll go to Cow Bay Road on our way to Oak Bluffs." Corey looked back at his map. "You know, this South Summer Street is really close to here. Do you feel up to a walk?" He looked at Tina. "We could walk there and back in fifteen minutes, pick up the car, and head to Oak

Bluffs. What do you say? It's pretty out and I'd like to see some of the sites."

"I'm game!" Tina said.

"Does it say which of those presents belongs to each address?" asked Corey.

Tina shook her head. "No," she said. "I think they're all the same. They don't even have names on them."

"Okay. Well, the address is in my phone," said Corey. "Grab one and let's go!"

"Tina looked into the bag and picked out a small parcel. "Okay. I think this one is the prettiest!"

The two of them stepped out of the car and into the lightly falling snow. Corey took Tina's hand, and they headed down Main Street toward the centre of Edgartown. Christmas lights were strung up on every lamppost and every home. Along the street, small Christmas trees were perched atop forest green lattice pedestals and lit with multi-coloured lights.

Tina looked around in wonder. "It's like a fairy tale! Isn't it, Corey?"

Corey found that he couldn't stop smiling himself. "It is," he agreed. "I feel like I'm in a movie. One of those sappy Hallmark Christmas movies that you're always watching." He laughed.

"They're not sappy—they're sweet!"

"They're sappy," he confirmed.

"Well, I like them," Tina said proudly. "They get me in the holiday spirit."

264

It wasn't long before they came upon South Summer Street. "This is it," Corey said. They turned right and headed down into the quiet of the Edgartown Village.

"Wow," said Tina. "Once you get off of the Main Street, there isn't a whole lot of foot traffic in here is there?"

Corey shook his head. "There sure isn't." He looked from Captain's house to Captain's house, trying to read addresses. "I think most of these really nice houses are summer people. A lot of them look shut up for the winter."

"Imagine having a house worth millions of dollars, and only using it for a few weeks a year," Tina snorted. "That's crazy."

"I think so too," said Corey. "But I guess, if you can afford it, life is a whole different ballgame." Corey looked down a gravel driveway at a house that was mostly hidden behind tall, sculpted, evergreen trees. "I think this is it," he said. Taking Tina by the hand, he led them down the drive to the large white home with black shutters. It looked empty.

"I don't think anyone is home, Corey," said Tina.

As they got closer, a large man walked around the corner of the house, carrying two gas cans. One he seemed to be emptying onto the lawn. He was filthy from head to toe. He stopped walking when he saw them. He set down the cans and wiped his hands on an oily rag. A grin spread across his face, exposing teeth that reminded Corey of Indian corn.

"Hi!" said Tina. "We have a present for the guy who lives here. What's the name again, honey?"

Corey put his arm out, trying to hold Tina back. He did not like the look of this guy at all.

"I'm the caretaker. You can leave it with me. I was just checking the meter. Making sure everything was running good, you know," The big man stood still. He continued to rub his hands on the rag. He didn't seem to blink. He just stared.

Corey cleared his throat, "I actually think that we have the wrong house," said Corey. "We'll keep going."

The big man started to walk forward. "Hold up now. No need to rush off. You said you're delivering presents? Who are you Santy Claus?" he laughed. "Is it a nice present? Leave it with me. I told you, I'll make sure they get it."

"What were you doing with those gas cans? You don't need them to check the meter," Tina said.

The big man turned his predatory glare onto Tina. "What do you know about those gas cans? What did you see?" he spat.

Tina stepped behind Corey. She shook her head. "I didn't see anything."

Tina and Corey started to back down the drive. "We're going to head out," said Corey. "You have yourself a good night."

The big man leapt forward with surprising agility. He grabbed Tina by the arm and twisted it. Tina screamed. Corey turned around and drawing his right fist back, hit the big man square in the jaw. The man stumbled backward,

266

releasing his grip on Tina's arm. Corey wrapped his arm around Tina and hurried them both toward the mouth of the driveway.

A single shot rang out into the quiet of Edgartown Village.

*   *   *

Mike and Trish climbed the stairs to the front door of the Edgartown Police Station. Trish opened the door and stepped aside for Mike to enter. His hands were full of coffee and doughnuts. "Thank you, ma'am!"

"Ma Pleashuh, kand suh!" Trish said mocking his Texas accent.

"You gals sure do love that accent, don't you?" Mike grinned at her. "Y'all think it's sexy!"

Trish rolled her eyes. "Oh lord!" she said. Trish held one of her hands up to her forehead, as if to indicate she was going to faint. "Lawd, yes! Why, I just about go weak in the knees every time you speak, Mike Walker! Pass me my smelling salts!"

Mike blushed. "Alright, that's enough making fun of the southern boy," he laughed. "Hey, I saw that in an old movie once. What is that?"

"What is what?" asked Trish.

"Smelling salts. What are smelling salts?" Mike asked in earnest.

"I think it was just a small vial or bottle of ammonia. Ammonia has a really strong odour. I guess it brings you back to consciousness if you pass out," said Trish. "It's not high on my list of things to discover firsthand."

"Yeah," said Mike. "No kidding." He looked around. "Where is everyone?"

"I'm here!" called out Sergeant Dan Thomas. "What's going on guys?"

"We have the coffee and doughnuts," said Trish. "You were regular coffee with a blueberry scone, right?"

"God love ya!" said the Sergeant. Trish passed him his order from the bag in Mike's arms and he accepted it hungrily.

"We have coffee and fritters for everyone else," said Mike. "Are they in the back?"

Dan shook his head—his mouth already full of scone. He sipped some coffee to wash it down. "They're out. You just missed them. There's an emergency out on Chappaquiddick and a missing girl and a friend of theirs is in the hospital over in Vineyard Haven."

"Good lord!" said Trish. "We weren't gone that long!"

"You can wait if you want to, but I don't know how long they'll be or what kind of time they'll have once they get here. I can call them if you want, but over coffee and doughnuts..." Dan trailed off.

"No, no, that's cool," said Trish. "We did want to see Jack though." Trish motioned toward Mike. "Mike lost my engagement ring last night. Well, we think he was mugged actually, and we now we think we know by who."

"Oh yeah, I heard about the ring," said Dan. He looked at Mike. "That really sucks. Sorry to hear that." He sipped at his coffee. It was hot and he made a slurping sound. "You were mugged?"

"I guess that's what you call it," said Trish. "Pickpocketed or whatever—you know?"

"Does Jack know this?"

Trish nodded.

"We were filling him in when we were going for coffee this morning. Then he had to come back for that G.B.C.," said Mike.

"So, who do you think it was?" asked Dan.

"A guy by the name of Joe Helm. Do you know him?" asked Trish.

Dan's face soured. "Unfortunately," he said.

"That's exactly what the bartender at The Shore Line Hotel said when I asked her about him," said Mike.

"Joe Helm is a particularly unpleasant individual," said Dan. "I'll tell Jack what you've told me. He'll be in touch for sure. If we got Joe Helm off the streets of Martha's Vineyard, I swear to you, every cop on-island would throw a party."

"Well, let us know when we can come back and talk to Jack," said Trish.

"Absolutely," said Dan.

"Should we just leave the coffee and doughnuts?" asked Mike.

"Absolutely," said Dan.

*　　*　　*

Edie sat in her hospital bed, staring at her hospital lunch. None of it looked appetizing—not the grey part, or the brown part. The only colour on the tray was the day-glow green of the dessert. Lime Jell-O. Edie wondered why hospital food always looked like this. The one place where you should be pumped full of nutrients to get you back on your feet as expeditiously as possible, you were always served something that looked like it came from the special effects department of a nineteen eighties horror movie. Wasn't there a movie called The Toxic Avenger? Edie didn't think she ever saw it, but for some reason, it kept leaping to mind. She could envision this tray being filled by someone in a heavy rubber apron and gloves, with a welder's mask over their face. Kind of like Homer Simpson in that power plant. Having sufficiently grossed herself out, Edie pushed the rolling table, and the tray, as far away from her spot on the bed as she could. She looked at her phone. Could she order a pizza? Was that a thing?

Chris Johns walked into Edie's room and held up a tray and a large paper bag. "Who's up for Fat Ronnie's?" he said with a smile.

"Oh my god! I could kiss you!" exclaimed Edie.

Chris shook his head. "You're beautiful, but that will get you nowhere." Chris stared down at the tray of food on the wheeled table. "Did they tell you what that was supposed to be?" he asked wrinkling up his nose.

Edie shrugged. "I'm not sure. The guy who brought it kind of mumbled. I don't think he was too sure either."

"Well, my plan had been to be here a little earlier so that you could have avoided that unholy mess altogether, but I went skating with Peter Jefferies, and then there was a line-up at Ronnie's. Do you like Fat Ronnie's?" Chris moved the lunch tray of horrors to the window sill, and set down the bag and tray he had been carrying.

"Absolutely!" said Edie. "The best burger on-island— maybe anywhere."

Chris reached into the bag, pulled out an onion ring, and popped it into his mouth. He moaned with delight. "I can't argue with you there," he said through batter and grease.

"What did you get us?" asked Edie. Instinctively, she wiped at her chin in case she was drooling.

"We got the exact same order, so there would be no fighting," said Chris playfully.

"You sound like my mother," said Edie.

"Well, I got it from my Nana," Chris said. He reached into the bag and pulled out a foil wrapped burger and set it down in front of Edie. "One Fat Ronnie's burger with roasted red peppers, fried onions, and old cheddar for you, *AND* one Fat Ronnie's burger with roasted red peppers,

271

fried onions, and old cheddar for me!" He pulled out a second burger for himself. "Also, not to be overlooked, we each get an order of onion rings."

"That onion ring that you just ate had better not come from my order!" Edie waved a finger at him.

Chris shrugged. "Delivery charge."

Edie shook her head in mock disgust. "All these hidden fees..." She shoved an onion ring into her mouth. "I guarantee there is more nutrition in this onion ring than there was on that entire tray." She nodded toward the tray still sitting on the window sill.

"Ha!" Chris laughed. "Definitely." He unwrapped his burger and grabbing it with both hands, took a huge bite. He moaned. "Jesus H Christ—that's good," he said. His words were almost impossible to make out, his mouth was so full. He kept chewing. Once he had swallowed, he said, "I almost forgot!" He reached down to the tray beside him and lifted up two wax covered paper cups with plastic lids and straws. "Two chocolate milkshakes!"

Edie's eyes widened and she moaned through her mouthful of culinary heaven. "Oh, my lord. Why did you have to be gay?"

Chris shrugged. "I've always been lucky like that." He winked.

A teenaged girl walked in carrying a bouquet of white and yellow flowers. She looked at Edie and smiled. "Edie Sparks?"

Edie nodded. "That's me."

"These are for you!" the girl bubbled. She passed them to Edie and said, "There's a card inside. Enjoy!" Then the girl spun on her heel and she was gone.

Chris put down his burger and inspected the flowers. "They're beautiful!" he said. "I love yellow flowers. Traditionally, they signify friendship or apology, but I'll take them on any occasion." He reached into the bouquet and pulled out the card. The envelope read, 'Edie' in an elegant script. He passed it to Edie. "Who are they from?"

Edie took the card. "I have no idea," she said. "Charles and Laurie probably." She slid her finger under the corner of the sealed envelope flap and tore it open. Gingerly, she pulled the card out. "They're from him."

"Who him?" asked Chris.

Edie was quiet for a moment while she read the card. "He's my husband's brother," she said. "At least, that's what he says. I can't see why he would lie about it, though. It's not like I'm up here sitting on the family fortune or anything. My house just burned down and now I'm in the hospital. My insurance is going to have a hairy fit. They'll probably drop me. God, I can't think about that right now. There's enough on my plate." Edie leaned back on her bed. "Sorry," she said. "These flowers have kind of killed my mood. I was really enjoying lunch too."

"Don't give up so easily. We're not done yet," Chris said. "So, this guy isn't here for your pot of gold. Why is he here? What does he want?"

"He says that he's here to connect with family. Apparently, Mark was the only family that he still had, or at least, thought he still had."

Chris shrugged and took a bite of his burger. "Sounds innocent enough," he said.

"I don't know, Chris," Edie said. She turned to look out the window at the falling snow. "Mark died a long time ago. I'm not sure that I want to open all of that up again."

"Can I read the card?" asked Chris.

Edie passed it to him.

Chris looked at the cover for a moment. "It's pretty," he said. He flipped it open and read the note inside. "So, he wants to take you out for supper. Doesn't sound so bad."

Edie didn't respond.

"Edie," Chris said. "Edie?" He put down his burger.

Edie turned from the window and looked at Chris. She could feel her eyes welling up. "Yes?"

"Do you have any other family?" Chris asked. "Are your parents still alive? Brother? Sister? Anything?"

Edie spoke softly. "No," she said.

Chris nodded. "I didn't think so," he said. "I'm just going to say this straight. I don't have any family that I'm close to at all. Jeff has his Dad, and that's it. We never really talk about it, but I know that we would both love to have a house full of family from time to time. It's obvious from the way we both enjoy our dinners with you and Charles and Laurie—you are our family. Our friends over

274

on Popponesset Bay have a huge family and they are always getting together. They laugh, and sing, and play instruments—they've figured it out. That's what life is all about, Edie. I'm sitting here looking at you and I can tell that you're afraid. Don't be. Family just came knocking on your door—let it in."

"But I don't know where this will end up going..." Edie said.

"It doesn't have to go anywhere," said Chris. "Think of it like a first date. He just wants to take you to dinner. So, let him. Pick your favourite restaurant, order the most expensive thing on the menu, and then go home." Chris shrugged. "That can be the end of it or not. It's entirely up to you."

21

Laurie drove along Litchfield Road on Chappaquiddick, checking the map on her phone as she went.

"I doubt there has been much traffic out this way other than Jack and the other officers," said Charles. "You can just follow their tire tracks."

Hating to admit it, but realising that he was right, Laurie turned off her phone and threw it on the dashboard.

There was something about Chappaquiddick, thought Laurie. It didn't matter what season it was, the little island had a magic all its own. The farther you got from America, the closer you came to Martha's Vineyard, there was a feeling that came over you. It was a combination of purging city life, and embracing island life.

It was exchanging seventy-five mile-per-hour highways for twenty mile an hour roads, giving up fast food chains for farm to table eating, tuning out booming manufactured radio for public broadcasting. Leaving Martha's Vineyard for Chappaquiddick is a more concentrated version of the same thing. Chappaquiddick was almost entirely one lane dirt roads. It had one store with a few odds and ends. The year-round homes were few and far between. The small island was six square miles of nature and wildlife preserve, sandy beaches, and a lighthouse. Laurie made a mental note to get out this way more often. She knew that the trustees had trails out this way. That would be a great thing to do on her day off. Charles would probably love it too. That was definitely his sort of thing.

"Have you ever been hiking out this way? Like on one of the trails, I mean," Charles asked as if reading her mind.

"I was just thinking that very thing," she said. "No, I haven't, but I would love to. I love Chappaquiddick, but I never seem to get out here. Oh sure, I've walked through Mytoi Gardens a couple of times and swum on East Beach, but there's a lot more to Chappy than that."

"I agree," said Charles. "Why don't we promise ourselves that, on a sunny day, we'll make a point of coming out here over Christmas and hiking one of the trails."

"It's a promise," said Laurie. Laurie steered the cruiser to the right, following the other cars that had gone

277

before her. The road was long and thickly wooded. "Is this a driveway or another road?" she asked rhetorically. The trees on the left stopped and were replaced by a short stone wall that enclosed a snow covered field.

"It's so pretty," said Charles.

"There's the house," said Laurie as they took another curve in the drive. There were two police cars and a van parked in the circular drive in front of the pillared entrance. "They're over there," she said, pointing across the wall and the field. "At the end of the stone wall."

"I see them," said Charles.

Laurie parked behind the other cars and the two of them stepped out into the cold winter air. In spite of the goings on of the other officers, it was quiet. The winter wind acted as a vacuum ensuring that they were surrounded in silence. Laurie imagined that peace and quiet were the real reasons people bought this far out on Chappy. For the most part, they just wanted to be left alone. Laurie figured that there were probably just as many celebrities per square foot on Chappaquiddick as there were in Beverly Hills. Without waiting for Charles, she headed toward the other officers. Jack, who had seen her drive in, had already started walking casually in her direction.

"Hey Chief," he said. "We still haven't dug her up. We're waiting for the forensics team to finish going over the area, then we'll go over it with the radar just to see what we're dealing with. They have taken moulds of the

278

boot tracks, and they are looking for hair and fibre, anything really that we can find. There's not a chance that she's alive. We did get a positive I.D. though—it's Karen Malone."

"How do we know that?" asked Laurie.

"A dog—I don't know—smelled her, or saw her, or something, jumped down into the hole, and dug into the corner of the hole, exposing her hand. We took a chance and took fingerprints. We ran 'em. The Shore Line Hotel requires that all employees have fingerprints on file for security purposes. Karen came up."

"Crap," Laurie said. "Well, that's not too surprising." She looked around the estate. "Any sign of Amelia?"

Jack shook his head. "None. We searched the house. The front door wasn't even locked. All of her belongings are there—at least as far as we could tell. It looks like she was living in the servant's apartment. Makes sense really, it's smaller and self-contained. That's a big house for one young woman," he said. "Do you know if she had any place else? Maybe a small apartment in town?"

"Not that I ever heard," said Laurie.

"Where did Charles go?" asked Jack.

They both looked around, but there was no sign of Charles from where they were standing.

"Who knows," she said. "He's always into something. If there's a clue to what's going on around here, he'll find it. That's why I bring him along. Don't ever tell him I said that."

"Oh hell, Chief, everyone already knows that!" Jack grinned.

Laurie snorted, and turned back toward the forensics team who had mapped out the hole and surrounding areas. "Have they found anything?"

Jack said, "No. Just footprints. It's hard in the snow and the cold. The ground is frozen and the snow changes everything. It also means that anyone out here probably wore a hat and gloves, maybe even a snowsuit. If this was summer, we'd be picking up hair and tissue all over the place."

"Well, I guess for the time being, I will cancel the general broadcast for Karen and put one out for Amelia. The other towns are going to wonder what the hell is going on down here in Edgartown," Laurie said. "Oh, Jack, by the way, I found my truck."

"You did?" exclaimed Jack. "Where?"

"In the parking lot of the Martha's Vineyard Hospital," she said. "It was Jeff who noticed it actually. We went up to see Edie because she passed out up at her place and was rushed to the hospital."

"What?" exclaimed Jack. "How is she?"

"She's a little shaken up but she's okay," said Laurie. She has a lot on her plate and it got to be too much for her. After she gets some rest, she'll be fine."

"Jesus," Jack said. "Some Christmas."

"No kidding," Laurie agreed. "Anyway, we went up to see Edie, and then Jeff came in to check on her too. That's when he told us that he was at the hospital for a shooting. On our way out, Charles and I checked out the truck and I think that his victim used it to drive themselves there. His victim is a pregnant woman and it looks like she bled out, and her water broke, all over my front seat. Now that I think about it that would mean that the shooting took place in Edgartown Village. They must have been close to the truck when the shooting took place or they wouldn't have used it. Jesus." Laurie took off her uniform hat and ran her hand over her hair. "I'd better talk to Jeff."

"I don't remember ever having a Christmas In Edgartown like this one, Chief," Jack said.

"Keep me posted, Jack. Okay?" Laurie started walking back toward her cruiser. "I'm going to put out that G.B.C. on Amelia and find out if she has another address. I'm also going to have to tell Sam that we found Karen...Then, I'll talk to Jeff about my truck."

"Good luck Chief," said Jack.

"You too, Jack," she said. "Good work—really."

Laurie strode across the lawn toward the big house. She was moving in the general direction of her car, but definitely moving in a round about way. She was looking for Charles. Like the dog that had dug out the hand of Karen Malone, if Charles had sniffed something out, there was a good chance it was important. Laurie walked past the cars in the circular drive, and around the house. It was impossible not to be impressed by the home. It was big without being ostentatious. It still had a homey feel to it. Laurie loved its traditional grey shingles and white trim. As she walked around to the ocean side of the house, she admired the large, screened-in porch. Laurie loved the thought of families sitting out on the porch in rocking chairs and lounge chairs enjoying morning coffee. Hanging from a large tree, at the other end of the house, was homemade swing crafted from an old mooring buoy. It made her smile. It was so Martha's Vineyard. The summer views must be amazing. There was movement down on the beach. It was Charles. Laurie followed Charles' footsteps in the snow down to the private beach. Once there, Laurie looked out over the water. The house was on Edgartown Harbor, down toward Katama Bay.

"How far do you figure that is?" asked Charles.

Laurie looked at Charles. His arm was stretched out and pointing across the bay. She shrugged. "I don't know. I'm terrible at judging distance over water. Two hundred metres?"

Charles nodded. "That's what I figured too," he said. He looked around. "It's beautiful here," he said.

"It is," Laurie agreed. "Did you find anything interesting?"

Charles shook his head. "No."

Jack came running down the path. By the time he got to them on the beach, he was out of breath. "Chief!" he panted. "The team started scanning the ground with the radar. They found a second body."

Corey woke up to the realisation that he was still in the hospital. It's not that he thought he could have been released, and brought back to The Ashley Inn, and slept through the entire process, but there was always the hope that everything after arriving at the idyllic inn had been nothing but a horrific nightmare. If he was in the hospital, it wasn't. Everything that he could remember was real.

"Good afternoon," said a man's voice.

Corey's eyes sprang open, his body jerked, and his muscles tightened. Corey heard a small scream, and then realised that he had made it. He struggled to his elbows to see who was in his room. There was a tall, slim, man in a uniform—a police officer's uniform.

"I'm sorry, Corey. I didn't mean to frighten you," the officer said. "My name is Chief Jefferies. I'm the Police Chief in Oak Bluffs. Please, lie back down. Actually, here. This should help." Chief Jefferies picked up the bed remote and the bed started to hum. In moments, Corey was sitting at a forty-five degree angle.

"Am I in Oak Bluffs?" asked Corey.

"Yes," said Jeff. "But it seems that you've upset the police in Edgartown as well."

"How?" Corey asked. The conversation was already becoming too much for him. "Have they doped me? Why am I so groggy?"

"I'm not sure actually," said Jeff. "They probably gave you something for a little pain relief and to help you sleep. Apparently, you were in pretty rough shape when you came in," Jeff grabbed hold of a chair with metal legs and vinyl padding, and swung it closer to Corey's bed. He sat down. "That's why I'm here. Corey, I need you to tell me what happened last night, buddy. You walked into this hospital, dragging a pregnant woman with a gun shot wound, and it looks like you got here in a truck that you stole from the Edgartown Police Chief."

"*Where's Tina?*" Corey blurted. "*Is she dead?*"

"No," said Jeff. "She's not dead, but she's not good either."

"What about the baby?" he asked.

"I think the baby's okay too, but you're really going to have to talk to the doctor," said Jeff.

"I want to see her."

"I know you do, Corey, but you can't even sit up. How are you going to go see Tina?" said Jeff. "Besides, she's in intensive care. I'm not entirely sure you'd even be allowed to see her at the moment." he smiled a fatherly smile even though he wasn't all that much older than Corey. "I need you to stay as calm as you can, and tell me what happened last night," Jeff sat back in his chair. "Corey, did you shoot Tina?" he asked point blank.

Corey stared at him in horror. "No!" he shook his head. "It was the man with the gas cans."

"When did you and Tina get to Martha's Vineyard?"

284

"Yesterday afternoon," said Corey.

"Okay, that sounds good. Why don't we start there. Tell me everything that has happened to you and Tina since you got to the island."

Corey stared up at the hospital ceiling and remained quiet for several minutes. Chief Jefferies didn't speak either. The two men just sat in the quiet room lit only by the light on the wall above Corey's headboard, and the quickly fading light coming in the window. Corey turned his attention to the falling snow outside, and began to speak. He started with the reason for the whole trip. He told him about delivering packages for his boss, Cameron—Christmas presents. Chief Jefferies took notes as Corey spoke. He didn't ask a single question, he just let Corey talk. Corey told him how it had been a Christmas bonus for Corey. He told him how excited both he and Tina had been. Corey told him how they had been having the time of their lives. He told him how he had never seen Tina smile and laugh so much. Then, Corey started to cry. He felt the emotion and stress drain out of his body with every convulsion. He brought his hands up to cover his face. The shame of showing this emotion in front of this stoic, older man—an authority figure, and a total stranger—was almost too much to bear. Chief Jefferies seemed to understand this. The Chief seemed to know that if he consoled Corey, it would only make the situation more upsetting, more humiliating; therefore, the Chief didn't offer any comfort, or words of sympathy. Again, he just

285

stayed in the background, and let Corey go. Corey reached for the box of tissue on the bedside table, wiped his eyes, and blew his nose. Without looking at the Chief, Corey said, "I'm sorry."

"No need," said Jeff and then quietly, pen in hand, waited for Corey to continue.

Taking a deep breath, Corey said, "We walked down South Summer Street to the address where we were supposed to drop off the first gift, at least I think it was. To be honest, I'm not sure. There didn't seem to be anyone at the house. It looked locked up and dark. A lot of the houses seemed to be in that neighbourhood. Anyway, we didn't even get close enough to knock on the door when this big, dirty-looking guy walked around from the far side of the house with two gas cans. Not only that, he seemed to be pouring one of them. But that doesn't make sense. Does it? Maybe they didn't actually have gas in them, but even still—what would you be pouring on the lawn and house at this time of year? There was something wrong with that guy.

When he saw us, he froze. He was not expecting anyone. He froze like we caught him doing something that he didn't want anyone to see. I don't think Tina saw him doing that funny thing with the cans though. I don't think she clued in right away. She just started talking to him. I wanted to get the hell out of there right away, but Tina was smiling and talking. She's too trusting—always has been. She's so sweet and good-natured. It wasn't until the

286

guy said that he was reading the meter that she started to figure things out. Tina asked him why he needed gas cans to read a meter. She practically called the guy a liar. Then, the guy wanted the gift we were delivering. He wanted to know what was in it. I think he was hoping it was expensive. We were already backing out by then, but there was no way that guy wanted to risk us leaving and telling what we saw. Finally, we started to run, but the guy jumped at Tina. He grabbed her arm, and he twisted it hard. She screamed. So, I hauled off and clocked him in the jaw," Corey looked down at his hand, and noticed for the first time, that it was bandaged up. "We turned and ran down the driveway. That's when I heard a shot. I wasn't even sure what was going on until Tina slumped down against me. She looked at me with a confused look in her eyes. She said my name, but she said it like a question." Corey's voice started to shake. "Then, I noticed the stain on her dress getting bigger, and I knew what had happened. I picked her up as best I could." Corey wiped his eyes with the back of his hands. "I remembered that there was a parking lot just a couple of houses down. I never been here before. I don't know where the cop stations are, and there was no one hardly on the streets at all. We got to the parking lot and it was full. I looked at one car, but it was locked. Then, I tried the truck. It was open and the keys were in it. I couldn't believe my luck. I remembered that the hospital was by the ferry. We had passed it on the way in. I figured that I could get there faster than waiting for an ambulance, or a cop anyway—no offense." Corey shook his head. "I wasn't thinking clearly. I just saw Tina bleeding from her belly, and I thought of the baby. I didn't want anyone to stop us because that would take time. I'm sorry about your friend's truck. I work on cars for a living. I can probably get him a new seat and I'll do the work for free."

Jeff smiled for the first time since entering the room. "Don't worry about that right now." He stood up.

"I didn't shoot my girlfriend, Chief Jefferies," said Corey.

Jeff nodded. "I believe you," said Jeff. "Did you ever find out what was in those presents you were delivering?"

Corey shook his head. "No."

"With your permission, I'd like to go back to The Ashley Inn and open a couple of them up," he said.

Corey nodded. "Sure. No problem."

Jeff put the chair back where he found it and started out of the room. "Get some rest, Corey. I'll be back."

"Chief?"

Jeff turned around and looked at the Corey.

"Can you check on Tina for me, please?" he asked.

"I'll send the doctor in to talk to you," Jeff said.

*   *   *

Victor drove up to Memorial Wharf in time to see Chief Laurie Knickles drive off of the Chappy Ferry in her police cruiser. Victor pulled over into the wharf's parking lot and got out of his truck. The snow was falling and the sunlight had long been clouded over. The only sounds were the waves lapping at the harbour, the hum of the ferry engine, and the Memorial Wharf flag clanging against the flag pole. The wind was out of the North East. It swept across Nantucket Sound and the outer harbour, forcing the temperature on-island to drop. Victor shrugged his shoulders up close to his ears as he walked toward the ferry.

"Ryan!" Victor called.

Ryan looked up at the voice calling his name. There were no cars in line to get on the ferry on either side, so he poured coffee out of a Thermos and waited. "Hey Victor, what's up?"

"That's what I was going to ask you," Victor said. "What was the Chief doing over on Chappy this time of year? There's hardly anyone even living over there, much less causing problems."

"I know, right?," Ryan said. "It's crazy. A whole bunch of cops are over there though. They won't answer any of my questions, but they don't mind askin' them though." Ryan snorted and took a sip of coffee from the cap of his Thermos, which doubled as a cup. "They wanted to know about that girl Amelia who lives over there. You know, the one from the hotel?"

Victor nodded.

"They asked me about that other girl from the hotel too—Karen Malone. I don't know why they want to know about her though. She doesn't live over there. She lives to hell and gone over in West Tisbury." Ryan motioned west with his arm. "Well, you know—she's out by you." Ryan took another sip of coffee. "I ain't seen the news or nuthin' though. I either been on this ferry or in bed for the last two days. That's it."

Victor stared through the snowfall at the other side of the harbour, the ferry dock, Chappaquiddick Road, and beyond. He stared through the white and grey blur that was the curtain of snow. It was easy to see why they called it snow when you switched to a television channel that had no reception. That was exactly what it looked like. It was a wall of shimmering white, and grey, and silver that hid Chappaquiddick from his line of vision. He still stared. He stared as if on a clear day, he would be able to see what was going on, what the police were up to. Of course, that was impossible. The wheels in his head were spinning nonetheless.

"Why'd you park?" asked Ryan. "Aren't you coming over?"

Ryan's words snapped Victor back. "Huh?" He shook his head. "Oh, no. I was just driving by and I saw the car. Chalk it up to islander's curiosity." Victor smiled. "I'll see you around."

"Yeah, see ya Vic," Ryan said. "It will probably be easier to finish that wall when this snow's gone anyway, right?" But Victor was already in his truck and driving away.

22

Victor looked up at his West Tisbury home. This was the home where eight generations of his family had lived before him. It was one of the oldest homes on Martha's Vineyard. One of the oldest that was still being used as a homestead, anyway. It was simple. There hadn't been a lot of renovation to the original design except for an addition on the back, and even that had taken place a couple of generations ago. Of course, heat had been added and running water updated. Renovations like that had come along here and there, but from the front, from the outside looking in, the house had stayed virtually unchanged. That was the way people liked things to be on the Vineyard. That was the way Victor liked things to be too. This house had never been enough for Violet—not ever. Looking back, he could see that now. Standing in front of his home, he knew it was never going to change. It hadn't changed in over three hundred years. It wasn't going to change now. Violet wasn't going to change either. He had figured that out too. Now, the years of fighting and lack of emotional stability had created Joey. Violet had been hateful and vicious; Victor had been aloof, distant, or just not there. Together they had created a monster. Victor didn't even know what his son was capable of at this point. That was a terrible thing to think about his own son, and he knew it, but that was just the way things were.

Victor walked in the side door like he always did, but this time, he did not take off his boots in the covered porch. He kept them on, and walked straight into the kitchen. The burner was still on, and the chili he had taken out to cook was still in the pot. It was mostly thawed and would be fine to eat a little later. He had a few things to get done first. Victor felt calm. His mind had been reeling when he had last left the house, but he barely remembered that now. A door had closed. His brain was no longer accepting deliveries. It had all that it could handle for the moment.

"Victor? Joey?" Violet called from upstairs.

Victor walked out into the hall to find Violet at the top of the stairs in her pink robe. The robe was terrycloth and tied in the middle with a matching belt. Her hair was sticking up like one of those troll dolls that people won at fairs or bought at cheap toy stores. Her eyes were bleary and unfocussed.

"It's me, Violet," Victor said. He wasn't even sure if she could see him.

"That figures," said Violet in a voice that was trying for nasty, but it was too weak. There wasn't enough power in it. Her usually acerbic barb, fell sort of the mark. She spoke again, but this time, her tone had changed, "I don't feel so good."

Victor didn't reply. He turned and walked back down the hall, toward the kitchen. Victor pulled on the wood door and then pushed out on the screen door window. It protested with a rusty yawn. There was a crash and several thumps behind him. A grunt like that of an over-the-hill football player being tackled by someone much younger. Victor didn't turn around, he continued out to the shed. He returned a moment later with the shovel he had cleaned earlier in his hand. When he returned to the hall, Violet was sprawled on her back at the bottom of the stairs. Her arms and legs were splayed almost cartoon-like on the floor. The belt of her robe had come undone. She was naked and exposed. Her entire body was almost colourless, raw, and pale pink. Her bunions, heels, and toes were red from long days in cheap shoes. There was a fiery, red ring around her waist from wearing pants that were two sizes too small. Her spread legs exposed a vagina that was red and swollen from rough, dry, sex. Violet stared up at him, and tried to speak. All she managed was

294

a gargle that forced spit out of her mouth, and down her cheek. She reached up toward him with her right hand.

Victor swung the shovel high above his head, and brought it down as hard as he could on Violet's face. There was a loud crunch as her skull collapsed under the blow. Her body twitched, paused, then twitched again. Then, it was over.

*　　*　　*

No sooner had Charles and Laurie walked into the Edgartown Police Station, than Sergeant Dan was on top of them. "Chief!" He called, running across the station to meet her. "Chief!"

"Hey, Dan," said Laurie. "Has Jack called in about the second body on Chappy yet?"

"No, Chief," Dan said. "I'll let you know as soon as he calls, but Chief, I've been waiting for you to get back. I would have called you but I knew what you were dealing with out there."

"What's going on?" Laurie asked.

"Mike and Trish were in here, and they say they know who stole Trish's ring," said Dan.

"What ring?" asked Charles.

Laurie looked at him and shrugged. "Don't look at me. This is the first I've heard of it."

"Mike was supposed to propose to Trish last night at the lighting of the Edgartown Lighthouse, but he lost the ring. At least, he thought he lost the ring. He actually thinks that it was stolen," Dan told them.

"By whom?" asked Charles.

"Joey Helm," said Dan.

"Christ!" said Laurie. "Of course, it was." Laurie shook her head. "Well, call Chief Riggs. He's the Chief in West Tisbury."

"I did," said Dan. "But he has two guys out with pneumonia and everyone else is working on hunting down that fire bug they've got out that way. They even have Peter Jefferies helping them out." Dan took another breath. "He asked if you could talk to him—what with the ring being stolen in Edgartown and all."

"This isn't about the ring being stolen in Edgartown; this is about nobody wanting to deal with Joey Helm!" Laurie sighed. "Fine. Charles and I have to go out to West Tisbury to talk to Sam Jones about discovering Karen's body anyway. The Helm place isn't far from there. They're just on Edgartown-West Tisbury Road." Laurie paused for a moment and stared at Sergeant Dan. "Dan, they're going to call in about the identity of that second body, if it's identifiable at all. If not, they're just going to bring it here so that it can be shipped off to Boston. I want an update either way. Charles and I are headed out to West Tisbury to see Sam and then we will bring in Joey Helm for questioning."

Dan nodded. "Okay, Chief."

"Would you please cancel the G.B.C. on Karen Malone?" asked Laurie.

"Sure, no problem," said Dan.

Laurie and Charles turned to walk out of the station.

"Oh, Chief!" called Dan.

"Yes?"

"Mike and Trish brought in apple fritters and coffees for everyone. Do you want to take some with you?"

Laurie's face showed no expression as she stared at the bag of pastries and the tray of coffees. "Definitely," she said.

* * *

Jeff drove his police cruiser into the driveway of The Ashley Inn, parked, and turned off the engine. He sat in the car for a moment, trying to remember the name of the man who owned and ran the inn. He knew that Laurie had introduced them once. He didn't really need to know it, but it wouldn't hurt. Then it came to him—Paul—the man's name was Paul. Jeff remembered that he liked him. He was a nice man.

Jeff stepped out of the car and made his way up the freshly shovelled path. The snow was still falling, fairly heavily actually, but Jeff was grateful that Paul or one of the inn's employees—Jeff would bet a paycheque that it had been Paul himself—had shovelled. He took the two front stairs briskly, and opened the front door.

The front room of The Ashley Inn was everything that a country inn on Martha's Vineyard should be. It was comfortable and classic. It was decorated in that elegant New England style that made all homes look like they had money but didn't want to brag about it. That always made Jeff chuckle. He remembered going to Florida and being overwhelmed by the opulence. The two styles were polar opposites. Jackie Kennedy versus Melania Trump. To each their own, thought Jeff. The room had been decked out with Christmas decorations. An enormous Christmas tree stood in front of the windows and the mantle was decorated with pine and ornaments. Jeff grimaced. He couldn't wait for this season to be over.

"Can I help you, Chief?" Paul walked into the room wiping his hands on a dish towel.

"Hi Paul," Jeff smiled his work smile. "How's your day?"

"It's a good day. Christmas In Edgartown keeps me busy," Paul smiled broad and genuine. "I'm not full, but I'm busy. What about you? The season keep you hopping?"

Jeff shook his head. "You don't know the half of it. These last couple of days have been nuts. Actually, that's why I'm here. I need your help."

Paul opened his arms in a welcoming gesture. "I'm all yours."

Jeff looked around. "Are we alone?"

Paul nodded. "All the guests are out enjoying the festivities." His bright demeanour greyed. "Is there something wrong, Chief Jefferies?"

"You had a young couple check in yesterday, Corey Johnson and his girlfriend Tina," Jeff said.

"Yes, I did," said Paul. "They seemed like real nice kids, although I asked them not to park out front, and their car is still out there. I haven't seen them yet today. When I do, I'll remind them to move it."

"You won't see them for awhile. They've run into some trouble on-island and I need to take a look in their car. I've spoken to Corey and I have his car keys, but his car is on your property, so I thought that I would just tell you why I'm here—as much as I can anyway—and what I'm doing." Jeff smiled pleasantly. "I really don't think that I'll be long."

"Well, I appreciate you letting me know, Chief," said Paul. "Are they okay?"

"Corey is doing alright. Tina isn't out of the woods yet, I'm afraid."

"Oh no. That girl must be eight months pregnant if she's a day!" Paul said. "She'll be in my prayers."

Jeff smiled and shook his head. "I'm sure she'd appreciate that, Paul. Thank you. I'll let myself out." Jeff turned back toward the front door.

When Jeff had parked in front of The Ashley Inn, he had blocked in a 1970 Firebird. He figured that it was Corey's. The boy spent his days fixing up cars; an old

299

sports car sounded like it would be just his speed. Jeff laughed at the pun. He slipped the key into the lock and turned. With a lift of the handle, the heavy door swung open without much coaxing. Jeff knew that cars weighed approximately the same now as they had fifty years ago— no matter what the car companies told the car buying public, but they seemed heavier. The doors almost seemed solid. The trunk and hood had to be lifted with a lot more force. There was a strength in the old American muscle car. Jeff grinned. He could see why Corey liked them.

Jeff slipped into the driver's seat, and he closed the door beside him. Even with the car off, it was a little warmer. There was a cardboard box on the passenger seat. The top flaps were open. Jeff peered inside. The box was about half-filled with small Christmas presents. On top of the presents was a list of addresses. Jeff skimmed the list, noted that the Summer Street address where Tina had been shot was on it, and set the paper aside. He picked up a box and unwrapped it. He had a pretty good idea what was in it—drugs. Cocaine or heroine were his big guesses. The first present that he had picked up was wrapped in a shiny green foil with gold ribbon. It had been very prettily wrapped. Jeff gave Corey's boss that much. The foil paper tore away easily, revealing a holiday patterned gift box. Jeff lifted the lid and found a crystal snowman. It was beautiful—probably worth a pretty penny too, thought Jeff. *A snowman?* Jeff reached into the cardboard box on the passenger seat and pulled out another Christmas present. This one was blue foil with a white ribbon. Jeff tore at the paper and lifted the lid on another Christmas box. This time, there was a crystal Santa Claus inside. His little red suit sparkled in the light that shone through the windshield. His beard looked like cut-diamonds. Had Corey and Tine really been delivering Christmas presents for his boss? Not drugs? They had truly, and innocently, been doing this guy Cameron a favour during the busy Christmas season. Corey and Tina had come to Martha's Vineyard, only to be attacked and shot. A young couple expecting their first baby were now lying in the hospital.

Somehow, this made it all much worse. No one deserved to go through what Corey and Tina were going through, but if they had been delivering drugs, it would have taken the edge off of it, Jeff thought. He'd be able to ask Corey what he thought this guy was doing paying him so much money to deliver these gifts? If it had been drugs, he knew that there would have been an undertone of "you should have known better" in everything he said to the boy. Corey would have felt it too. That was how society worked. But now, all they had been doing was delivering presents for a good employer, who wanted to show his employee his gratitude. There had been nothing but altruism and joy. And it had been destroyed.

*   *   *

Victor picked Violet up, and slung her over his shoulder like a sack of fertilizer. Her neck snapped when she bounced off of his back, and blood sprayed from the red and white pulp that had been her face. The wood door was still open. Victor pushed open the screen door, and it caught in Violet's brassy blonde hair, now streaked pink and burgundy. Either unaware or indifferent, Victor walked on without losing pace. Wet, pink, and yellow hair tore from Violet's scalp, and started to freeze to the metal doorframe. He lumbered down the stairs, and walked toward the back of his pick-up truck. He tossed his shovel onto the flatbed. It landed with a metallic clang. With his free hand, Victor lifted the latch that opened the tailgate. Using his entire body, Victor heaved Violet's corpse forward, and she fell back like a teenager falling excitedly onto a waterbed for the first time. Her head bounced on the cargo bed. The belt completely untied, her pink fluffy robe was still open. Violet's body was slowly greying from blood loss. Her heavy breasts slid into her armpits. What remained of Violet's mouth was slack. Her tongue lolled out to the side like raw liver. The top of her jaw had collapsed from the blow with the shovel. Her teeth were missing. What had been her nose—attached to her face by nothing but sinew and torn skin—fell into her now expanded oral cavity. The bridge of her nose was gone. Her brow, eye sockets, and cheeks were all one purple, black, and red piece of meat. Blood no longer pumped from her wounds, but it still leaked out of her ears—the only feature not altered by Victor's shovel.

Victor closed up the tailgate, and walked over to the driver's side. He opened the door, slipped behind the wheel, and turned the key in the ignition. The truck roared to life. The headlights automatically shone into the darkness. Snow flakes danced in their beams. Slowly, Victor eased the truck forward and turned onto the main road.

As the house disappeared into the night behind him, Victor drove into the dark. The road was barely visible through the thick snow. He tried to stay focussed on the road, but it was difficult. He had so much to think about.

For the first two practice holes, he had planned ahead. He had even planned to do one more practice run—he had even dug the goddamn hole! But the police were out on Chappy and asking questions. He couldn't take a chance. Digging that third hole had been a complete waste of time and energy. Now, he had to think of another spot. Where could he dig another hole? Here he was at the main event—this was no practice run—and he didn't even have a hole dug. This was not how this was supposed to play out.

Edie's. He hadn't finished the wall out at Edie's. The snow had surely forced all of the fire fighters in. The cops were long done whatever they were doing. He'd go there. He could dig up a hole and then put the stone wall in place over top. That had been the plan with the first two.

He had managed to replace the wall after filling the first hole, but he hadn't finished with the second. He should have done that before starting the third hole. That was foolish. Victor looked contemplatively out the window at the snowfall. The snow might actually work in his favour. It would keep people away from the house, and off the roads almost entirely. The island practically shut down in this kind of weather. Victor sighed. He felt better. At least now, he had a plan.

A pair of headlights, that had sprung to life just as Victor had exited his drive, shone into the snowy darkness. Approximately one hundred feet behind him, it was the only vehicle on the road, and it had been following Victor since he left the house. The driver stayed close enough to maintain eye contact with Victor's tail lights, but no closer.

23

Edie sat in Charles and Laurie's den. It was her favourite room in the house. The overstuffed burlap cushions on the wooden framed furniture were earthy and comfortable. Floor lamps with ivory shades bathed everything in a warm glow. The walls were almost entirely windows, affording anyone in the room an unobstructed view of Vineyard Sound. There wasn't much to be seen tonight though. It was a dark night. The heavy snowfall and cloud cover had blocked out the moon entirely. Short waves lapped up onto the icy shore no more than forty feet from where she was sitting. Edie knew this because she could hear it, not because she could see it. She loved that sound. It was a soothing sound. She would be lying to herself if she didn't admit that the sound of the ocean sweeping over the rocky beach below hadn't played a major part in her deciding to make Martha's Vineyard her permanent home. Almost exactly that sound. There had been other factors of course, but she had been sitting on one of the benches at the foot of the East Chop Lighthouse when she had decided to stay. That was only a couple of properties away from where she was now.

Edie sat on the soft couch in her friends' den with a glass of Kim Crawford Sauvignon Blanc in one hand, and a business card in the other. William Singleton's business card.

Chris Johns' words had really hit home. Edie had been ready to completely ignore William's note. She had had enough. There was more than enough to keep her occupied for the time being. She didn't even technically have a home! The last thing she needed was trying to reconnect a complete stranger with the memory of his brother, her husband, who had been dead for more than two decades. She had buried her husband, and the memories of their life together, a long time ago. She had moved on. Now, thanks to the fire, she didn't even have any photos of him. Unless, she had something stored at the inn. That was possible. She had boxes in the basement of The Edgartown Inn that she had completely forgotten about. The inn basement was large, cool, and bone dry—perfect for storage. Those boxes had been down there for a long time. Edie had no idea what was in them. Now that they were all of her worldly possessions, she had better take a look. One more thing to add to her list of things to do.

Chris had been right. She didn't have any family to speak of. She had wonderful friends, but she spent a good part of her time alone. She told people that she liked it that way—she told herself that she liked it that way—but there had definitely been times when she would have enjoyed some company. Wasn't that true of everyone? Didn't all of the research show that the actual secret to a long and healthy life was companionship? There was a direct correlation between the number of positive and healthy relationships that a person had and how long that person lived. So, why was Edie so reluctant to allow this person into her life? Was it just because he had been a jerk at The Old Whaling Church? That didn't seem right. We all have our off days. Edie took a mouthful of wine. "Lord knows there are people in this world who think I'm a bitch on wheels just because I was having a bad day," she said aloud. Edie laughed. The vibrations stirred Bubbas The Cat, who had seen fit to curl up in her lap. Bubbas sounded a quick purr, and looked up at her. The tone of the purr had gone up at the end, as if it were a question.

"Sorry, Bubbas," Edie said, petting the feline's soft back. "I don't know what's wrong with me." The sound of voices brought Fenway The Beagle scampering into the room. "Jesus, it's like being Marlon Perkins in here!" Fenway sat down on his haunches and looked up at Edie. He thumped his tail on the hardwood floor. Bubbas looked down at the dog, shook her head in what Edie took to be disgust, and went back to sleep.

"So, Fenway, do you think I should call Mr William Singleton?" Edie looked at the dog. Fenway thumped his tail harder on the floor and let out a single yelp. "I knew you were going to say that," she said. "Alright, I'll meet him for supper, but that's it." Edie set down her wine. She reached over to the end table, careful not to disturb the cat in her lap, and picked up the phone. Holding the business card out so that she could read it, she dialled the number. The phone rang twice before it was answered.

"Hello William," she said. "It's Edie." She took a deep breath. "I'd like to take you up on your offer for supper. Have you been to Rockfish? It's on North Water Street in Edgartown. Tomorrow at six p.m.? Does that work for you?" She waited for his response. "Fine. I'll see you then. I'm looking forward to it too. Good night." She hung up and picked up her glass of wine. She took a mouthful that was a little larger than she had intended. She swallowed. Bubbas looked up at her and gave her a low brief purr. "I know," said Edie. "I'm not looking forward to it at all."

*   *   *

William Singleton pressed the red phone symbol on his screen, and ended the call on his iPhone. It's funny, he had expected that he would be happier if Edie agreed to meet him for supper. Finding family, sitting down and
308

connecting with them, was the whole reason for his trip to Martha's Vineyard. Now that he was faced with it, that it was actually happening, he was terrified. That didn't make sense. William was a man who had walked into board rooms and given unpleasant talks to important men and women. He had walked into their companies as the man who had just bought them out, and told them how things were going to be. That never went over well. People hated change. William had walked into halls of thousands of people and lectured on the business world. He had explained to thousands about the world of investment banking. William had even gone to suppers attended by Presidents of the United States. None of those meetings had filled his stomach with butterflies like meeting this short, middle-aged woman, with honey blond hair. The last time William had felt like this, he had been sixteen and going out on his very first date. A lot was riding on this. This supper would change the direction of his life. He didn't even know which direction he wanted his life to take exactly, but he knew that after this supper, things would be different. For the first time since he had come to the island, William wondered if coming to Martha's Vineyard had been the right thing to do.

William collected a handful of ice from the ice bucket, and poured himself two-fingers of scotch. He then crossed the room and took his place in the wingback chair in front of the fire crackling on his hearth.

His brother was dead. William hadn't planned for that. It hadn't even occurred to him that it would be a possibility. He had braced himself for a brother who wanted nothing to do with him. He had been willing to accept that fact. William had only very briefly been a part of his life. William had been much older than Mark. He had left and moved on with his life when Mark was very young. William had also thought that maybe Mark wouldn't even know who he was. His family had always been the type to bury difficult times, not talk about them. His people just moved forward. When William had immersed himself in business, he had separated himself from his family. It hadn't happened overnight, but slowly and surely, there had been fewer birthdays remembered, and more often holidays were skipped. Eventually, William lost touch completely. It hadn't been intentional. He harboured no ill will against any of them. He just...got busy. The more successful he became, the more expensive his time was. The more expensive his time was, the more foolish it seemed to miss a week of work for something as trivial as a birthday party or Memorial Day. Eventually, he received a note that his mother had passed. That had been difficult to process. Possibly, because in his mind, she had died years ago. Not sure what to do with the information, he did the only thing that he knew how to do—he kept working. He kept working until he couldn't work anymore. So, it wouldn't surprise him if his name never came up in the house that Mark grew up in. The memory of the son who had abandoned the family—no matter how successful he had become—would be extinguished.

Now, he had a lot of money. Money had been how he had ranked the importance of every minute of his life. The value of his life had been based on how much each moment either cost him or made him. The money had been the reason that all of his other priorities had been rescinded. Now, he could watch his money go up in value on a daily basis. He continued to buy and sell real estate all along both coasts. The irony was that it all felt worthless. Money was worthless when you had no one to share it with. William knew this to be true better than he knew anything else. So, this supper tomorrow night was important. William was banking on it.

*   *   *

Charles and Laurie pulled up in front of the Helm house. The house was a beacon of light in the surrounding darkness. Street lights were almost non-existent on this side of the island. They were certainly few and far between. The lights on the main floor were all on. The light shone across the lawn, reaching out to the street, but then faded to black behind a curtain of falling snow. The second storey was dark. The Chief and her Deputy stepped out of the police cruiser, and into the freshly fallen snow. There was one car in the driveway. Laurie looked at Charles. "That's Violet's car," she said.

"Somebody else was just here," said Charles. "These tire marks are fresh. Looks like a truck."

"Victor and Joey both drive trucks," said Violet. "Along with almost everyone else on the island."

"Seems quiet," said Charles. "It doesn't look like the front door gets used much." He pointed at the pile of snow that had accumulated in front of the door. "Is this a side door house?"

Laurie nodded, and started down the driveway toward the kitchen door. The house was old but very well maintained. She looked casually in the windows as she walked by. She figured if someone was home, they would have heard her drive up, and looked out the window to see who it was. Laurie had prepared her pleasant but on duty face and was ready to motion whomever caught her eye to meet her at the kitchen door. She saw no one. No movement. She didn't hear anything either. "It is quiet," she said. "All the lights are on though. That's odd."

"Laurie. Stop," said Charles.

She stopped.

"Take out your flashlight and scan the snow around you," Charles said calmly.

Laurie did as instructed. The snow was covered in a dark spatter that sparkled red in the beam of her flashlight. Laurie remembered her great-grandmother making candy for her when she was a little girl in Northern Canada. She would boil maple syrup and other sugary concoctions in a pot, and then throw it onto the pure,

312

white, country snow. It would harden instantly and Laurie and her friends would eat it with delight. That's what this looked like. This haphazard spatter that trailed from the house to the fresh tire marks of an absent truck. Frozen, dark, glimmering trail of blood. A lot of blood. Almost as if a hunter had exsanguinated a deer. Some of the blood had pooled into heavy boot tracks. Laurie wondered if the boot prints would match those that were found on Chappaquiddick that afternoon. There was a frozen puddle the size of a dinner plate at the tire tracks.

Laurie looked at Charles. His face was blank and his eyes wide. "Go back to the cruiser, please Charles. Call Jeff and ask him to get out here now."

Watching his step, Charles turned around, and went back to the car. He opened his door and slipped in.

Satisfied that Charles was safe for the time being, Laurie turned back toward the house and followed the trail of blood to the kitchen door. She shone her light on the door and noticed the blonde and pink clump of hair caught in the door frame. There was a piece of skin about an inch square holding the hair in a clump. Laurie took out her phone and took a photo. She returned it to her pocket. Then, with a gloved hand, she opened the door. She removed her forty calibre Glock from its holster. She cocked it. Her chest tightened. Her chest always tightened when she pulled out her gun. Laurie was not a gun fan, and did not take their use lightly. She took a deep breath and stepped into the Helm kitchen. The blood splatter continued into the house. Their were no footprints. Whomever or whatever was doing the bleeding had been led out of the house. The man in the boots was in front.

"Victor? Violet? Joe? This is Chief Laurie Knickles of Edgartown. Is anyone home?" Silence. No response. The blood continued into the hall and Laurie followed it cautiously.

In the centre of the hardwood floor, in the main hall, the blood stopped. Or rather, this was where it had begun. There was an explosion of blood and a large smear. Laurie tried to make out the outline of what had happened, but it was impossible. Whatever had happened in this house, she had missed it. Walking around the blood, Laurie peeked into the den. It was empty. There was a half-consumed bottle of wine on an end table and a single wine glass beside it. Laurie turned toward the stairs.

"Victor? Violet? Joe?" she yelled. "Is anyone upstairs?" Again she was answered only with silence.

Laurie pulled out her iPhone again and snapped photos of the gruesome scene surrounding her. When she was finished, she opened up the phone and called Jeff.

"Jeff, are you on your way? Are you bringing anyone with you? We're going to need a complete forensics team out here. I'm not sure what happened, but I missed it. I'll call Dan and put out an A.P.B. for Victor, Violet, and Joey Helm. It's possible there was an accident here, but that's not the feeling I get, Jeff. Someone died in this hallway and not at their own hand. I've got a lot of blood here and it

314

leads all the way out to the driveway. I want to follow the tire tracks before the snow covers the trail completely. What's your ETA? Never mind, I can hear your sirens, see you in a minute." She ended the call and headed back outside.

When she reached the foot of the drive, Jeff pulled up in his squad car with another squad car in tow. He stepped out and walked over to Laurie.

"I didn't check upstairs," she said.

"We'll give it a full sweep," Jeff said. "Go!"

"Are you sure?" Laurie asked.

"Definitely," he said. "This snow is only going to get heavier. Follow those tracks. He's not going to make much of an escape leaving a trail like that."

Laurie jumped into the car and drove silently down Edgartown West Tisbury Road.

24

Victor drove his truck up onto Edie's property and parked in front of the charred carcass of her home. The fire was completely extinguished and had been for some time. The charcoal black was now layered with white snow. The whole scene was colourless and slightly blurry behind the blizzard. The whole property looked like a photo that would have appeared in The Vineyard Gazette before colour photography was commonplace.

The hill was just high enough that Victor didn't think anyone passing on the road would notice his truck. He stepped out and walked far enough down the drive to get a look at the stone wall that he had been building for Edie. It looked fine, he thought. The wall started by the driveway and wrapped around the property to the side of the house. Like everything else, a thick layer of white snow

316

iced it like a layer cake. Scrub oak and pine trees surrounded the wall by the house; he would have plenty of cover to dig a hole, and then fill it. No one was going to be looking for him on a night like this anyway. The only person who would know whether or not he was home would be Joe, and Joe wouldn't care either way. Joey would be grateful that he was out. Victor walked over to the flatbed and opened the tailgate. He needed to get started.

With one hand, Victor grabbed Violet by the ankle and dragged her down toward the open end of the pick-up. Her naked body slid out of the loose robe. When she was close enough, Victor let go of her ankle and with a strong grip, grabbed the fleshy side of her thigh, below her hip. With his other hand, he grabbed a breast. He hauled her up, and threw her over his shoulder. She had stiffened slightly. Victor felt like he was hauling mannequins for a department store, or maybe this was what one of those real life sex dolls felt like that you could buy on the internet nowadays. Once she was balanced properly, Victor reached for his shovel, and closed the tailgate. He marched across Edie's sloping lawn, toward the stone wall, crunching in the snow as he went.

When he had reached the wall, Victor let Violet drop to the ground. Her limbs slapped out straight into the snow. There was no longer any heat in her body. The ride in the flatbed had seen to that. Snow fell on her and did not melt. Victor took his shovel in both hands and sliced it into the ground. The ground was more earthy here than on Chappaquiddick. There were fewer stones. That would make for easier digging. He sliced another shovelful, and tossed it over his shoulder. He sliced again...and again.

With a loud crack, Victor was hit hard from behind. He tripped forward, and fell on the handle of his shovel. He exhaled hard as the wind was knocked out of him. He tried to regain his balance, but his boots slipped in the snow, and he fell onto his stomach. As soon as he realised what had happened, Victor rolled onto his back. He prepared to be hit again. Joey ran at him. His eyes were wild. His mouth frothing between peeled lips over clenched teeth. With a gas can gripped in both hands, he swung high above his head. Victor held up his shovel in defence. The boy was bigger than Victor, but he was overweight and out of shape. Victor was strong. Joey's gas can hit the shovel. Sparks flew as the dented can screamed against the shovel blade. Victor pushed Joey backward. This time it was Joey who lost his balance. He rolled in the snow and scrambled up to face his father.

"What did you do?" screamed Joey. *"What did you do?"* Joey looked at his mother's naked body, lying in the snow. He wailed and doubled over as if consumed by an unbearable physical pain.

"It's too late, Joe," said Victor, scrambling to his feet. "She had to go. She was done. I couldn't take it anymore. She was a miserable person—so unhappy. I couldn't let her go on like that Joe. I just couldn't." Victor stared down

318

at his faceless wife. Her eyes were still intact. One was covered in snow and the other stared comically inward. "It was like when we took the dog to the vet, Joey. This was an act of kindness. That's all." Victor turned to his son and scowled. His tone changed. It deepened. "I guess you're going to have to *get it when you need it* somewhere else."

Joey froze in his tracks. *"I don't know what you're talking about."* He said. He was wheezing already.

"I saw you Joe. *I saw you!*" Victor said. "You drugged your own mother so you could fuck her. You fucked her Joe! Upstairs—in my bed. You drugged her wine, and then carried her upstairs, and you fucked her. What did you use Joey? What is in that little bottle in your coat? The date rape drug? Is it GHB? I was there. I saw you! *Oh Christ—I heard you!*" Victor covered his ears with his gloved hands at the memory. He felt his stomach start to twist. "How long has that been going on?" Victor vomited into his mouth, and he spit it out.

"You're lying," Joey said, unable to meet his father's eyes. "You're a goddamn liar!"

Victor stared at him and for a moment, he saw the little boy that Joey used to be. Somewhere in that pure terror of being caught, there was a child-like quality that had been gone for decades.

Joey swung the gas can back over his head, but he knocked the cap and poured gas onto his face and shoulders. He let out a high-pitched cry as the liquid slipped under his eyelids. Joey dropped the can, clawing at his eyes. Victor swung his shovel at his son's chest. The shovel scraped the gas can as it fell. Again, sparks flew into the winter air as metal scraped on metal. Almost in slow motion, Joey went up in flames. He made a guttural, animalistic howl that Victor had never heard come out of a human being. His nylon coat ate up the flames like kindling. Victor watched as the outer lining disappeared, exposing the cheap, synthetic filling underneath. In a matter of seconds the coat had all but disappeared. The flames got larger. Joey pulled his hands away from his swollen, red, eyes. Frantically, he beat at his chest, but that only served to increase the flames. The sleeves of his coat caught next. As it fell, the can doused Joey's pants and boots in gasoline. The filthy cotton work pants lit him up like one of the Christmas trees at The Shore Line Hotel. Briefly, Victor saw his son's eyes widen, and then disappear as his skin blackened and lifted in layers. The air was filled with the smell of burning meat. It reminded Victor of the pig roast that he had attended the summer before. Joey fell to his knees and then onto his back.

Victor smiled. He picked up the gas can, and poured the remainder over Violet. Then, he made a trail connecting her to his still burning son. He stepped back and watched the body of his wife light up. The open wound of her face sizzled like bacon. He threw his shovel onto Joey's burning corpse, and walked back to his truck.

320

None of this had been according to plan, but Victor couldn't be more pleased with how things had turned out. He figured now, all he had to do was drive home, and call the police. His story would be simple enough—he had been out for the evening, he came home, and found blood all over the house. He called the police immediately. Eventually, they would find Violet and Joey. They would think that Joey had killed his mother and accidentally set himself on fire when he was trying to cremate and bury her. Wasn't that the most logical answer? As he slipped behind the wheel, Victor started to whistle. He couldn't remember the last time that he felt this good.

Victor put his pick-up in reverse. He slowly gave it gas and turned the wheel as far as it would go. Moving the gear shift into drive, he looked up just in time to see a set of headlights coming up the hill. The car stopped at the end of the drive, and Chief Laurie Knickles stepped out of the driver's side. She wasn't more than fifty feet away, but she spoke into the speaker. "Turn off your vehicle, please."

Victor remained in the car. He hadn't planned on this either, but this wasn't good. Victor tried to think of a story that would explain the burning corpses of his wife and son behind him in the snow, but he could think of nothing.

"Turn off your vehicle, and step out with your hands up, please," said the Chief.

Victor could hear fire trucks in the distance. That was it. It was over. The pick-up was facing directly at the squad car. There was nothing else to do. Victor pressed his heavy boot to the floor as hard as he could. The truck leapt toward the chief, and her squad car.

Chief Knickles raised her gun, took aim, and fired a single shot. The almost inaudible cracking of glass immediately followed the sound of the gun. The truck slowed and veered to the left. It bumped the squad car, but not hard enough to move it.

Laurie ran over to the truck and pulled the driver's door open. Victor fell out onto the ground. There was a bullet hole in his forehead, just above his left eye. "It's Victor! It's not Joey!" she said.

Charles ran toward the fires with the fire extinguisher from the squad car. He sprayed the two flaming lumps with the white chemical foam. He grimaced. "I think this is Joey and Violet," he said. "What the hell happened up here?"

25

Doctor Nevin walked into Corey's hospital room and pulled the chair that Chief Jefferies had sat in closer to the bed. The doctor sat down and leaned in toward Corey. "How are you, son?"

Corey looked at the old man. His face was kind and his brow was furrowed up in sympathy. Corey had seen this scene before. He had seen it play out in E.R. and on Chicago Hope. He had even seen it on that Grey's Anatomy show that Tina loved so much. This scene was never a good scene. There was something wrong. Corey knew it. He could tell. Doctors didn't do this. Doctor's would send in a nurse to deliver good news. If the doctor was taking the time to come in to see him personally, come in pull up a chair and call him son, then something was up. The cop.

That cop didn't answer him when he had asked about the baby. What was wrong with his baby?

"Corey? How are you?" the doctor repeated.

Corey struggled to sit up. He reached for the remote control and the bed hummed into an upright position. "Well, I don't know, Doc. You tell me. What's wrong? There's something wrong with my baby, isn't there? Even when I asked that cop, he wouldn't answer me. What's wrong? What happened?"

Doctor Nevin reached out and lay his hand on Corey's arm, but Corey drew back. "Corey, I need you to try and remain as calm as you can. Okay? Look at me." The Doctor spoke in a low voice. "Your baby is fine. You have a beautiful little girl, Corey. She's as healthy as can be."

Corey's mouth dropped open as he took in what the Doctor was telling him. "I have a little girl?"

The Doctor nodded. "Yes. She's beautiful, Corey."

"Can I see her?" asked Corey. "Has Tina seen her? Is she with Tina now? Tina so wanted a little girl. She said it didn't matter but I know she really wanted a girl."

"Corey," said the Doctor. "Tina didn't make it."

Corey stared at the Doctor. He felt the blood leaving his feet and hands. Cold spread across him. "Tina..."

"I'm sorry, son," said Doctor Nevin. "Corey, I think that I should call someone for you. I don't think that you should be alone right now. Do you or Tina have some family that we can call? Someone who can come out to the island and meet you?"

Corey didn't say anything. He was shaking. He didn't look down at his hands, but he could feel them shaking. His heart was pounding. Sweat was running down his face and down the back of his neck. Was he blinking? Corey wasn't sure. He thought he might have stopped. His eyes were burning, but he didn't want to move. Somehow, just maybe, if he didn't move, then none of this would be real. If he was really careful, and didn't move, this would all just stop.

"Corey, Tina's surgeon did everything that he could, but she had just lost too much blood. In a situation like that, the priority is always the baby. I want that to be your focus too, son. Your daughter needs you now. You need each other," said the Doctor.

My daughter, thought Corey. He hadn't even thought that word. He had a daughter. He was a father and he had a daughter. He turned to look at the Doctor. "I'd like to see my daughter, now," said Corey. "I'd like to tell her about her mother."

The Doctor smiled weakly and nodded. "I think that's a good idea."

*   *   *

Edie walked into Rockfish on North Water Street. She scanned the main floor for William, but did not see him. The main floor was entirely made up of high tables with bar seating and a large bar, like the one in Cheers in the centre. Actually, thought Edie, It kinda looked like Cheers. The proper dining area was upstairs and that's where she wanted to eat, but William hadn't been there before, so she just wanted to make sure that he wasn't waiting downstairs by mistake. Once she was certain that he wasn't there, Edie told the hostess that there would be two of them for supper, and she was escorted upstairs. The restaurant was relatively quiet. Not off-season quiet, but it wasn't hopping like the summer either. There were two tables available at the large windows overlooking Edgartown.

"May we sit at one of the window tables?" she asked.

"Of course!" said the hostess. The hostess was young and slim with long hair and a wide smile. Edie wondered if they made restaurant hostesses in any other model, or if this was it. The girl placed two menus and a drink menu on the table. "Your server will be with you shortly," she said.

"Thank you," said Edie, pulling her scarf from around her neck and taking off her coat. After draping them across one of the chairs, Edie sat down in one of the chairs closer to the window. Below, the winter scene on North Water Street was picture perfect. Snow blanketed the sidewalks, the coniferous trees, and the lawn of The Sydney Hotel across the street. Christmas lights trimmed the lamposts and the small Christmas trees topped the

326

green lattice pedestals that the city of Edgartown put up every year. Edie had always loved the town's Christmas decorations. She smiled as she remembered how excited Charles had been when he told her that they were the same decorations they used in the movie JAWS: The Revenge. Edie hadn't seen that film, nor did she intend to, but she had to admit, she liked the idea of the Edgartown decorations being immortalised on film.

With all of the drama that had hit her over the last twenty-four hours, she had almost entirely missed the Christmas In Edgartown celebration. The parade had been yesterday morning, but she had been too busy fainting to attend. The chowder competition had been yesterday afternoon—the chowder competition was always a highlight for Edie. The best lunch on-island—but she had been in the hospital. At least, Chris had brought her a Fat Ronnie's burger and onion rings. That had been good. Even when eaten in a hospital, Fat Ronnie's had the best burger on-island in her opinion. Edie had really enjoyed Chris's visit. Chris was a good man. She always enjoyed his company. Now, thanks to Chris, she was here waiting on a supper companion whom she wasn't all too sure she wanted to see.

William came up the stairs in a long black wool coat, with a red scarf tied at his throat. On his head was a black fedora. On his hands were black leather gloves. When he got to the top of the stairs, William scanned the room. Their eyes met and he smiled broadly. He bent slightly at

327

the waist in a bow, and touched the rim of his hat. Without thinking about it, Edie smiled back. She may have even blushed. Until know, she wasn't really sure if she had ever noticed how handsome William was—she was too busy being angry with him—but he was. He was very handsome.

William walked over to the table, pulling off his gloves finger by finger. When one hand was free of the lined, black leather, he motioned for a server. "One hot tea, please." He turned his attentions back to Edie. "Good evening, Edie," he said. "You look well."

"Better than the last time you saw me, anyway," Edie said.

"Well, you're upright!" William said still smiling. "Don't worry, you didn't actually look that bad. I could hardly see your face at all through all of your winter clothing. In fact, I didn't even recognise you at first." William undid his coat and scarf and draped them over the chair with Edie's. "In fact, I think it was your anger that I recognised first."

Edie knew she was blushing now. She turned her eyes down toward her lap, "I'm sorry about that. It's been a trying couple of days."

"Please," William said, waving her away. "No need to apologise. I'm the one who owes you an apology. I acted very badly in the church. I thought I was being funny and it got out of hand. I'm hoping we can start again, now. This evening."

328

"Well, there's just one problem with that," Edie said.

William's smile dropped a little. "What's that?"

"If we start tonight, then we omit the flowers you sent me yesterday. They were lovely. Thank you. Yellow flowers are probably my favourites," Edie smiled.

William's smile quickly broadened again. "That's good to know."

The server came with William's hot tea. She looked at Edie. "Can I get you a drink? Have you looked at our wine list at all?"

"Were you planning on drinking this evening?" Edie asked William.

William shook his head. "I don't think I will, but you go ahead."

"I'll have a hot tea as well, please," Edie said. The server smiled a smile that reflected the drop in tip she had been calculating, and walked to the kitchen. "She's not going to get rich off of us tonight, is she?"

"I'll make it up to her," William said.

"They serve the best Brussels sprouts here," said Edie. "Do you like Brussels sprouts?"

"They're my favourite vegetable," William said.

"I think they're mine too," said Edie. "They were Mark's favourite too. We ate them a lot." She looked around. "He would have loved this place. He passed long before it was around. It's only been here for maybe five years? It was a restaurant called David Ryan's before this."

The server came with Edie's tea. "Do you know what you'd like to order?" she asked.

"We haven't even looked yet," William said. "We have a lot to talk about."

The server smiled. "No problem. Shout if you need anything."

Edie put her tea bag in the small metal pot and noticed for the first time that William had both hands wrapped around his mug. His knuckles were swollen and misshapen. They looked sore. "Arthritis?" she asked and then caught her breath. "I'm sorry. That's none of my business."

William lifted a hand from his mug and straightened his fingers as best he could. "Yes. For quite sometime now," he said. "The heat of the mug makes it feel better. You want to know something?"

"What?"

"I don't even like tea!" he said with a chuckle. "I just order it to warm my fingers. I drink it so I don't look like a crazy person. I like coffee, but for whatever reason, tea seems to hold its temperature longer than coffee." William shrugged. "I could be making that last part up, but that's how it seems to me."

Edie liked how William spoke. His speech was clear and concise. It was almost like a British accent, but not quite. "Where did you grow up, William?"

"New York and then Boston," he said. "I went to Harvard. What about yourself?"

330

"Florida," she smiled. "I did not go to Harvard."

"No, I realise that," he said. This time it was his turn to catch his breath. "I didn't mean that to be as insulting as it sounded."

Edie blushed again. She felt her defences rising. "How did you mean it?" She was trying not to glare at him, but she knew that he could feel that the energy at the table had changed.

"It wasn't meant to mean anything derogatory. There is an Ivy League tone, and inflection. If anything, all I meant was you don't sound like a snob...like me."

Edie relaxed a bit. "That was a pretty good save," she said. She paused before she spoke again. "My lack of education has always been a sore spot for me." Edie said. "I started college, but I didn't finish. My mother never let me forget it either."

"May I ask what happened?" asked William.

"Martha's Vineyard happened," Edie stated. She took a sip of her tea. "Your brother happened."

"How do you mean?" William asked.

"I came out here for the summer, and I never went back," she said. "That happens a lot out here. People come to Martha's Vineyard and they never leave. There's something special about this place. Sure, a lot of people come out here and enjoy the beaches. They have a bunch of drinks at The Seafood shanty or The Newes From America. They eat lobster rolls in Menemsha and watch the sunset. They might even go sailing with Catboat

331

Charters, but when they go home—they go home. They start planning their next vacation to Mexico or Orlando, but they never think of Martha's Vineyard again. But there's another group of people. This second group gets hit and hit hard as soon as they start walking down the gangplank of the Ferry. They know that they've come home, even if they've never been here before. Every turn on North Road, every path to Moshup Beach, every Nancy's sunset, and every street in Edgartown is almost too much for them to take. Emotionally, they just know that this island is where they are supposed to be. Leaving is gut-wrenching. Some of them, some of us, can't leave, and we don't." Edie looked out the window at her island home.

"When I came here," she continued. "I thought I was coming for a couple of weeks before I went back to school. I fell in love with the place. I ended up getting a job at The Edgartown Inn. Then your brother came and worked on the roof."

"I thought he was a fisherman?" asked William.

"Not at first," Edie smiled into the past. She could see Mark unloading his ladder from an orange Volkswagen van. He was wearing low slung jeans and white running shoes. Workmen in the seventies didn't wear much else, especially on Martha's Vineyard. Edie laughed. "He had an afro when we met. Hey—it was the seventies. If you were black, you had an afro."

"I didn't have an afro," said William.

332

Edie grinned and raised an eyebrow. "Yeah, but I'll bet dollars to doughnuts, that you were what Mark would have called an *Oreo* for sure. You know, black on the outside but white on the inside?"

William grimaced slightly. "I am familiar with the term."

"Sorry," Edie continued. "There was nothing *Oreo* about Mark. He introduced me to a lot of things that I had never heard of before. Good things—exotic things. At least they seemed exotic to a white girl from Florida. Food and music—Mark was the one who introduced me to Bob Marley. He used to cook for us too. He learned from his—your—mother. My curried goat still is nothing like his. Mark's ackee and saltfish? Forget about it. Mine doesn't even come close. I don't know what I'm doing wrong. I still pick up the ackee in Boston and I get the cod right here in Menemsha but still..." Edie stopped. She could feel tears streaming down her cheeks. "Oh, I'm so sorry, William. I haven't thought about any of this for so long." She looked across the table. William was weeping.

Edie reached across the table and pulled one of his hands away from the mug of tea. She held it. "Are you okay?" she asked.

William shook his head. "I'm so embarrassed," he said. "I'm ashamed...I'm so ashamed."

"Don't be," Edie said gently. "Cry as much as you want." She passed him a tissue from her purse.

"Oh, I'm not embarrassed about that, although..." William looked around the room. "I probably should be." He cleared his throat and looked up into Edie's eyes. "I'm ashamed because I let this all pass me by. I am ashamed because I wasted my life making money. My mother never taught me how to cook. She probably tried. I don't even remember. I cannot remember if my mother even tried to teach me how to cook. I was so indifferent to her or anyone else. My only brother and I let him just slip through my fingers," he chuckled miserably and looked at his hands. "My fingers. I'm now a withered, old man at the end of the line and I have missed out on it all."

Edie squeezed his hand a little tighter. "William, I never thought that I would say this, but why don't you stay?"

"Stay where?"

"Here," she said. "On the island. Stay through Christmas and New Years. I get the feeling you don't have anyone to go back to and you can afford that house for the month, right?"

"Yes," he said.

"Then stay," said Edie.

"Why?" asked William.

"Because I'd like you to," she said.

It had been a long time since anyone had wanted William to do anything that wasn't for financial gain. "Alright, I'll stay," he said.

Chris pulled a batch of sugar cookies out of the oven just as he heard Jeff come in the front door. He set the cookie sheet down on the stovetop. Pulling off his oven mitt, he reached for the glaze of icing sugar and water, and began brushing it onto the hot cookies. Chris moved fast. Once the cookies were glazed, he reached for a bowl of green sprinkles, and covered half of the cookies. Then, he picked up a bowl of red sprinkles and covered the other half.

"You were moving at a good clip there," said Jeff from the archway that led into the kitchen from the front hall.

"Well, I have to get the glaze on fast, because if I don't get the sprinkles on while the cookies are still hot, they won't stick," explained Chris, admiring his handiwork. "They look pretty good. Don't you think?"

Jeff walked over to the stove and inspected the cookies. "They look delicious, is what they look." Jeff moved quickly and before Chris could protest, he shoved half of a cookie into his mouth. A moment later he screamed in agony. "Jesus Christ!" he muffled through a mouthful of cookie. He desperately tried to inhale air to cool his mouth. "It's hot!"

Chris laughed. "Well, it serves you right!" he scolded. "These are for kids at the Teddy Bear Christmas. What were you thinking? You saw me take them out of the oven and glaze them."

"I was thinking I was hungry," said Jeff. "I'll be so glad when all of this Christmas crap is over."

Chris took a glass from the overhead cupboard. Pressing it into the dispenser on the front of their refrigerator, he filled it halfway with ice. Then, with the dispenser beside it, filled the glass with water. He passed it to Jeff.

"Thank you," said Jeff. He slipped an ice cube into his mouth.

"Jeff," Chris spoke in a gentle almost tentative voice. "I went skating with your Dad today."

"Oh yeah," Jeff said. "Better you than me."

"Jeff, your Dad's a good guy. I like him," said Chris.

Jeff sat down in one of the family room chairs that faced the fireplace, but backed onto the kitchen. He exhaled an exasperated sigh.

"We should spend more time with him. He's the only family we have on the island," Chris walked over and sat on the ottoman in front of Jeff.

Jeff looked at Chris with a weary stare. "He's a good guy, I know. We're just not that close. That's all. There's no need for you to go all *cats in the cradle* on me over this. Just leave it alone. I don't want to talk about it."

"Well, that much is clear," said Chris. "Jeff, I'm not trying to upset you."

336

"Well, congratulations then, because you've managed to do it with almost no effort," Jeff snorted.

Chris positioned himself square in front of Jeff. He leaned forward and put a hand on Jeff's thigh. "Jeff, why didn't you ever tell me about your mother?"

Jeff's face went slack. His eyes opened wide. He looked like a child who had just been told his birthday party had been cancelled. "What about my Mom?" His voice was almost a whisper.

Chris rubbed Jeff's thigh slowly with one hand, and reached out with the other to hold his husband's hand. "Jeff, you told me she died."

Jeff didn't say anything.

Chris continued. "Jeff, she's not dead. She left. Your Dad told me today. She left just before Christmas when you were a teenager. I can't imagine how hard that must have been for you. How old were you? Fifteen?" Chris felt Jeff squeeze his hand tight. "Why did you tell me she was dead? Did that make it easier for you?"

With his free hand, Jeff wiped at his eyes. "We had just started dating. I didn't want to get into the whole thing. Then, it never really came up again; I didn't want to talk about it anymore, so I just left it. Dad and I don't talk about her so there was no worry that it would ever come up."

"And that's why you hate Christmas?" asked Chris.

"Did Dad tell you then rest of the story?" Jeff asked.

"I don't know," said Chris. "Why don't you tell me? I'd like you to tell me."

"My mother left a week before Christmas, and she didn't say good-bye. I got no explanation. I'm not even sure if he did either, actually. I was just told she was gone and she wasn't coming back." Jeff stared straight into Chris's eyes. "Then, on Christmas, there were still presents for me under the tree from her that I had to open. I don't know if he thought it would make things easier for me, if he thought that I would feel better getting gifts from my Mom, my Mom who had just decided that life would be better if I wasn't in it, but it didn't. All it did was drive the point home. I think Dad realised his mistake, because it got so uncomfortable that he couldn't look at me. Then, he left the room. I just sat there, alone on Christmas morning, opening presents from the mother who had left me the week before."

Chris knelt down on the floor and leaned in toward Jeff. He took him in his arms and held him tight. "Jeff, I am so sorry that happened to you." Chris pushed Jeff back, and placed his hands on Jeff's shoulders. "I'm going to ask you to do something now."

"What?" asked Jeff.

"I'm going to ask you to forgive your mother," Chris said.

"Why the hell should I do that?" asked Jeff.

"Jeff, wherever she is, I guarantee you, she is beating herself up over this every minute of every day," said Chris.

"Good," said Jeff. "Then why do I need to forgive her? It's not like she's going to hear me. It won't make a damned bit of difference to her."

"You're right. It won't make a damned bit of difference to her. She won't know if you've forgiven her or not," said Chris. "But it will to you. Jeff, if she won't know whether or not you've forgiven her, she also won't know if you're walking around angry with her either. The only person you're affecting by doing that is you. Let it go. Forgive her. Your anger is only a burden on your shoulders, not hers."

Jeff stared at Chris with childlike fear.

"Jeff, I want to be able to enjoy the holidays with the man I love. I want us to love Christmas together. Don't you? Don't you see the holidays as a possibility for us to do new and exciting things together? I'm sorry about your Dad, but put yourself in his shoes. His wife had just left him—the woman he loved according to him—with a teenage boy. He was hurting and probably scared to death. He feels awful about your childhood. He loves you very much, but every time he looks at you all he sees is everything he did wrong. He blames himself. Now, I'm going to tell you what I told him this afternoon—your mother leaving doesn't say anything about you or your

Dad. It only says something about her. So, you two need to stop blaming yourselves and each other."

Jeff smiled meekly at Chris. "You know you talk pretty smart for a hockey player," he said.

"The was a recent study ranking professionals by how much of the brain was used at one time. Hockey players came in second. Chefs came in first. I'm both. You're screwed."

*   *   *

Corey watched the nurse push a Plexiglas crib on four wheels into his room. Gently, she picked up the soft, pink bundle and passed it to Corey. Corey reached for her and brought her gently to his chest. She was sleeping. Corey looked down at her little red face in wonder. Did she already look like her mother? Was that possible? Corey marvelled at each and every eyelash. Gently, with one finger, he stroked her nose. She sighed.

"Hi," he said softly. "I'm your Daddy."

Corey brought the warm bundle up closer to his face. He could smell her. He could smell that baby smell. Softly, he kissed her on her forehead. "You're so soft," he said. "You're like a little lamb...but I can't call you lamb." Corey smiled for the first time since he'd been told about Tina's death. "I'd call you Tina after your Mom, but she would never forgive me. She hated that. So, I know I'm not

340

allowed. I'll have to give it some time." Corey looked at the nurse. "What time was she officially born?" he whispered.

"First thing this morning," she said. "Just after seven, I think?"

"You're an early riser, are you?" Corey said. "Your Mom was too."

The nurse smiled. "Yep. I remember it was right at the crack of dawn."

Corey looked down at his daughter. She wiggled in his arms, and curled into his chest. "Dawn...I like that," he said. "Dawn Marie."

Epilogue

Charles walked into the living room with another tray of Chris John's sugar cookies—red and green sparkle covered cookies cut into the shape of Martha's Vineyard. He carefully stepped through his guests, some of whom were sitting on the floor. The Christmas tree was lit and there were presents stuffed to capacity underneath. Laurie sat on her favourite chair laughing with Chris Johns. Beside Chris was his husband, Chief Jeff Jefferies and his Dad, Peter Jefferies. Peter and Jack were deep in conversation. Charles stared at them, narrowing his gaze. If they were talking shop, he was going to have to break them up. Mike and Trish sat on the floor, talking to Virginia. The doorbell rang, and Fenway The Beagle barked his traditional greeting. "Fenway!" Charles scolded. "Fenway! Be quiet!"

Laurie looked up at Charles and laughed. "You're the one who thought we should have a dog!"

"Oh please," said Charles. "Who sneaks him treats at the table every chance she gets? He's getting fat because of you."

Laurie rolled her eyes. "Are you going to get the door?"

Charles walked over to the front door and opened it. He stepped aside so that Edie and William could come in. Charles shook William's hand and leaned in to give Edie a hug and kiss. "Hello you two!" he said. "Happy Christmas Eve!"

"Happy Christmas?" said William. "What happened to *Merry Christmas*?"

Edie rolled her eyes. "He's Canadian and he doesn't like us to forget it."

He's crazy is what he is!" Laurie made her way through the crowded room and gave the new arrivals a hug and kiss. "How did you get here?"

"William collected me at the inn," Edie said. "I came with him."

Laurie gave Charles a sly look.

"You wipe those looks off your face, or Christmas or no Christmas, I will slap them off faster than you can say *Mrs Kintner*!"

"Alright! Alright!" said Charles. Both he and Laurie started to laugh.

"You two are impossible," Edie said.

343

"There is rum and egg nog in the punch bowl in the kitchen," said Laurie.

"Who the hell is Mrs Kintner?" asked William.

Charles put his arm around William, "William, my man, have I got the movie for you!"

"*We're not watching JAWS!*" said Laurie emphatically.

"Well, not tonight," said Charles.

The music stopped and Charles listened for the next song. When it didn't come, he looked at Chris. "Chris, you always have a good playlist on your iPhone. Do you have a Christmas playlist? You must."

Chris nodded with a mouthful of eggnog. "I do!" Chris got up and made his way over to the iPhone dock that was connected to the speakers.

Jeff rolled his eyes. "How many times do I have to hear Madonna sing Santa Baby this month?"

Charles laughed. Trish waved at Charles and winked. Charles winked back. "Chris, hold off on the music for a second, would ya?" Charles winked at Chris.

Chris looked down onto the floor and nodded. He winked back.

"Edie? William? Laurie? Can you guys come in from the kitchen for a moment, please?"

Having heard their names, Edie, William, and Laurie walked into the living room and stood in the archway that led back to the kitchen. They stared down at Mike and Trish, grinning from ear to ear.

344

Mike looked around the room realising that all eyes were on him. Trish got up on one knee and took one of his hands.

Mike looked at her, bewildered. "What are you doing, babe?"

"Mike, when I first saw you, I knew right away that you were the one for me. I knew even before you spoke that you were supposed to be in my life. I've never had that feeling before. I love you so much," Trish's eyes became glassy. Her chest heaved as she gasped for breath. "That's why, now, in front of all these people," Trish looked around the room. "In front of all of these beautiful people, I'd like to ask you," Trish wiped at her nose. "Would you marry me?" Trish reached into her sweater sleeve and pulled out a small Christmas present. It was a small box wrapped in shiny red paper and a gold bow. "Open it," she said.

Mike wiped at his own tears and took the box in a shaky hand. He tore off the paper and found a small ring box. Mike went a bit limp, but managed to stay sitting on his haunches. He opened the box. It was his great grandmother's ring. "Oh, Trish!" he said. "Oh my god!" Mike looked around the room. "Did you all know?"

Everyone nodded as they wiped their eyes and sniffed.

"Best kept secret on Martha's Vineyard!" said Virginia. Everyone laughed at that.

"Probably the only kept secret on Martha's Vineyard," Peter Jefferies chimed in.

"But I don't understand?" said Mike. "How?"

"It was sent back last week with the autopsy report," Laurie said. "It looks like Joey Helm had it in his back pocket."

Edie shuddered. "I don't even want to hear the names of any of them," she said. "I still don't understand why Joey Helm would burn down my house. I never even met him."

"It wasn't about you," said Charles. "A pyromaniac is someone who sets fires to experience an instant tension or stress release. I don't think we'll ever know exactly what was going on in that house, but I'd say that Joey's home life gave him plenty of stressors."

"Poetic justice that the firebug should burn to death," said Peter. "He accidentally set himself on fire?"

"We're not really sure yet. It's clear that the fire was the result of a fight between Victor and Joey. When Joey lost consciousness, he fell backward," Laurie said. "When he fell backward, he smothered the flame, and saved the ring. When it came back to us, Jack saw it. He took a photo of it, and showed it to Virginia. She confirmed that it was your ring. We were going to hand it back to you, but then Charles suggested this idea, and we all conspired against you!"

The group laughed.

"Well?" asked Trish.

346

"Well, what?" asked Mike.

"You didn't answer my question!"

Mike's cheeks flushed. His eyes welled. He leaned in toward her and when he was close enough to taste her, he said, "Yes. In front of all of these beautiful people, Trish McKenzie, I will marry you."

THE END

Martha's Vineyard Mysteries

By

Crispin Nathaniel Haskins:

The JAWSfest Murders

Deadly Catch

White Shark

Pretty Vineyard Girls

Dead And Buried

Made in the USA
Middletown, DE
22 December 2020